THE 37th
HOUR

THE 37th HOUR

HOUR

Jodi Compton

Delacorte Press

THE 37th HOUR
A Delacorte Book / January 2004

Published by Bantam Dell
A Division of Random House, Inc.
New York, New York

Book design by Lynn Newmark

Delacorte Press is a registered trademark of Random House, Inc., and the
colophon is a trademark of Random House, Inc.

Library of Congress Cataloging in Publication Data
Compton, Jodi.
The 37th hour / Jodi Compton.
p.   cm.
ISBN 0-385-33713-2
1. Police—Minnesota—Minneapolis—Fiction. 2. Minneapolis (Minn.)—
Fiction. 3. Missing persons—Fiction.   I. Title: Thirty-seventh hour.
II. Title.

PS3603.O595T47 2004
813'.6—dc22
2003055270

Manufactured in the United States of America
Published simultaneously in Canada
10 9 8 7 6 5 4 3 2 1
BVG

acknowledgments

This book is a work of fiction, with the usual amount of narrative license taken. Although real government agencies are named within, nothing here is meant to represent the actual workings of those agencies or their employees.

Having said that, there are several people who helped me understand the world in which Sarah Pribek works, and they deserve mentioning. Particularly I wish to thank an officer of the Las Vegas Metropolitan Police Department and lawyers Beth Compton of Indiana and David Lillehaug of Minnesota. All remaining errors, or dramatic license taken, are to be laid at my doorstep, not theirs. Also helpful was reporter Carol Roberts of *The Tribune* in San Luis Obispo (when you retire, Carol, can I have that Rolodex?).

I also want to thank some extraordinarily supportive people

in the publishing business: Barney et al. at the Karpfinger Agency, and Jackie and Nita at Bantam.

Lastly, I wish to thank my father for leaving thousands of crime novels around the house (fortunately not all at once) when I was growing up; my sister, whose opinion I seek first on story and character; and a teacher who learned me and a lot of other kids how to read. Thank you, Bethie.

THE 37th HOUR

Every cop has at least one story about the day the job found them. It's not uncommon. Out on the streets, on duty or off, suddenly an officer sees two guys in baseball caps and sunglasses run out of a bank as if their heels were afire. By pure luck, there's an officer on the scene even before Dispatch takes the call.

With missing-persons cases, though, it's a little different. The people you're looking for, generally, are already dead, out of town, out of state, or in hiding. As a rule, they're not in highly visible places, waiting for you to all but run into them. Ellie Bernhardt, fourteen, was to be the exception that proved the rule.

Yesterday, Ellie's sister had come to see me, all the way to Minneapolis from Bemidji, in northwest Minnesota. Ainsley Carter was 21, maybe 22 at the outside. She was thin and had that tentative, nervous kind of beauty that seems proprietary to blondes, but today, and probably most days, she hadn't chosen to accentuate her looks save for some dark-brown mascara and a little bit of concealer under the eyes that didn't erase the shadow of a poorly slept night. She wore jeans and a softball shirt—the kind with a white body and colored long sleeves, blue in this case. A plain silver band rode her right hand; a very small diamond solitaire the left.

"I think my sister is probably in town somewhere," she said, when I'd gotten her settled before my desk with a cup of coffee. "She didn't come home from school the day before yesterday."

"You contacted the police in Bemidji?"

"In Thief River Falls," she said. "That's where Ellie still lives, with our dad. My husband and I moved after we got married," she explained. "So yes, they're looking into it. But I think she's here. I think she ran away from home."

"Does she have a suitcase or bag that's missing?"

Ainsley tipped her head to one side, thinking. "No, but her book bag is pretty large, and when I looked through her stuff I thought that some things were missing. Things that she wouldn't take to school, but would want if she were leaving home."

"Like?"

"Well, she had a picture of our mother," Ainsley said. "Mom died about six years ago. Then I got married, and Joe and I moved away, so it's just her and Dad."

It seemed an anecdote was forming out of what had started to be generic background information, so I said nothing and let it unfold.

"Ellie had the usual amount of girlfriends growing up. She was a little shy, but she had friends. But just in the past year or so, I don't know, Dad says they've kind of cooled off," she said. "I think it's just because Ellie has gotten so pretty. All of a sudden, within almost a year, she was tall, and she was developing, and she had such a lovely face. And that same year she was out of grade school and into junior high, and that's a big change. I think maybe the girls felt differently about her, just like the guys did."

"Guys?" I said.

"Since Ellie turned thirteen or so, boys have been calling. A lot of them are older boys, Dad says. It worries him."

"Was Ellie seeing someone older, someone your father didn't have a good feeling about?"

"No," Ainsley said. "As far as he knew, she didn't date at all. But I don't have a good feel for her life." She paused. "Dad's nearly seventy. He doesn't talk about girl things with us, he never has. So I can't get a good idea from him what Ellie's life is really like. I try to talk to her on the phone, but it's not the same. I don't think she has anyone to confide in."

"Ainsley," I said carefully, "when you talk to Ellie, when you visit the house, do you ever feel something isn't right about her relationship with her father?"

She understood immediately what I was asking. "Oh, God, no," she said, and her tone left me no room to doubt she meant it. She picked up her coffee; her blue eyes on me suggested she was waiting for another question.

I licked my teeth speculatively, tapped a pen against my notepad.

"What I hear you saying is that you worry because she doesn't have any friends or nearby female relatives to talk to. Which is unfortunate, I guess, but what I don't see here is a crisis that caused her to run away. Can you think of anything?"

"I did," Ainsley said more slowly, "talk to her friends. Her classmates, I mean."

"What did they say?"

"They didn't say much. They were kind of embarrassed, and maybe feeling guilty. Ellie's run away, and I'm her sister, and probably they felt like I was there to blame them for not being kinder or more supportive of her."

"They didn't say anything useful?" I prompted.

"Well," she said, "one of the girls said there were some rumors."

"What kind?" I asked.

"That Ellie was sexually active, I guess. I tried to get her to say more, but the other two girls jumped in, and said, 'You know, people just talk.' Something like that. I couldn't get anything more out of them."

I nodded. "But you said Ellie didn't date. It seems like there wouldn't be much grounds for those kinds of rumors."

"Dad would let her go to sleepovers." Ainsley lifted her coffee cup, didn't drink. "He thought they were all-girls parties, but sometimes I wonder. You hear things, about what kids are doing at earlier and earlier ages...." Her voice trailed off, leaving the difficult things unsaid.

"Okay," I said. "None of this may be relevant at all to why she ran away."

Ainsley went on with her train of thought. "I wish she could live with us," she said. "I talked to Joe about it, but he says we don't have enough room." She twisted the diamond ring on her hand.

"Why do you think she's in the Twin Cities?"

"She likes it here," Ainsley said simply.

It was a good enough answer. Kids often ran away to the nearest metropolis. Cities seemed to promise a better life.

"Do you have a photo of Ellie I can use?"

"Sure," she said. "I brought you one."

The photo of Ellie did show a lovely girl, her hair a darker blond than her sister's, and her eyes green instead of Ainsley's blue. She had a dusting of kid freckles, and her face was bright but somewhat blank, as is often the case with school photos.

"It's last year's," she said. "Her school says they just took class pictures, and the new one won't be available for a week or so." It was early October.

"Do you have another one that you can use?"

"Me?" she said.

"I have a full caseload right now," I explained. "You, though, are free to look for Ellie full-time. You should keep looking."

"I thought . . ." Ainsley looked a little disillusioned.

"I'm going to do everything I can," I reassured her. "But you're Ellie's best advocate right now. Show her picture to everyone. Motel clerks, homeless people, the priests and ministers who run homeless shelters . . . anyone you think might have seen Ellie. Make color photocopies with a description and hang them up anywhere people will let you. Make this your full-time job."

Ainsley Carter had understood me; she'd left to do what I'd said. But I found Ellie instead, and it was just dumb luck.

At midmorning the day after Ainsley's visit, I'd driven out to a hotel in the outer suburbs. A clerk there had thought she'd seen a man and boy sought in a parental abduction, and I'd been asked to look into it.

I handled all kinds of crimes—all sheriff's detectives did—but missing persons was a kind of subspecialty of my partner's, and along the way, it had become mine, too.

The father and son in question were just packing up their old Ford van as I got there. The boy was about two years older and three inches taller than the one I was looking for. I was curious about why the boy wasn't in school, but they explained they were driving back from a family funeral. I wished them safe driving and went back to the registration desk to thank the clerk for her civic-mindedness.

On the drive back, just before I got to the river, I saw a squad car pulled over between the road and the railroad tracks.

A uniformed officer stood by the car, looking south, almost as if she were guarding the tracks. Just beyond her, those tracks turned into a trestle across the river, and I saw the broad-shouldered form of another officer walking out onto it. It was a scene just odd enough to make me pull over.

"What's going on?" I asked the patrolwoman when she approached my car. Sensing she was about to tell me to move along, I took my shield out of my jacket and flipped the holder open.

Her face relaxed a little from its hard-set position, but she didn't take off or even push down her mirrored shades, so that I saw my own face in them, distended as if by a fish-eye lens. I read her nameplate: OFFICER MOORE.

"I thought you looked familiar," Moore said. Then, in answer to my question, she said succinctly, "Jumper."

"Where?" I said. I saw Moore's partner, now standing out on the train tracks mid-bridge, but no one else.

"She climbed down on the framework," Moore said. "You can kind of see her from here. Just a kid, really."

I craned my neck and did see a slender form on the web-work of the bridge, and then the flash of sunlight on dark-gold hair.

"A girl? Like, around fourteen?"

"Yeah, she is," Moore said.

"Where can I park?"

The trip out onto the railroad bridge kept taking me through sun and shadow, sun and shadow, not just from the bridge's overhead structure, but also from the sun dipping behind a cloud and then back again. It was a day of broken cloud.

"I thought we radioed for the water patrol," Moore's partner said in greeting, mildly perplexed, as I neared him.

I knew him by sight but couldn't quite remember his name. Something with a *V.* He was a few years younger than me, 25 or so. Handsome and olive-complected.

"Nobody sent for me, Officer Vignale," I said, my memory delivering the name to me before I had to read his tag. "I was just passing by. What's going on?"

"She's still down there, Detective . . ."

"Pribek," I said. "Sarah Pribek. Have you tried to talk to her?"

"I'm afraid to distract her. I don't want her to lose her balance." I turned, leaned against the railing, and looked down. Sure enough, the kid was right there, standing with her feet braced and her hands up on a diagonal strut. The mild breeze ruffled hair exactly the color and texture of Ellie Bernhardt's.

"She's a runaway from Thief River Falls," I said. "At least, I'm pretty sure she is. Her older sister was downtown reporting her yesterday."

Vignale nodded. "Water patrol is sending out a boat. Just in case we have to fish her out."

I looked down at Ellie and the water below that.

Ellie had picked a particularly low bridge to climb out on, and that in itself was interesting. I'd never learned a whole lot about psychology, but I'd heard that when people make survivable suicide attempts, it's often a way of asking for help. Then again, Ellie could simply have been confused, angry, and impatient and rushed out to the first structure across the Mississippi that she could find.

Either way, it was a fortunate situation. Up to a point: The river she was over was still the Mississippi.

I had grown up in New Mexico, and in the high country where I'd lived, the terrain had been crosshatched with creeks, but we'd had nothing like the Mississippi. At the age of thirteen I'd come to live in Minnesota, but even then I hadn't lived near the river. The Mississippi had been an abstraction to me, something to be seen from a distance or crossed on the occasional road trip. It wasn't until years later that I'd gone down to the river to check it out at close hand.

Down at the bank, a kid had been pretending to fish with plain string tied to a long branch.

"Does anyone ever go in?" I'd asked him.

"I saw a man go in once with a rope around his waist," the kid had said. "The current took him under so fast that both his friends, they were both grown-ups, had to pull just to get him out."

Since then I'd heard dissenting opinions on the strength and the malice of the river that divided Minneapolis. The Twin Cities' police and emergency blotters have recorded the stories of people who have survived jumps and falls from all of its bridges. But these survivals aren't the rule. Even sober, healthy adults who can swim and aren't suicidal get in trouble in the river, largely due to the current. It drags you in the wrong directions: downward, where people get caught up in submerged trees and roots, and toward the river's center, where the current flows fastest over the deepest part of the bed.

The fall from this structure might well be survivable, and the water might not be the paralyzingly frigid temperatures of midwinter. But all the same I thought it was best if things didn't get to that point.

Holding on to a railing, I put one experimental foot out onto the edge.

"You've gotta be kidding me," Vignale said.

"No kidding," I said. "If she didn't want someone to come talk her out of it, she would have jumped already." *I hope.* "I'm worried about *you*, Officer Vignale," I said. "If your partner didn't radio ahead to keep train traffic off the bridge, I'd think about going back."

The bridge's framework wasn't really any more difficult to climb down than a child's jungle gym at the playground, but I negotiated it a lot more slowly.

"You got company, but don't be scared," I said when I got down to the kid's level, keeping my voice low and modulated. Like Vignale said, I didn't want to startle her. "I'm just coming down to talk."

She turned to look at me and I saw that she was indeed Ellie. More than that, I saw the beauty that had so worried her older sister. Ellie had in fact changed since the taking of last year's class picture.

She was one of those people who seriousness, even unhappiness, makes far more lovely than a smile. Her green-gray eyes were heavy-lidded, her skin clear, her lower lip very full. The freckles from the photo, fading already, were the last vestige of her child's face. She wore a gray T-shirt and black jeans. No pastels, no ribbons, no girl stuff for Ellie. If I'd seen her from a distance, I might have taken her for a petite 21-year-old.

"Give me a minute here, Ellie," I said. On her level now, I was cautiously switching my handholds around so that instead of facing inward in my climbing stance, I could stand sideways, toward her, to talk.

"That's better." My feet were braced and I could lean back against the webwork. "That's not an easy climb for a grown-up," I told her. There were times when I liked being five-foot-eleven, but this wasn't one of them.

"How did you know my name?" she asked.

"Your sister came to see me yesterday," I said. "She's very worried about you."

"Ainsley is here?" Ellie glanced up and toward the road, from where Vignale and I had both come. I couldn't tell if she was hopeful or unhappy at the prospect.

"Uh, no. But she's in town," I said.

Ellie looked down again, toward the water. "She wants me to go back to Thief River Falls."

"We both just want to know what's bothering you," I said. When she didn't speak, I tried again. "Why'd you leave home, Ellie?"

She said nothing.

"Was it the kids at school?" I said, floating the broadest, gentlest question possible, so she could pick up on it or not, as she wanted.

"I can't go back there," she said quietly. "They're all talking about me and Justin Teague. He told everyone, the shithead."

Somehow I liked Ellie just a little more because she'd used that word. Besides, it sounded like it might be warranted.

"Was he telling lies about you?" I asked her.

She shook her head. "No, it was all true. I did sleep with him. I had to."

"Because you liked him and were afraid of losing him?"

"No," she said flatly.

I'd thought this was what you were supposed to do with jumpers, talk to them about their problems until they felt better and agreed to come in. That didn't seem to be happening here. Ellie Bernhardt didn't appear to be feeling any better.

When I was her age, I was still new to Minnesota, separated from what remained of my family, feeling I would never belong anywhere. It wouldn't help to tell Ellie any of that. When-I-was-your-age stories invariably fail to pierce the walls and barriers and defense systems of troubled kids who think all adults are, if not the enemy, at least useless civilians.

"Look," I said, "there seem to be things in your life that need straightening out, but I don't think the underside of a bridge is the place to do it. So why don't you come with me, okay?"

She sniffed loudly. "I slept with him because I *didn't* like him. And I wanted to change things."

"I don't understand," I said.

"Ainsley doesn't, either," she said quietly. "I . . . I like girls."

"Oh," I said. *This just in from left field.* "That's all right."

Angry tears stood in Ellie's eyes as she stared me down. "All right for *who?*" she demanded. "For *you?* Some cop in Minneapolis?"

As if her rage had freed her, Ellie jumped.

And I did, too.

If it had been January, the river at its most frigid, my decision might have been different. Or maybe I would've stayed where I was if I'd done everything right, instead of making

Ellie talk about her problems and getting her upset enough to jump.

Or maybe I was lying to myself when I called it a decision. I don't really remember thinking anything. When I let go, that is. In between the time when I realized I had really let go of the framework and the time I hit the water, I thought of several things in very quick succession. The kid on the bank with his ridiculous pretend fishing pole. My brother, holding my head under the water in a trough when I was five.

Last of all, I thought of Shiloh.

I learned something that day that I'd only thought I'd known: the river you stick your feet in on a summer's day, with a little shiver at its coldness even in June, is not the same river God throws at your body when you fall from even a moderate height. I felt almost as if I'd hit a sidewalk; the impact was so jarring I bit my tongue, drawing blood.

Most of the first moments after I jumped passed too quickly for me to remember much of them. My lungs were burning when I finally broke the surface again, and almost immediately I was breathing like a racehorse. The environment was so different from the tame, cool, chlorinated waters of the lap pool in which I'd been taught to swim that I was reduced to struggling in the current like someone who'd never learned at all. It was pure coincidence, I think, that I bumped Ellie and got hold of her.

She'd either knocked herself out hitting the water wrong or had gone motionless from shock. Either way, she wasn't struggling, which was a blessing. I got an arm around her and rolled onto my back, breathing raggedly.

Anxiety stabbed me when I noticed how rapidly the railroad bridge was disappearing, and how quickly we'd been carried to the center of the river. The current kept pulling at my scissoring legs, particularly my flooded boots, which felt as heavy as cinder blocks.

I kicked for the shore, and paddled weakly with my free arm. I did that for a minute or two. And then I realized something: I wasn't going to be able to save Ellie. I wasn't a strong-enough swimmer.

I could keep us both above the surface, if I kicked hard enough. But that was all. And how long could I do that? After a certain point, Ellie might be dead, because I wasn't at all sure I was keeping her face above the surface enough to keep her from inhaling water, filling her lungs.

And if I remembered my geography right, before too much time we'd be at the spillway, the lock and dam near the Stone Arch Bridge. That was, by far, the greatest hazard in the area. I'd heard that someone had gone through it once and survived. The word I'd heard in connection with that incident was *fluke*.

I could let go of Ellie and swim for the bank in my service-able crawl stroke, and live. Or I could stay with her and drown.

I don't think I really weighed that choice much. Rather, my cold arms wouldn't let go of Ellie's frame. We went under, briefly. I swallowed water, came up coughing, and saw in the sky above me that the sun had gone behind another cloud. The cloud was dark gray and wet-looking, but its torn edges were turned a fiery gold from the sun behind it.

God, that's beautiful.

And then something on the periphery of my vision distracted me. It was a boat. A towboat, actually, but one without a barge before it.

It was all luck for Ellie and me that day: luck that the towboat was stalled in the water where its crew had time to notice us, that its powerful engine wasn't going, kicking up a current that would have made a rescue impossible.

The crew had seen us. They were yelling at us, but my ears were too full of water to hear anything, turning them into the cast of a silent movie, animated, gesturing. One of them was throwing something.

It was a line, with an empty, sealed two-liter soda bottle tied to it to keep the far end from sinking. I kicked up great splashes on the surface as I headed for it, and with great relief got my free hand on the floating bottle.

Something strange had happened to my flesh in the water. Usually, when the weather is frigid and even warm winter clothes aren't enough, the fingertips and toes go numb first, followed by the whole of the hands and feet. But when they pulled me out, I could still feel my fingers, but the skin of my upper arms and chest had lost sensation, so that I barely felt the edge of the deck as many hands pulled me ungracefully onto it. It was then I realized I'd shrugged off my jacket; at least, I wasn't wearing it anymore.

Ellie was already lying on her back next to me, eyes closed. The skin of her face was so white from the cold water that the freckles I had seen as fading now stood out in stark relief. I sat up.

"Is she—"

"She's breathing," the oldest of the crew told me. As if to prove it, the semiconscious Ellie turned to her side and vomited up some river water.

"Jesus," a young Hispanic deckhand said, watching.

"Are you all right, miss?" the old one asked me. His doubtful eyes were a piercing blue, although the rest of him was grizzled and faded. He looked Scandinavian, like a Minnesotan of old, but I heard Texas in his voice.

"I can't feel the surface of my skin," I said, pressing my shaking fingers into my triceps. It was a very disconcerting sensation. I got shakily to my feet, thinking that walking might help.

"I have rye," he said.

In my first-aid training, our instructor had advised against offering or accepting "field medicaments" in time of trauma: alcohol, cigarettes.

But at that moment I wasn't thinking about my training, the fact that I'd mostly quit drinking a few years back, or that the water patrol's boat was on the horizon now, its prow bouncing on the water as it approached. A little rye whiskey sounded eminently reasonable at that moment.

But it was my own weak flesh that saved me from myself. When the riverman put the bottle in my hands, it slipped right through my shaking fingers and shattered on the deck.

chapter 2

Fallout from Ellie Bernhardt's attempted suicide ate up most of my afternoon.

We were both taken to Hennepin County Medical Center. After they took Ellie away, a middle-aged physician's assistant looked at me and said, "I'll have a look at you in the second exam room down the hall."

"Me?" I said, startled. "I'm fine."

"Probably," she said. "But I got to look at your ears and check—"

"My ears feel fine," I said, ignoring the faint but telltale cool heaviness that meant there was water in one of them. At her skeptical look—medical people take challenges to their authority nearly as badly as cops—I said, "Really. I don't do exams."

I meant it. Few things frighten me. Doctors' offices do. "Just point me toward your showers, all right?" I said.

She gave me the skeptical look a moment more, and then said, "Fine, at this time of year I doubt you've even got mild hypothermia." There was a definite fox-and-grapes sound to her dismissal, as though she hadn't really wanted to examine me anyway.

In the doctors' and nurses' locker room, I took a fifteen-minute shower under very hot water and put on a set of nurse's scrubs they'd provided me, a flowered top and sea-green pants. My wet clothes I balled up and put in a plastic bag. When I came out, I peered into the examining rooms, looking for Ellie. A young nurse saw me.

"We already took her over to the crisis unit," she said, meaning the psychiatric ward. "She's going to be admitted overnight, at least. We gave her a chest X ray to see if she inhaled a lot of water, and it hasn't come back yet, but I think she's fine, physically."

Officer Moore had been dispatched back to headquarters to retrieve the change of clothes I kept in my locker there. Detectives don't get bled on and vomited on nearly as much as patrol officers do, but we do spend time at crime scenes that are muddy or still smoldering from a suspicious fire, and I'd figured a change of clothes might come in handy sometime. That day had definitely arrived.

When I got out into the waiting room, Moore wasn't there yet. Ainsley Carter was. She jumped from her seat quickly, but the hug she gave me was very tentative, shoulders only, as though I were sick or injured.

"Do you have children, Detective Pribek?" Ainsley asked me.

"I'm sorry?" I said. I'd expected a question about Ellie's situation. "No, I don't."

"Joe and I have been talking about it," she said. She twisted her solitaire, the way she had yesterday when talking about her husband's unwillingness to have Ellie move in with them. "We want kids, but after this, a child seems like"—she shook her head—"a terrifying responsibility." For the first time I saw the dried trails on her cheeks from the tears I'd heard over the phone.

Officer Moore was coming through the sliding double doors, carrying clothes on a plastic hanger in one hand and boots in her other.

"You're going to be at the same phone number, the same motel, right?" I asked Ainsley quickly. "I'm going to have to touch base with you later."

"I'll be at the same place," Ainsley said. "And...thank you," she added quietly.

I met Officer Moore halfway across the room and cleared my throat. "Thanks," I said awkwardly. I hadn't been a detective very long, and I felt uncomfortable having a patrolwoman run this kind of errand for me.

"Sure," she responded as I took my things from her. "You were Genevieve Brown's partner, weren't you?"

"Yes," I said. "I still am."

"How is she?"

"I don't know," I said. "I haven't talked to her recently."

"Well, a lot of us miss her."

"She's coming back," I told her quickly.

"Really? When?"

I had to backpedal. "She hasn't mentioned a date yet. I just meant, it's compassionate leave. She'll be back."

Moore shook her head. "Sure, it'll take time. It was just awful, what happened."

"Yeah," I said. "It was."

———

Genevieve Brown had been my first friend in the Twin Cities. I wasn't surprised that Officer Moore had known her; Genevieve knew everyone.

Her roots were in the Cities, and she'd spent her entire career with the Sheriff's Department: first on patrol, then in community relations, and now in the detective division. Her real strength was interrogation. Genevieve could talk to anyone.

No criminal ever really feared her: She was short and not imposing, with a low voice soft as suede. She was logical, educated, reasonable; before the perpetrators knew it, they were telling her things they wouldn't have told the guys. A few of the detectives called her the Human Polygraph.

I'd known her from way back in my patrol days, and had learned a lot from her. I paid her back for her shared wisdom by training with her in the gym, pushing her, keeping her at a physical peak as she went into her late thirties. When I lived alone in a cheap studio in Seven Corners, Genevieve used to invite me to dinner from time to time at her place in St. Paul.

It might have been the happiest day of my life when I got my shield and went to work with her. She was a good teacher and mentor, but more than that, she was fun to work with.

We used to get coffee in the skyways, the interconnected second-story warren of shops, restaurants, and newsstands that served the businesspeople of Minneapolis. She'd stop sometimes in one of the glassed-in passageways, usually on a morning when the weather was at least ten degrees below zero. Holding her paper cup of French roast in both hands, she'd look out at the city beyond, where white steam escaped from every building vent and the sunlight bounced with deceptive brightness off every heap of snow and icy surface.

"Today's the day, kiddo," she'd say. "We're going to turn the radio off and drive south until we get to New Orleans. We're going to sit in the sun and eat beignets." Sometimes, for variety, she'd say we were going to San Francisco instead, to drink Irish coffee by the Bay.

But she was never serious. After more than a decade of police work, she still loved the job.

Then her only child, her daughter, Kamareia, was raped and murdered.

I'd known Kamareia since she was a child, from the early days of my career when Genevieve had first begun inviting me home for dinner. Born of Gen's early, interracial marriage to a law student during her college days, Kamareia had been mature beyond her years, generally supportive of her mother's demanding job.

Sometimes, we'd listen to other detectives talking about their teenagers: tales of incomplete homework and teacher conferences and coming home to messy houses. Afterward, Genevieve would say, "God, sometimes I don't know how I got so lucky."

I had been there the terrible evening Genevieve came home to find her daughter badly injured but still alive. I'd ridden to the hospital with Kamareia and held her hand until the ER crew had taken her away. I'd stood around in the waiting room until a doctor came out to say that Kamareia, who wrote poetry and had applied to the early-admission program at Spelman, had died of massive internal bleeding.

Genevieve had come back to work two weeks after Kamareia's death.

"I need to be working," she'd told me, the Sunday night that she'd called me and told me she'd be at work the following day. "Please make everybody understand."

The next morning Genevieve had turned up fifteen minutes early, eyes reddened but neatly dressed, with a clean herbal scent clinging to her damp hair, ready to work. And she'd done okay, then and in the weeks to come.

It seemed to help that there'd been an arrest made right away: a housepainter working on a place in Genevieve's St. Paul neighborhood. Kamareia herself had identified him as her attacker. While he was in the system, and Ramsey County prosecutors built their case, Genevieve was all right. She buried herself in work, concentrated on the job like a white-knuckle passenger on a rough flight or an alcoholic drying out with nothing but willpower.

Then the case was dismissed on a technicality, and Genevieve lost her way.

I carried her for a month. She lost weight and came in with violet shadows under her eyes testifying to her sleepless nights. She couldn't concentrate at work. Questioning witnesses and suspects, she could only ask the most basic questions. Her powers of observation were worse than those of the most oblivious civilian. She didn't make even the simplest logical connections.

I couldn't bring myself to tell her to hang it up, and in the end, I didn't have to. Genevieve was just together enough to realize she wasn't doing any good to the department, and asked for an indefinite leave of absence. She left the Cities and went south, to stay with her younger sister and brother-in-law at a farmhouse just south of Mankato.

When had I last called Genevieve? I tried to remember as I drove back downtown. The thought caused me a pang of guilt and I set it aside.

Back at the station, I wrote up a report of the morning's events, trying to make my leap into the water sound like rational behavior, something any detective would have done. Had I "pursued" Ellie into the river? That sounded weird. I backspaced and tried *followed* instead. Writing was my least favorite part of the job.

"Pribek!" I looked up to see Det. John Vang, my sometime partner in Genevieve's absence. "I heard something pretty strange about you this morning."

Vang was a year younger than me, only recently promoted from patrol. Technically, I was training him, a situation I didn't feel entirely comfortable with. It didn't seem so long ago to me that I was trailing behind Genevieve, letting her take the lead on investigations....I glanced toward her desk. It wasn't exactly cleaned out, but Vang used it now.

He had put up two framed photographs on her desktop. One was a picture of his wife and nine-month-old baby, a close shot with the infant in arms; the second showed just the baby girl at a playground. She was in a kind of swing, a sling that held her at an angle with her head and chest forward, her arms waving in the air. I was sure that she felt she was flying when that picture was snapped.

One day, while Vang had been out, I had tipped the photo so I could see it from my desk. When the miseries of the Ellie Bernhardts of the world piled up on my desk, I liked to look up and see the flying-baby photo.

"If what you heard was about me and the river, it was true," I said.

"You're kidding."

"I didn't say it was smart, just that it was true."

I moved my hand, self-consciously, to my hair. At the hospital I'd pulled it back in a ponytail that I'd doubled back up onto itself, so that it hung in a heavy but not-very-long loop on my neck. Touching it now, my hair felt not quite dry: It wasn't damp but, rather, cool to the touch.

After my report was finished, it was time to request a new pager. The old one had been in my jacket, and my jacket was now in the river. I was grateful that my billfold and my cell phone had been elsewhere during the morning's insanity.

Before I could go on that errand, my phone rang. It was Jane O'Malley, a Hennepin County prosecutor.

"Come on up," she said. "The testimony's been going faster than we expected. We're probably going to get to you today."

O'Malley was prosecuting a case that told a common, sad story: a young person with an ex-boyfriend who just couldn't let go. But this was an old story with a twist: The missing person had been a young man. He'd left the Gay 90s, a nightspot popular with both gays and straight people, by himself and sober after dancing with friends. That was the last anyone had ever seen him.

Genevieve and I had investigated the case. Later, as the ex-boyfriend's evasions and quasi-alibis grew increasingly thin, we'd been joined by a detective from Minneapolis Homicide. We never found the victim or his body, just a lot of his blood and one of his earrings in the trunk of the car his ex had reported stolen the following day and not disposed of very well.

As I crossed the atrium of the Hennepin County Government Center to the elevators, a familiar voice hailed me.

"Detective Pribek!"

Christian Kilander fell into step beside me. He was a Hennepin County prosecutor, imposingly tall and fiercely competitive both in the courtroom and on the basketball courts where I sometimes went up against him in pickup games.

If Genevieve's voice was suede, his was something lighter

yet, like chamois. And nearly always arch, a quality that made his everyday speech sound teasing and flirtatious and his cross-examinations sound ironic and disbelieving.

Basically, I liked Kilander, but an encounter with him was never to be taken lightly.

"It's nice to see you on dry land," he said. "As usual, your innovative policing techniques leave us all in awe."

"All?" I said, lengthening my stride to match his. "I only see one of you. Do you have fleas?"

He laughed immediately and generously, defusing the joke. "How is the little girl?" he asked as we came to the elevator bank.

"She's recovering," I said. A pair of double doors slid open to our left and we followed a pair of clerks into the car. As we did, I reflected that I'd probably heard the last of Ellie Bernhardt. I had done what I could for her; the rest of her troubles would be someone else's to help her with, not mine. Whether those efforts were successful or not, I'd probably never know. That was the reality of being a cop. Those officers who didn't like it quit to get degrees in social work.

The clerks got off the elevator at the fifth floor. I rubbed my left ear.

"You have water in your ear, don't you?" Kilander said as we began ascending again.

"Yes," I admitted. Even though I knew it was a harmless condition, I wasn't used to it. The slight crackling of water in that ear was disconcerting.

The elevator came to a halt at my floor, and in the brief lapse between the car's full stop and the opening of the door, Kilander gave me a thoughtful look from his six-foot-five height.

Then he said, "You're a wide-open girl, Detective Pribek. You surely are."

"Thanks," I said noncommittally as the door slid open, not sure that it was the answer that was called for. A few years ago I would have bristled at being called a girl and tried in vain to think of a cutting response, which would have come to me about fifteen minutes after Kilander and I parted ways. But I was no longer an insecure rookie, and Kilander had never been a chauvinist, no matter how he appeared at first glance.

The hallway was empty, and I walked slowly to the doors of the courtroom. I settled my shoulder bag, and then myself, onto a bench. I was to wait for O'Malley to come out and get me. I knew the drill.

Only once had I been called to testify in a criminal case in a capacity other than my official one, and that hadn't been here in Minneapolis. It had been in St. Paul, at the pretrial hearing of Royce Stewart, accused killer of Kamareia Brown.

It was to me that Kamareia had identified him as her attacker, in the back of the ambulance.

The afternoon she'd died, Kamareia had been home alone. But she'd actually been attacked in the house of some neighbors who had been redoing their interiors. The two painters working there had finished around four in the afternoon, but only one of them was alibied for the time after that.

The other one was Stewart, a 25-year-old laborer from downstate. His car's license plate reflected his nickname, SHORTY. He wasn't that short, actually, about five-nine, with a wiry frame and a shaggy blond ponytail. But Kamareia had called him by his nickname, appropriate or not. She'd never even known his name; she'd only seen the license plate on the car that he drove.

Genevieve had told me, a week before Kamareia's death, that Kam had noticed "Shorty" looking at her, and that it gave her a creepy feeling.

No one ever figured out how he got her to come over to the neighbors' property.

Stewart's juvenile record was sealed, and since I was not an official part of the investigation and prosecution, I never got to see it. As an adult, he'd been caught furnishing alcohol to minors and exposing himself to teenage girls near a high school. Shorty, by all accounts, liked young girls.

Jackie Kowalski, the public defender who'd represented Stewart, told me later how Stewart had disclosed to her that he was making support payments for a child by a "black chick I only did one time."

Stewart didn't believe the baby was his. He had believed that the paternity test results were faked by sympathetic hospital staffers, who naturally took the side of a young, unmarried mother against a man. " 'Cause you know, guys don't have any rights anymore," Shorty had explained.

He'd told Kowalski this story more than once, and she'd realized he felt it was part of his defense. The fact that he was making the support payments, for a half-black child, no less, proved that he was a good guy who wouldn't have hurt Kamareia, who was biracial.

Shorty had also suggested to his lawyer that she present the theory that a black man had killed Kamareia with the express plan in mind of having a white guy take the fall for it.

If only Shorty had taken the stand, he would have repulsed any jury ever impaneled and all but convicted himself.

But the case never got to a jury, and that was my fault.

I was on the stand at the Ramsey County Government Center, during a pretrial hearing. Stewart's public defender had asked for the case to be thrown out, as Mark Urban, the Ramsey County prosecutor, had predicted she would.

Urban sat at the table nearest the empty jury box, but it wasn't him my eyes went to. Christian Kilander was also there, seated in the spectators' benches. He must have taken the morning off to see me testify. It surprised me, though perhaps it shouldn't have. Kamareia's death caused quite a stir among the many people who knew and liked Genevieve.

Kilander acknowledged my gaze with the slightest of nods, which I couldn't return, and his face was unusually serious.

Jackie Kowalski stood in front of me, a slight young woman fresh out of U of M Law School, with light brown hair and an inexpensive catalog suit.

I more or less knew—Urban had warned me—what she was going to ask me, but it didn't make things any easier.

"Detective Pribek—can I call you Ms. Pribek? Since you aren't involved in this case as an officer of the law."

"You can."

"Ms. Pribek, you were at the house shortly after the crime, as you've said. And you rode in the ambulance with Miss Brown, correct?"

"Yes."

"Why you and not her mother?"

"Genevieve was being treated for shock at the scene. She was still distraught when they were taking Kamareia away. I felt someone should go with her who wasn't so upset that it would increase Kamareia's distress."

"I see. How did it come about that she identified her assailant? Did you ask her?"

"No, she volunteered the information."

"What did she say?"

"She said, 'It was Shorty. The guy who was always watching me.' "

"And you took this to mean Mr. Stewart?"

"Yes. It was his nickname."

Jackie Kowalski paused. Had we been at trial, before a jury, she most likely would have pursued the matter, trying to poke holes in Kamareia's tenuous identification-by-nickname. But there was no jury here, only the judge who Kowalski was asking to dismiss the charges. She had a legal point to make, and so she moved on.

"What else did she tell you about the assault?"

"She had gone on to say she should have been more careful, or something to that effect. And I said, 'It's okay, you couldn't have known.' "

"Was that the extent of your discussion of the attack?" She knew it was. She'd read the deposition.

"Yes."

"So you never asked her a question."

"No."

"Did you come to the scene as an officer of the law?"

"I'm always an officer of the law."

"I recognize that," Kowalski said. "But you were at your partner's home socially, weren't you?"

"Yes."

"The two of you see a lot of each other outside of work, and consider yourselves friends?"

"Yes."

"And you saw a lot of Kamareia Brown in this capacity, as a friend of her mother?"

"Yes."

"And so, when Genevieve Brown was too distraught to go along to the hospital with her daughter, you went in her place because you were 'composed.' That indicates to me that your purpose was to keep Kamareia Brown calm, to comfort her. Would you agree?"

"My primary purpose was to make sure Kamareia was not alone at that time."

I wasn't going to make it easy for her.

"Did you ever remind her of your status as an officer of the law?"

"Kamareia grew up around—"

"Please answer the questions I put to you."

"No, I didn't."

Kowalski paused, signaling a change in direction. "Ms. Pribek, the ambulance attendant who was in the back with you and Miss Brown has said in her deposition that you made efforts to comfort Miss Brown. In fact, she said that she heard you say 'You'll be all right' twice. Is that true?"

This was the question all the others had been leading up to.

"I don't remember if I said it twice."

"But you know that you said, at least once, 'You'll be all right.' "

I met Kilander's eyes and saw him seeing the case fall apart. He knew what the question meant.

"Yes."

Genevieve, a potential witness, had been barred from attending this hearing, and at the moment I was grateful my partner was not among the spectators.

"And in general you made comforting statements to Miss Brown, leading her to believe she would survive her injuries."

"I don't feel I was leading her to believe anything."

Kowalski raised her eyebrows. "Could you explain, then, what other understanding she could have taken from the statement 'You'll be all right'?"

"Objection," Urban said. "Counsel is asking the witness to speculate."

"I'll withdraw it," Kowalski said. "Ms. Pribek, did you say anything to Miss Brown that would indicate to her that her injuries were fatal?"

Genevieve, I'm so sorry. I was trying to do the right thing.

"No, I didn't."

Dying declarations are notoriously tricky. They rely on the understanding that someone who knows she is dying has no reason to lie. For this reason, the paramount issue in court tends to be whether the dying person in fact believed he or she was dying.

On the stand, Kowalski had made it clear to the judge that Kamareia did not see me as a criminal investigator, hence Kowalski's insistence on calling me "Ms. Pribek," instead of using my rank. More importantly, Kowalski established that I had led Kamareia to believe she would not die of her wounds.

Kilander had told me about dying declarations once, long before Kamareia's death. It wasn't as if I'd never heard about the legal aspects of point-of-death accusations; they simply had not crossed my mind, not even remotely, that day when I'd been watching a young woman die.

Jackie Kowalski was right about one thing—I had gotten into that ambulance as a friend. I had tried to be a good friend to Kamareia, to do what her mother would have done, to comfort and reassure her. All these things compromised Kamareia's accusation, and in doing so jeopardized a case that was shaky in its other aspects.

Despite the rape, there had been no semen recovered, an occurrence more common than many people realized. Maybe Shorty wore a condom, maybe he simply didn't ejaculate. It was an academic point to me. I considered Kamareia's murder a hate crime in its simplest definition: the result of hatred. As far as I could see, Stewart had raped Kamareia because it was just another way of beating her.

But the end result was that there was no DNA to recover. Other hair and fiber evidence wasn't useful, because Stewart had been all over the house, working, for two weeks. And Kamareia's fingernail scrapings yielded nothing useful. She'd clearly been too stunned, attacked too abruptly, to put up a good fight.

The whole case revolved around Kamareia's point-of-death accusation. When the judge threw out Kamareia's statement, the rest of the case collapsed like a house of cards. The judge found insufficient grounds to go to trial, and the worst that happened to Royce Stewart in the Cities was that he lost his driver's license in an unrelated DWI.

"Sarah?"

The courtroom door had swung open almost soundlessly. Jane O'Malley was looking at me. "Are you ready?"

"Yes," I said.

chapter **3**

While O'Malley had said the people's testimony had been moving faster than expected that day, it took time for me to recount my part of the story. It was after five when I returned. Vang was still at his desk, and once again on the phone. He must have been on hold, because he slid the lower end of the receiver away from his mouth and said, "Your husband was here, looking for you."

"Shiloh was here?" I repeated, stupidly. "Is he—"

But Vang had snapped his attention back to his phone conversation.

"Hello, Commander Erickson, this is—"

I tuned him out. Shiloh had obviously been and gone, and even though my day was over and I'd be home soon, I was oddly disappointed at having missed him. Up until two weeks ago, Shiloh had been a detective with the Minneapolis Police

Department. While we hadn't technically worked together, our jobs used to overlap at times. Now I never ran into him downtown anymore, and I missed it.

It was something I'd have to get used to. Shiloh was leaving next week for his FBI training at Quantico, which would last for four months.

I glanced down, making one last check for messages. There were none, so I set the phone to go to voice mail on one ring and picked up my bag. I gave Vang a little finger wave on my way out, which he acknowledged with a nod.

My 1970 Nova was the first car I'd ever bought. Some of the guys at work winced to see it; I knew they were imagining the restoration work they'd do on it, if it were theirs. Its gunmetal gray paint had faded without the regular waxing a car aficionado would have given it, and thin cracks ran through the dashboard. Yet it was surprisingly reliable, and I was perversely attached to it. Every winter I imagined trading it in for something more surefooted on the snow and ice, an SUV or 4WD truck like many of my fellow officers drove. But now it was fall again—October—and I still hadn't given serious consideration to placing an ad.

I didn't go straight home. The Nova's fuel gauge needle had slipped below the quarter-tank mark, and I filled it at the cheapest gas station I knew, then took my boots to a repair shop. They were going to need professional attention if they were going to survive their unexpected soaking in the Mississippi. My errands cost me more than a half hour before I turned onto the quiet street in Northeast Minneapolis where Shiloh and I lived.

Nordeast, as locals still sometimes called it, used to be a

heavily Eastern European part of town; it had grown more integrated through the years. Bisected by the railroad, it was a place of weather-beaten old houses with big screened porches, light industrial businesses, and corner bars whose signs advertised meat raffles and pulltabs. I'd immediately liked it here, liked Shiloh's old house with the rumbling trains that ran behind the narrow backyard and the dreamy, undersea quality it had in the summer from the dappling of sun and shade created by the overhanging elms. But I also knew that in this neighborhood Shiloh had taken a switchblade knife away from an 11-year-old kid, and last Halloween someone had scrawled antipolice slurs in red chalk on our driveway. It was a city neighborhood, no mistake.

Old Mrs. Muzio, our next-door neighbor, was coming out of her house with her old wolfhound-mix dog, Snoopy. I considered waving, but it was often necessary to stand right in front of Nedda Muzio to get her attention, so instead I cruised past her place to ours. Shiloh's old Pontiac Catalina was absent from the driveway, so I pulled in to occupy that place.

Perhaps he'd taken his car to the shop. Like the Nova, it was a first car, never replaced. More out of laziness than sentimentality, Shiloh maintained. It was a 1968 model and heir to all the problems older cars had—most recently, the timing was off. From time to time Shiloh mentioned selling it and buying something more reliable, but he hadn't yet.

I went in through the back of the house. The kitchen door didn't, technically, open directly onto the kitchen but onto an entryway with a perennially dirty linoleum floor and a washer and dryer on the right. I tossed my plastic bag onto the surface of the dryer and decided to wash my clothes then and there.

I had thrown them into the drum of the washing machine,

and was just about to pour in a half measure of detergent when I saw someone watching me, an outline against the white of the opposite wall.

Startled, I jumped; my gun hand in particular leapt into the air, spilling some of the laundry powder from the cup I held. Then I realized who it was and turned to face Shiloh directly.

"Holy shit," I said. "Don't sneak up on me like that." I took a steadying breath. "I thought you weren't home, your car—"

I broke off, unnerved suddenly.

Although he was over six feet tall, my husband had never been the most intimidating physical presence among the cops he'd worked with; he had a long and lean frame. His features helped to make up for that. Shiloh had a face I thought of as Eurasian, with pale skin but strong and sharp bones. Most unusual were his eyes: they had a slight epicanthic fold, as if generations ago his forebears had lived on the steppes. The eyes made him hard to read. But right now I thought I saw disapproval in them.

"What's wrong?" I said.

Shiloh shook his head slowly, definitely a rebuke. "You dumb shit," he said quietly.

"What are you talking about?" I said, but he just kept giving me his level, reproving look.

Shiloh and I had never worked any cases together, so I'd never got a chance to see his interrogation technique. I thought I might be seeing it now.

"Do you know how many people die in that river every year?" he asked finally.

"Oh," I said. "Vang told you?" My voice was a little high. The anger of people who rarely get angry is deeply unnerving. "I'm fine," I said.

"What were you thinking?" he said.

"You would have done the same thing," I said.

He didn't deny it. "I didn't first learn to swim at age twenty-three."

"I was twenty-two," I said.

"That's not the point."

I turned my back on him and swept the spilled laundry powder into the machine. Cranked the dial over to the warm-water setting, heard the muffled hiss as the cycle started.

Shiloh came up behind me and laid his hands on my hips. "I almost had a heart attack when Vang told me," he said softly.

Forgiven, I felt a relieved, retroactive urge to apologize. Instead, I said, "I could've used you out there today." He'd had experience with suicidal people; more than experience, a good track record. "She was my first jumper."

I'd given him an opening to say, *And nearly your last,* but he seemed to have forgotten the issue. He leaned closer to my ear and said instead, "I can smell the river in your hair." Then he lifted the half ponytail up and kissed the nape of my neck.

I knew what that gesture meant.

In our bedroom afterward, Shiloh was so quiet I thought for a moment he'd fallen asleep. I lifted my head off his chest and looked at his face; his eyes were closed.

Then he stroked my back with one hand, still not opening his eyes. If I hadn't known him better I would have thought that was the way he took everything: languid and easy.

I knew better. I'd been observing Mike Shiloh for years, at both long and close range. Sometimes I thought that Shiloh deliberately took the course of most resistance, refusing to ever take the easy road.

Shiloh's career had taken a more circuitous path than mine. When I'd met him, he'd been an undercover narcotics officer. Later, he'd applied for special training as a hostage negotiator. He wasn't chosen for negotiation training. Instead, he'd been given an assignment he didn't ask for or want, a role adjunct to Homicide. Shiloh became a cold-case detective.

Cold-case reviewers are something of a luxury. In good economic times, with budget surpluses and falling homicide rates, many metro police departments could afford to assign detectives to analyze and reinvestigate old unsolved cases, usually homicides. In many ways it was an ideal job for Shiloh, who liked intractable intellectual puzzles. He understood, however, that his assignment to cold-case, noticeably lacking a partner, was a thinly veiled criticism.

Shiloh was seventeen when he left his Utah home without finishing high school. He'd been on a logging crew in Montana when he did his first law-enforcement work as part of a sheriff's search-and-rescue unit.

His career had taken him across the Midwest. From patrol work, he'd gotten into undercover narcotics. Across the upper Plains and Midwest, he'd worked on narcotics squads that always needed an unrecognizable new face to come in and make buys. In cities like Gary, Indiana, and Madison, Wisconsin, he'd often worked alone. Sometimes his colleagues were decent. Other times they were bigoted, or trigger-happy cowboys. His superiors weren't always better.

By the time he arrived in Minneapolis to put down semi-permanent roots and get a degree in psychology, Shiloh was a loner who'd learned to trust his own instincts and opinions over those of others.

Underneath all that, Shiloh was a preacher's son. In the

heart of Utah's Mormon country, Shiloh's father had headed a small nondenominational church whose stern creed divided the world into saved and unsaved. And while Shiloh himself hadn't been inside a church on Sunday morning in perhaps a decade, I thought some of the rigid moralism of his youth lived on inside him, but now fused to a set of attitudes more politically liberal than the ones most cops held.

In the close and collegial quarters of a metro police department, Shiloh's opinions didn't win him a lot of friends. He'd had dustups with prosecutors and supervising detectives whose ideas and tactics he disagreed with. His sympathies raised eyebrows: he was compassionate toward drug users and prostitutes that his peers had no use for, and terse and unfriendly with white-collar informants that his superiors valued. An anonymous wit had once sent ACLU literature to him at work, as if it were a shameful form of pornography.

I'd argued with him more than once myself, getting angry and defensive when he pressed me on cop values and virtues I didn't like to question. Those kinds of debates between us were never rancorous, but if we had worked in the same department, it was unlikely we would have been assigned as partners, much less predicted to get married.

"Nobody 'gets' you and Shiloh," Genevieve had said once. "When I first met you, you said 'disorientated' instead of 'disoriented.' And Shiloh . . ." She'd paused for thought. "Shiloh once got in an argument with another detective who'd been feeding important information to a TV reporter—I think there was some suspicion this guy was sleeping with her. Anyway, Shiloh called him a 'goddamned quisling.' After the two of them left, the rest of us who'd overheard the fight all went to the dictionary to find out what a 'quisling' was. We all thought it was something dirty." Genevieve laughed. "Turned out, it means a traitor."

"That's Shiloh for you," I'd said, "getting in someone's face and talking over his head at the same time."

Nobody could fault the work he did, though. There were those in the department who appreciated the intelligence and the work ethic he brought to the job. But too many others thought it was time for Mike Shiloh to be slapped down, and he was.

Cold-case work provides few opportunities to shine. There's lots of fruitless rereading and reinterviewing. Breaks in cases more than a year old tend only to come when a witness comes forward years, even decades, later, after getting religion or being nagged by conscience.

Shiloh's career was flatlining at the same time that Genevieve and I were clearing cases at a remarkable rate. "It's luck," I told Shiloh then. "It'll turn."

And it had. He'd caught Annelise Eliot, a murderer and fugitive for more than a decade, and an FBI agent had suggested he fill out their application.

Our own relationship had taken a circuitous course toward marriage, over nearly five years' time. We certainly weren't an obvious match, as Genevieve had pointed out, and we'd seen each other, broken up, reconciled, and finally moved in together before marrying only recently. But through it all there was a certain inevitability that drew me to Shiloh. I'd had a hard time explaining it even to Genevieve, who understood the relationship between Shiloh and me better than anyone.

I'd told her early on that I was seeing him, but *told her* wasn't quite the phrase for it; it had been a slip of the tongue.

Back in the days when I was still on patrol, Genevieve was

always on the lookout for a way to help me up the food chain. One evening, when I'd been a guest in her St. Paul home, she'd reflected on one such opportunity.

"The head of the interagency narcotics squad thinks a lot of you," she'd told me. She was a short woman, with an apron partially covering the old sweater and jeans she'd changed into to cook. Although she was chopping tomatoes and olives for a pasta dish, she frequently glanced over to where I was sitting at her counter, her hazel eyes lively with thought and speculation. She was big on eye contact; a conversation without it was, for her, like driving without headlights.

"Have you ever thought about that kind of work?" she asked, looking my way. "Radich's got two veteran guys, Nelson and Shiloh, who are probably going to want to transfer out someday."

"Shiloh hasn't said anything about it," I'd said thoughtlessly, and then said to myself, *Oh, hell.*

"Why would Shiloh have mentioned it to you?" she'd said. I'd had a very brief assignment with the narcotics squad, but that was long over, and Gen knew it.

Then she'd understood. "Oh, my God. You've got to be kidding me."

"We've been keeping it under wraps at work," I'd said tersely, embarrassed at my slip.

"We're talking about the same guy, right?" she'd said, teasing me. "Six-two, reddish-brown hair, never says much of anything, regularly hands your ass to you on the basketball court?"

"That's not true," I said.

"Yes, it is, Sarah. You can't admit you're not good enough to guard him."

"No, about him not saying much of anything," I'd said. "He does. He does to me."

Her hazel eyes had widened, and a half-cooked tomato slid languidly, unnoticed, off the spatula she was holding. She believed me.

"I'll be damned," she said. "I would never in a hundred years have connected the two of you. You seem so different. Well, on the surface. I guess I don't know Shiloh that well." She paused, considering. "So what's he really like?"

My first impulse was to make a joke of it, saying, *You mean in bed?* But I couldn't, and instead I spoke without premeditation. "Shiloh is a deep river," I'd said.

It hadn't been an adequate summary. But what I couldn't quite explain to Genevieve was that I needed and wanted Shiloh not in spite of the fact that we were so different but because of it. Shiloh wasn't like me, and he wasn't like the men I'd usually felt comfortable with.

He didn't need to be holding my hand or touching me constantly when we were together. He didn't need me to share all his interests or like the same things he did. And from early on I'd seen that I'd have to stretch myself to keep up with the things he knew and the way he thought.

If I'd met him even a year earlier in my life, those things probably would have been sufficient to scare me off. But instead, I saw in Shiloh the possibility for a kinship based on something much deeper than common interests, something that made those old criteria seem irrelevant, even trite. There were depths in him that unnerved and excited me, made me feel like someone raised on a prairie seeing the ocean for the first time. After I'd met him, the kind of man I'd previously gone out with, that guy with the sidewall haircut and 4WD vehicle, seemed a little less dimensional, a little less attractive, to me.

Now Shiloh stirred and slipped out from under the arm I'd thrown over his chest. I watched as he went to the chest of drawers and dug out a pair of nail clippers.

"You're going to pare your fingernails? You already got your hair cut today, didn't you?" I asked, a little accusingly. He knew I missed the longish hair he'd had when I'd first met him. When he kept it short, the sun didn't have a chance to bring out the lighter russet tones in its dark-auburn color.

He ignored the gentle criticism. "No, I'm going to clip *your* nails," he said, settling on the edge of the bed and picking up one of my hands.

I pulled it away. "Why?"

"Because," he said, "you scratched me. I don't know if they have group showers at Quantico, but I don't want to turn up there with red marks on my back." He reclaimed my hand.

"My nails aren't that long."

"No, but they're ragged. Because you bite them."

"I don't anymore," I lied. When I felt the sides of the clipper against the first fingernail, my hand twitched involuntarily.

Shiloh glanced at my face. "Do you trust me to do this?"

"Yes," I said, not lying this time.

There was a metallic click as the clippers bit through my index fingernail; Shiloh released that finger and moved on to the next. A dissociative feeling ran through my body, a physical memory, and I closed my eyes to isolate it. Of course: In Shiloh's hands I felt my mother's touch. She'd been the only person ever to do this for me, back when I was a child. Even then ovarian cancer had been spreading through her insides like blackdamp through a mine.

Shiloh brushed parings from the Indian blanket of our bed onto the floor. I opened my eyes again. "All done," he said mildly.

"Thanks," I said. "I guess." I got off the bed and went to hunt for clothes. "We should start thinking about dinner," I said, pulling a T-shirt over my head.

Shiloh rolled onto his side and watched me get dressed. "Don't get too hungry," he said. "I don't want to start a panic, but the kitchen shelves were looking very bare the last I checked."

"No shit?" I said. "Well, this is bad."

I went out into the kitchen. Outside the window, I saw, twilight was deepening. When Shiloh came out, I was sitting on my heels, checking out the contents of the refrigerator. He'd been right: they weren't promising.

"I could walk over to Ibrahim's," I said.

"Ibrahim's" was our name for a Conoco gas station and mini-mart in the neighborhood. Despite the fact that there were plenty of full-service grocery stores in Minneapolis that were open late, if not all night, Ibrahim's seemed irresistibly convenient to us when we needed milk or wanted coffee at an odd hour. We went there often enough that Shiloh had once remarked that it was too bad we hadn't had a traditional wedding; we could have had the reception catered by Conoco.

"Maybe," Shiloh said. He sounded unenthusiastic about the kind of food available in the freezer section of a mini-mart.

"Or," I said thoughtfully, "we've got those slivered almonds and olives and some rice. If we went out and got some tomatoes and lemon—"

"And chicken, I know. I see where this is going," Shiloh interrupted.

Neither of us would ever put cooking very high on our list of skills, but Shiloh was better than I was. Of the several staple recipes that he made from memory, my favorite was a Basque-style chicken. Shiloh fixed it every second or third week, but he seemed to wait for me to ask him for it. I thought that he liked my prodding, liked it that I enjoyed his cooking so much, and that was why I suspected his current reluctance wasn't genuine. I wheedled a little more.

"I know it's kind of labor-intensive, with the prep work," I said.

As I'd thought, Shiloh shook his head negligently. "No, I'll do it. If you're willing to drive to the store and pick up what we need."

"I don't mind," I said, already heading back to the bedroom for my shoes. His words, though, reminded me of something. "Hey, where is your car, anyway?"

"Oh, yeah," he said from the kitchen. I could hear him taking a can of Coke from the refrigerator, fixing himself a drink. "I sold it."

"Really?" I was startled. "That was kind of sudden," I said. Despite his threats to get rid of it, Shiloh had seen his car through so many mechanical ailments that the news of its sale took me by surprise. I picked up my running shoes and a pair of socks and walked back to the kitchen doorway, where I sat on the floor to put them on.

"I didn't trust it to get me all the way to Virginia," Shiloh explained. "I'm just going to fly instead. I'll worry about a new car later, after I'm finished at Quantico."

"You've got some time left before you leave," I reminded him, lacing up my shoes. "You could buy a new car in that time."

"I've got a week," he said, peeling the papery husk off a clove of garlic. "I could buy a car in that time, but I can also live that long without one."

"I'd go nuts," I said, getting to my feet. "It's not that I mind walking, but just knowing I didn't have a car if I needed one, that'd bother me."

"I know what you mean," Shiloh said. "A car is a lot more than transportation. It's an investment, an office, a locker, a weapon."

"A weapon?" I said doubtfully.

"If people really thought about the physics of driving, the forces they control, some of them would be afraid to leave the driveway. You've seen the accident scenes," he said, rounding up stray pieces of chopped garlic with the flat of the knife.

"Yeah," I said. "Too many." Then another thought hit me. "When you were downtown, were you looking for a ride home?"

"Yes," he said. "I had to drive the car out to the guys who bought it, then I went to find you. But Vang said you were in court."

"You should have waited," I said. "That was a long walk."

"A couple of miles. Not so long." Then he said, "Have you heard from Genevieve?"

The question seemed to come out of nowhere. I picked up his glass of Coke and took refuge in a sip of it before answering. "No," I said. "She never calls me. And when I call her, she's nearly monosyllabic. I don't know if that's better or worse than how she was before. For a while, all she wanted to do was talk about Royce Stewart."

Genevieve lived an hour north of where her daughter's murderer had gone to ground in his hometown of Blue Earth. But she knew sheriff's deputies down there, and some of them were apparently willing to give her information on Shorty's whereabouts and activities. Genevieve had told me that he was working construction again by day. At night he was a barfly. Even though his driver's license had been revoked, and he lived outside of town, Shorty would drink in his favorite bar rather than at home. He could often be seen, Gen's sources said, walking home along the county highway late at night. No one had ever caught him driving without a license, and he was apparently a well-mannered enough drinker that he hadn't had any arrests for disorderly conduct or the like.

"I remember," Shiloh said. "You told me."

"She's stopped talking about him. I don't know if that means she's stopped thinking about him," I said. "I wish she'd come back to work. She needs to be busy."

"Go see her," Shiloh said.

"You think?" I said idly.

"Well, you said you were thinking about it."

And I had mentioned it to him. How long ago had that been? Weeks, I realized, and in the meantime I hadn't acted on the idea. I felt ashamed. I'd been busy, of course. That was the classic excuse, and cops used it as often as CEOs. *I'm busy, my job is demanding, people depend on me.* Then you realize that the needs of strangers have become more important to you than the needs of the people you see every day.

"You've got a couple of personal days coming up," Shiloh added.

I was warming to the idea. "Yeah, I'd kind of like that. When exactly did you think we should go down?"

"Not me. Just you." He was at the refrigerator, turned away from me, so that I couldn't see his face.

"Are you serious?" I was perplexed. "I asked for those days off to spend with you, before you leave for Virginia."

"I know that," Shiloh said, patiently, turning to face me again. "And we'll have time together. Mankato's not far away. You could just go overnight."

"Why don't you want to come along?"

Shiloh shook his head. "I've got things to do up here, before I leave. Besides, asking Genevieve's sister to put up one guest is one thing, two is something else. I'd be in the way."

"No, you wouldn't," I said. "You've known Genevieve longer than I have. You were a pallbearer at Kamareia's funeral, for Christ's sake."

"I know that," Shiloh said. A quick flash of pain registered behind his eyes, and I regretted bringing it up.

"I'm trying to say," I put in quickly, "that if you can't come with me, I'll put off the visit until after you leave for Quantico. I'll have plenty of time to visit Genevieve while you're in Virginia."

Shiloh looked at me in silence. It was a look that made me feel self-conscious, the way I had when I was trying to explain my jump from the railroad bridge.

"You're her partner," he said. "She needs you, Sarah. She's in a bad way."

"I know," I said, slowly. "I'll think about it."

Shiloh wasn't trying to shame me, I thought, watching him take a jar of olives from the refrigerator. He was just being Shiloh. Direct, on the verge of blunt.

"I don't want to hurry you, but I'm going to need that chicken and the other things fairly soon," he reminded me. Then he gave me an olive, wet from the jar. He knew I liked them.

Out on the street, as I drove toward the grocery store, the first electric light was shining from the windows of Northeast's tall, pale houses. They looked warm and inviting, and made me think of winter and the holiday season coming.

I wondered how we'd celebrate them this year.

"No, I'm listening," Genevieve said. "Elijah in the wilderness. Go ahead."

Genevieve's house in St. Paul had a big kitchen, with lots of room for several people to work, and plenty of tools for a serious cook. She lived only with Kamareia, which was why Shiloh and I had come over to make Christmas dinner with them.

While a roast crusted with a thick rub of herbs baked in Genevieve's old, speckled roasting pan in the oven, Shiloh was working on garlic mashed potatoes, and Genevieve was slicing red peppers and broccoli to be cooked at the last minute. I, the least talented in the kitchen, had been assigned to peel and quarter the gold-skinned potatoes, so my work was done. Kamareia, who had made a cheesecake in advance, had been likewise excused from further duty, and was now absorbed in a book in the living room.

Shiloh had mentioned to Genevieve that he had a theory of investigative work based on the Old Testament story of Elijah in the wilderness.

"Explain, please," Genevieve urged, cupping a glass of eggnog in one hand. It was nonalcoholic; the flush in her cheeks was kitchen heat, not liquor.

"Okay," Shiloh said, with the temporizing tone of someone mentally rounding up the elements of a story that he knows well but hasn't told in a while. "Elijah went out

to wait for God to speak to him," he began. "As he waited, there was a strong wind, and God was not in the wind. And there was an earthquake, and God was not in the earthquake. And there was a fire, and God was not in the fire. And then there was a still, small voice."

"And the still, small voice was God speaking," a soft voice said from behind us.

None of us had heard Kamareia approach, and we all looked toward the archway leading into the kitchen, where she stood watching us with her lambent hazel eyes.

Kamareia was taller than her mother, and slender where Genevieve had the roundness of muscle. In a heather-gray leotard and faded jeans—we'd all agreed we weren't going to dress for this dinner—and with her dozens of cornrows pulled back and tied at the nape of her neck, Kamareia looked more like a dancer than an aspiring writer.

"Exactly," Shiloh said, acknowledging her erudition.

Kamareia was generally confident and talkative around her mother and me. When Shiloh was with us, she was much quieter, although I noticed she tended to follow him with her gaze.

"And the point is?" Genevieve asked Shiloh.

"The point is"—Shiloh threw a small handful of garlic into the olive oil heating in a saucepan—"that a major crime investigation is kind of like a circus sometimes."

"A circus?" Genevieve repeated lightly. "Wasn't Elijah in a forest? I love freshly mixed metaphors."

"Well, actually, Elijah was on a mountain," Shiloh said. "But what I mean is, a major investigation is frenetic and distracting. In the middle of it all, you've got to ignore the fire and the whirlwind and listen for a still, small voice."

"You should have been born Catholic, Shiloh," Genevieve

said. *"You could have been a Jesuit. I've never met anyone who can quote the Bible like you."*

"Even the Devil can quote Scripture to his purpose," Kamareia interjected.

Apparently undisturbed by being compared to Satan, Shiloh winked at her. Kamareia quickly glanced away, pretending to take interest in the vegetables her mother was preparing, and I thought that if she had the pale skin of a white girl, her own audacity would have reddened her cheeks.

Then she surprised me by meeting Shiloh's eyes again. "Are you saying that in your work you try to listen to God?"

Shiloh poured milk into the saucepan, soothing the heat and noise of the browning garlic. He didn't answer right away, but he was thinking about her question. Genevieve, too, looked toward him for an answer.

"No," Shiloh said. "I think the still, small voice comes from the oldest and wisest part of the mind."

"I like that," Kamareia said softly.

Shiloh and I didn't discuss Genevieve again that night, nor work, nor his impending sixteen-week absence. His Basque chicken was as good as the first time I'd had it, and we ate in the near-silence of true hunger. Later we found *Othello* on one of the cable channels: the 1995 version, with Laurence Fishburne in the lead. Shiloh fell asleep before it was over, but I stayed awake in the darkened living room to see the tragic lodging of the bed.

chapter 4

Shiloh was a morning person. I tended to stay up late. As long as we'd lived together we'd pulled at each other like tides. I got up earlier because of him; he stayed up later because of me. The day I left for Mankato, though, he didn't wake me; I didn't feel him slip out of bed at all.

In the end, Shiloh's words had weighed on my conscience—*You're her partner*—and I'd taken his suggestion. I'd called Genevieve, and also spoken to her sister, Deborah. It was arranged: a quick overnight trip on Saturday, time enough to assess Genevieve's state of mind and, hopefully, raise her spirits. Not long enough so that the time would drag if nothing I said could rouse her from her dark mood.

When I came out of the bathroom, dressed and wet-haired from my shower, Shiloh was sitting at the living-room window, which had a wide sill and faced east. He'd opened it and the fresh air was making the room cold.

It had rained in the night. In addition, the temperature had dropped sharply enough to create sleet; there had been a brief ice storm. Outside the window, the bare branches of our trees were coated with silver shells of ice. The snows weren't due for another two weeks or so, and yet our neighborhood had turned into an icy wonderland, something a set dresser would be proud of.

"Are you all right?" Something about his stillness made me ask.

Shiloh looked over at me. "Fine," he said. He swung his legs down. "Did you get enough sleep?" He followed me into the kitchen.

"Yeah," I said. It was nearly ten by the clock over the stove. "I wish I'd woken up earlier."

"It's not like you're on a tight schedule. You've got all day to get there, and it's only about a two-hour drive."

"Yeah, I know," I said. "Look, it's not too late for you to come along." I poured water into the coffeemaker.

"No," he said. "Thanks."

"I'm just afraid I won't know what to talk about. You always know what to say in hard situations. I never do."

"You'll do fine." Shiloh rubbed the back of his neck, his gesture for stalling and thinking of how to phrase something. "I'm supposed to report at Quantico on Monday. I don't want to cut it that close, if we were to have trouble getting back. My plane ticket's not transferable. Or refundable."

"What kind of trouble would we have? I mean, you're already willing to count on me to give you a ride to the airport."

"I'm not counting on you. It's a two-thirty flight. If I don't hear from you by one, I'll call a cab."

The coffeemaker made its choked gurgling noises. I'd already known I wasn't going to convince him. When Shiloh made up his mind, it was like making water flow uphill to change it. He took my travel mug down from the shelf and handed it to me.

In the bedroom, I pulled my duffel bag out from under the bed and checked what I'd packed. A change of clothes, something to sleep in, something to wear if I wanted to go for a run. That was all I needed, but when I lifted up experimentally on the handles, the sides drew in, concave. The bag was about a third full, ridiculously thin.

I felt and heard Shiloh kneel down beside me on the bedroom floor. He scooped hair off the nape of my neck and kissed the skin underneath.

It was a quick thing. We didn't even get undressed, really.

A lot of things had changed for us in the past year: Kamareia gone, Shiloh heading to Virginia, his career to take him God knew where after that. He must have felt the world tipping out of balance as much as I did. It had been Shiloh who'd first brought up marriage, in the same conversation in which he told me he'd passed his Phase II testing and had been given a place in the next class at Quantico.

Shiloh's proposal had been an attempt to solidify at least one part of a world gone too fluid. I had understood that, and realized that in considering marriage we were probably grabbing too hard at something that was meant to be finessed.

Then I'd said yes and married him anyway. I'd never been a finesse kind of person anyhow.

Shiloh was still breathing hard when he said, "Just in case you do stay down there and I don't get to say goodbye."

"Goodbye to you too," I said, brushing a lock of hair away from my eyes.

Shiloh came out to the driveway with me and scraped ice off the windshield of the Nova, while I pitched my thin, light duffel bag into the backseat and unlocked the driver's-side door.

"I'll call if I won't be back in time to take you to the airport," I said when he came around to stand near me. "But I'm sure I will." I leaned over the open door and kissed his cheek.

Before I could pull away, Shiloh took my face in both his hands and kissed me on the forehead.

"Be safe," he said.

"I will."

"I mean it. I know the way you drive. Don't make me worry about you."

"I'll be fine," I told him. "I'll see you soon."

The freezing rain that had fallen on the Cities had also fallen on the southern part of the state, and I eased up on the gas once I got out into the countryside, because there were patches of ice still on the road, although they were shrinking and melting under the friction of car wheels. On the radio, the forecast called for more rains over southern Minnesota later, with the temperature likely to dip down to freezing in the night. But I'd be long off the roads by then. By noon I had shot across the line into Blue Earth County.

In one of those quirks of geography that drive newcomers to

an area up a wall, Mankato was the county seat of Blue Earth County, while the city of Blue Earth, nearly on the Iowa border, was the seat of Faribault County.

Blue Earth was where Royce Stewart, who'd killed Kamareia Brown, lived and walked around free. Best not to think about that.

Genevieve's sister and brother-in-law lived in a farmhouse south of Mankato, although they only had two acres and didn't farm. This was the first I'd been to their house, although I'd seen a lot of Deborah Lowe in the weeks following Kamareia's death. She'd come up to the Cities and helped with the needed arrangements, taking as much of the burden as she could from her sister.

Their family, of Italian and Croatian extraction, went back for four generations in St. Paul. Genevieve's parents were working-class liberals, both union organizers. They'd sent four of their five children to college and one into the priesthood as well. When Genevieve had become a cop, her parents had accepted her career the same way they'd accepted the marriage to a black man that had resulted in a biracial granddaughter.

Deb, I had learned, had flirted with becoming a nun in her teenage years before abandoning the idea. ("Guys," she'd explained succinctly.)

She'd become a teacher instead, starting in St. Paul and then moving outstate to find a kind of lifestyle her family hadn't known for over a century.

She and Doug Lowe didn't work the land, but they did have a sprawling kitchen garden and a henhouse to reduce the grocery bills and supplement the paychecks of two school-teachers.

It was Deborah who heard the car's engine and came out of

the farmhouse to greet me as I was pulling my bag from the backseat of the Nova, which I'd parked in front of the apple tree in their yard.

Deborah was a hair taller than Genevieve, a shade thinner, but otherwise they looked a lot alike. Both had dark eyes and dark hair—Deborah's was long, worn today in a ponytail—and a pale-olive complexion. Deborah descended the front steps, followed by a dog, a fat caramel-and-white corgi that yapped intermittently without a lot of interest. He stopped at the bottom of the steps, content to observe the interloper's behavior from a safe position.

Reaching the car, Deborah hugged me while I stood, a little surprised, in the circle of her hard-muscled arms.

"Thank you for coming," she said, releasing me.

I opened my mouth to say "How is she?" but even as I did, the screen door opened again and Genevieve came out to stand on the porch, looking at us.

She was letting her short, dark hair grow—or more likely, she simply hadn't thought to have it cut since Kamareia died. The few pounds she had on her sister weren't fat; they were muscle from the gym. Her physique reminded me of the hard roundness of ponies that used to work down in coal mines.

Shouldering my bag, I stepped around Deborah and walked to the porch. Genevieve held my gaze as I climbed the front steps.

It seemed only right to hug her in greeting, but she was as rigid in my arms as I had been in Deborah's.

From the front room came the sounds of a basketball game on television. Deborah's husband, Doug, lifted a hand in greeting but didn't rise from his place in an easy chair.

Deborah led me down the hall. "You can put your bag in

here," she said, gesturing through the doorway into a spare room.

Inside were two twin beds. The comforter on one was slightly rumpled as though someone had been lying on it in the middle of the day, and I realized that this was Genevieve's room that I would be sharing.

I set my bag down at the foot of the other bed. On the dresser, in an old-fashioned pewter frame, was a familiar picture of Kamareia. The photo was only a year old; a 16-year-old Kam looked at me with her wide-set hazel eyes. She was smiling, almost laughing, and holding the Lowes' corgi partly on her lap. The dog wanted to be set at liberty, and Kam was trying to hold on until the picture was taken; that was the source of her merriment.

I'd seen the same picture in Genevieve's house and wondered if she'd brought it with her or if the Lowes had always had the same one in their spare room.

"Can I get you something to drink?" Deb asked from the doorway. "We've got Coke, and mineral water, I think. Beer, if it's not too early in the day for you." It was approaching one in the afternoon.

"A Coke is fine, thanks," I said.

In the Lowes' big, sunny kitchen, Deborah fixed me a glass of Coca-Cola with ice. Genevieve was so quiet she might as well not have been in the same room with us. Deliberately I caught her eye.

"So," I asked her, "what do people do around here for fun?"

"I thought you were just down here for a day," Genevieve said.

A little bit of heat rose under my skin; it was embarrassment.

I'd been hunting around at random for a conversation starter and had seized on that one. "I meant, in general."

When Genevieve appeared to have no answer, Deborah intervened. "There's a cineplex in town, and that's about it," she said. "If we want nightlife, we have to go up to Mankato. There's a state university there, so they've got the stuff that keeps college kids happy."

"All college kids need are bars," I said.

"Bars and music," Deborah agreed.

A moment of quiet followed that. Then Deborah spoke up again. "How's your boyfriend...what's his name?"

I couldn't help but glance at Genevieve, to see if she'd correct her sister. She knew Shiloh and I were married. But she remained silent.

"Husband," I said. "Shiloh's fine." I sipped my Coke and turned back to face Deborah. It was clear that Genevieve didn't have much to contribute.

It wasn't as if Genevieve were catatonic, or even near-catatonic. She moved around, she answered questions, she performed tasks that were immediately at hand. But if anything, she was in worse shape than she'd seemed on the job in Minneapolis. Retreating to the countryside might help her in the end, but it hadn't helped her yet.

The conversation between Deborah and me, mostly about Twin Cities' crime and politics, limped along for another half hour. I drank my Coke. Genevieve just listened. Eventually, Deborah said she had some papers to grade, and Genevieve and I joined Doug Lowe in the living room, where he was still watching his game.

I did that for about fifteen minutes. I'd grown up playing basketball, but I couldn't find any interest in it today. As long as

I'd known Genevieve, she'd never shown any interest in sports, unless she was being asked to play, but now she kept her eyes on the screen, the same as Doug.

She didn't seem to care when I got up and slipped away.

Deborah was still in the kitchen, papers in two piles in front of her: marked and unmarked. A single paper was in front of her. Her eyes were skimming over it, a red pen ready in her hand. She looked up when I slipped into the chair opposite her.

"Do you think Genevieve's angry with me?" I asked.

Deborah set the pen down and licked her teeth thoughtfully. "She's like that with everyone now," she assured me. "You've got to practically kick her in the ass to get her to say anything."

"Yeah," I said. "I figured that. But you know about Royce Stewart and the hearing, don't you?"

"What about it?"

"Kamareia's identification of Stewart, on the way to the hospital," I said. "It was my fault that it got thrown out."

Deb shook her head. "I know what you're talking about," she said, "and it's not your fault."

"If I'd handled things right, in the ambulance, Stewart would be in prison now."

She set the pen down and gave me a level look. "If you'd handled it right—'right' for a cop—what would that have been? Telling Kamareia she was going to die?"

I said nothing.

"Do you think that's what Genevieve would have done if she'd been with her daughter?" she persisted.

"No," I said, shaking my head.

"See? And if you'd done it, Genevieve would never have forgiven you. Ever."

"I'm not sorry about what I said to Kam on the way to the hospital," I said slowly. "But . . ."

"But what?"

"Genevieve might not be thinking straight."

Deborah reached across the table and squeezed my closed fist. "She doesn't blame you. I'm sure of that," she said.

"Well," I said, "I guess that's good. Sorry I interrupted your work."

"I think she's glad you're here," Deborah said. "You've got to be patient with her."

Around ten-thirty, after a quiet evening, I found myself in the guest bedroom with Genevieve.

I'd undressed in front of her dozens of times in the locker rooms at work and the gym, but this sisterly, intimate context made me feel exposed and shy. I tried to take my clothes off entirely from a sitting position on the narrow twin bed, head lowered.

"Damn," I said, rolling a sock over my callused heel, "in bed at ten. Now I know I'm in the country."

"Sure," Genevieve said, as if reading from a script.

"Doesn't it get boring, being out here?" I said, pulling my shirt over my head. Hoping, I suppose, for *Yes, it does; I think going back to the Cities would do me good.*

"It's nice out here. It's quiet," Genevieve said.

"Well, yeah," I agreed lamely, pulling back the covers on my bed.

"Do you need the light any longer?" she asked.

"No," I said.

Genevieve clicked the bedside lamp off.

She was right about one thing: it was quiet. Despite the early hour, I found sleep beginning to tug at my body. But I resisted. I wanted to stay awake long enough to hear Genevieve's breathing change. If she could fall asleep in a normal amount of time, that at least was a good sign.

I don't know how much time passed, but she must have believed me asleep. I heard the susurrus of the bedsheets, then padding footsteps as she left the bedroom. It took a few minutes after that for me to realize she hadn't just gone across the hall to the bathroom. I got up to follow.

The light from the kitchen spilled, increasingly narrowly, down the hall. There was no need to wonder where she'd gone. I walked carefully on the plastic carpet runner and my steps were audible only to me. I stopped just short of the kitchen doorway.

Genevieve sat at the broad table where Deborah had corrected papers, her back to me. A bottle of scotch and a glass with about two fingers in it sat in front of her.

How do you counsel your own mentor, be an authority to your authority figure? I had a sudden desire to go back to bed.

You're her partner, Shiloh had said.

I stepped into the kitchen instead, pulled up a chair, sat down with her. Genevieve looked at me with no great surprise, but there was a dark light in her eyes that I didn't think I'd seen before. Then she said, "He's back in Blue Earth."

She meant Shorty. Royce Stewart.

"I know," I said.

"I have a friend in the Dispatch office down there. She says he can be counted on to be at the bar every night. With his *friends.* How does a guy like that even have any friends?" Her speech wasn't slurred, but there was a certain impreciseness in it, as though her gaze, her speech, and her thoughts weren't entirely in line with each other.

"What do you think it is?" she demanded. "You think they don't *know* he killed a teenage girl? Or that they just don't care?"

I shook my head. "I don't know."

Genevieve lifted her glass and drank, a deeper draft than people usually take with hard liquor. "He walks home late at night, even though he lives outside of town, on the highway."

"You told me this before. Remember?" I said.

And she had. It was understandable, her obsession with Stewart, but it made me uncomfortable.

"Let her talk about it," Shiloh had counseled, shortly before I left. "She'll probably work it out of her system and move on in her own time. Kamareia's dead, he's alive and free . . . she's not going to come to grips with that overnight."

But I had a more immediate concern.

"Gen," I said, "it's starting to worry me, the way you talk about him."

She drank again, lowered the glass, and gave me a questioning look over the rim.

"You wouldn't be thinking of paying him a visit, would you?"

"To do what?" Her face was open, as if she really didn't know what I meant.

"To kill him." *God, let me not be planting a seed in her mind that wasn't there before.*

"I turned in my service weapon up in the Cities."

"And nothing is stopping you from buying one. Or getting one from a friend. There're lots of guns in these parts."

"He didn't kill Kamareia with a gun," Genevieve said softly. She refilled her glass.

"This is important, damn it. Don't go flaky on me," I said. "I need to know you wouldn't go down there."

She waited a moment before speaking. "I've had to counsel the survivors of murder victims. They don't get retribution, even when we catch the guy who did it. There's no death penalty in Minnesota." She thought. "I probably wouldn't get away with killing him, either."

These were stock answers, and not entirely comforting.

"There's such a thing as revenge," I pointed out. "Call it closure, even."

"Closure?" Genevieve said. "The hell with *closure*. I want my daughter back."

"Okay," I said. "I understand." There was so much bitterness in her voice that I believed she was telling the truth: she didn't want to kill Royce Stewart.

Genevieve looked at the empty space in front of me, as if just now realizing I hadn't been drinking with her. "You want me to get you a glass?" she asked.

"No," I said. "We should probably go back to bed."

Genevieve ignored me and put her head down to rest her chin on her arms, which were folded on the table. "Are you and Shiloh going to have kids?"

"That's, uh ..." I was surprised into stammering, "... that's a long time in the future." The question reminded me of something, and in a moment my mind retrieved it: Ainsley Carter asking, *Do you have children, Detective Pribek?* "I'm sure we'll have one," I said.

"No," Genevieve said, shaking her head emphatically as if

she'd asked a yes-or-no question and I'd answered it incorrectly. "Don't have one. Don't *just* have one." She hit the *s* a little too hard in *just.* "Have two. Or three. If you have just one child, and you lose her . . . it's too much."

"Oh, Gen," I said, thinking, *Help me, Shiloh.* He would have known what to say.

"Make sure Shiloh agrees you guys are going to have more than one," Gen went on. She reached out and pressed my arm hard, with an almost-proselytic fervor. "I know I'm not supposed to be saying this," she said.

"Saying what?"

"I'm supposed to be saying that I'm glad I had Kam for the time I did. Like at the funeral, they don't call it a funeral anymore when it's a young person, they call it a 'celebration of life.' " Her eyes were still dry, but clouded over somehow. "But if I had it to do over again, I wouldn't have had a child at all. I wouldn't have brought her into the world just to have this happen to her."

"I think," I said, struggling for the right words, "I think someday you're going to feel differently about that. Maybe not right away. But someday."

Genevieve lifted her head and took a deep breath, closed her eyes, and opened them again. She seemed clearer. "Someday is a long way away," she said. She looked at the scotch bottle, found the cap, and screwed it back on. "But I know you mean well."

"Listen," I said. An idea was coalescing even as I spoke. "Shiloh's going to be at Quantico for sixteen weeks. You could come back up to the Cities and we could be roommates. It might be easier than going straight back to your place." I paused. "You wouldn't have to go back to work right away. Just keep me company while Shiloh's gone."

Genevieve didn't respond right away, and to close the deal, I said, "I know he'd like to see you before he leaves."

For a moment I thought I had convinced her. Then she shook her head. "No," she said. "I'm just not ready."

I rose and she followed suit. "Well," I said, "the offer's going to stand."

She put the scotch away, and instead of setting the glass in the sink the way people did with late-night dishes, she rinsed it and put it away in the cabinet. It was an action that suggested to me that drinking had become a common ritual that she was trying to hide from her sister and brother-in-law.

When we were back in bed, Genevieve dropped off to sleep almost immediately, aided undoubtedly by the whiskey. Not me. I was keyed up from our conversation. I closed my eyes, thinking surely my previous lassitude would return soon.

It didn't. I lay awake for a long time in the narrow twin bed, breathing the Clorox scent of the sheets. The room had an old-fashioned digital clock, with white numbers that rolled over, and every ten minutes the first of the two minute place-holders rolled over with an audible click. There'd been a clock like that in the main room of the trailer I'd lived in as a child.

When 11:30 rolled over, lit from the side with an orange light, I sat up in bed and was nearly surprised to feel my feet reach the floor.

I'd lived too long in cities, gotten too used to a little light and a little noise at any hour. I hadn't lived in a place like this since New Mexico. Beyond the sheer curtain I brushed aside with one hand was the country-dark sky I knew I'd see, richly spangled with stars despite the pale wash of light from a full moon. The last time I'd looked out a bedroom window to a sky like that, I'd never held a gun, I didn't have any money of my own, had never had a lover to share my bed.

I lay down again, rolled over to lie on top of the pillow, wishing for Shiloh. If he were here, we could do something wicked and adult to hold this child's feeling at bay.

In the distance I heard a train whistle. Probably a freight at this hour. This train was too far away for me to hear the three-part rhythm of its passing on the tracks, but the whistle blew again, a faint comforting sound of Minneapolis.

Genevieve agreed to go for a run with me in the morning, two easy miles. We returned to find Doug and Deborah getting ready to go out, to meet friends for a late Sunday breakfast. "There's coffee on," Deborah advised me, hurriedly, when Genevieve and I arrived in the kitchen, and its scent did fill the house.

In the kitchen, shortly before Deborah and Doug left, I managed to talk with both of them while Genevieve wasn't in the kitchen.

"Listen," I said carefully, "I was talking about something with Genevieve last night....Do you keep any guns in the house?"

"Guns?" Doug said. "No. I don't hunt."

"Why?" Deborah asked.

"I'm just worried about Genevieve," I said. "You live awfully close to Royce Stewart. And sometimes I wonder if she's always thinking straight."

Doug gave me an incredulous look. "You can't seriously think—"

"No," I said. "I'm probably just being paranoid. Goes with the job sometimes."

Genevieve drifted back into the kitchen, and I fell silent. Deborah busied herself before the refrigerator, surveying its contents.

"Honey," she told Doug, "I thought we had more Diet Coke than this. Don't let me forget to stop on the way home, all right?"

While her husband was warming up their car in the garage, Deborah pulled me aside.

"Come upstairs with me for a minute," she said.

I followed her up to their bedroom and watched as Deborah pushed aside the hanging clothes in her closet and took a small black purse from a peg in the back. Although the bag looked empty to me, with its sides caved slightly in, she handled it with delicacy. Sitting on the bed, she unzipped it and reached inside. Made curious by her caution, I moved closer.

She paused with her hand in the purse and looked up at me. "I guess Doug didn't know I had this," she said. "So I'm sure Genevieve doesn't, either."

She withdrew a small handgun from the bag, a .25 with cheap, bright plating.

"When I had my first teaching job in East St. Louis," she said, "the school was in kind of a rough neighborhood. A friend who'd lived there all his life gave this to me. It's not registered to me. . . . I don't know who it's registered to, actually."

Deborah Lowe wore a white blouse and a black straight skirt, and her lips were limned tastefully with pale red lipstick. I marveled.

"Teacher's got a Saturday-night special," I said.

"I know, it's awful. That's why I wanted you to take it. It's not necessarily because of Genevieve. I just want it gone, and I don't know how to get rid of it." She offered it to me.

Doug's voice echoed up the stairs. "Deb! We're burning daylight!" he yelled.

I took the little gun from her hand. "Sure," I said. "I'll take care of it."

I stayed awhile with Genevieve after they had gone. I tried to interest her in department news and gossip, to the extent that I knew any. The truth was, I'd always counted on her for that sort of thing. She'd been my branch of the grapevine.

When I left, Genevieve followed me as far as the front porch. I stopped there and spoke to her. "If you ever want to talk, just give me a call. You know I'm up late."

"I will," she said quietly.

"You should think about coming back to work," I added. "It might help you to be occupied. And we need you."

"I know," she said. "I'm trying." But I could see in her eyes that she was in a dark place and a few rallying words from me weren't going to help.

The first raindrops speckled my windshield only minutes after the house disappeared from my rearview mirror.

I thought I'd left in plenty of time to get back to the Cities. I should have known better. You should always expect bad luck on the road. Particularly when it rains.

The bad luck turned up twenty minutes north of Mankato. Traffic on the 169 slowed to a thick automotive sludge. Impatient, I turned down the radio, which suddenly seemed loud, and turned up the heat to keep the idling engine cool.

For twenty-five minutes, we all inched along. Finally, the cause came into view: a jackknifed truck in the road. Two highway patrol officers directed traffic around it. It didn't look like an injury accident. Just a nuisance.

Past the obstruction, as the traffic broke up, I urged the Nova up to 87, ignoring the rain. I was going to have to really move if I wanted to catch Shiloh in time.

A little over an hour later, I turned into the long driveway outside our house. It was a quarter to one. Good, I thought, I was in time.

I made enough noise, banging the kitchen door open, that Shiloh would surely hear, wherever he was in the house. But the only answering noise was the ticking of the kitchen clock.

"Hey, Shiloh?"

Silence. Half the living room was visible from the kitchen, and unoccupied.

"Shit," I said. I'd considered calling from the Lowes' place to make it clear I'd be home in enough time to take him to the airport. Perhaps I should have done so.

It only took a moment to satisfy myself that he wasn't home. But it seemed early yet. He shouldn't have left already.

The house looked the same inside as it usually did, not really clean, not dirty, either. Shiloh had straightened up just a little. There were no dishes in the sink, and in the bedroom the bed was made, the Indian blanket pulled smooth.

I set my bag down on the bedroom floor and went out to the front of the house. In the front entryway, the hook where he hung his key ring was bare. His everyday jacket was gone as well. He'd erred on the side of caution and left without me.

There was no note.

Generally, Shiloh and I were well matched in our lack of sentimentality. But Shiloh's abruptness, his lack of concern for convention, sometimes had the power to sting me a little. It did then.

"Well," I said, aloud and alone. "Goodbye to you too, you son of a bitch."

chapter 5

You always pay for time off with extra time at work, either before or after. On Monday I went to work early, knowing I'd need time to make up for my personal days.

Vang wasn't there when I got in, but he'd left reports on the recent disappearances on my desk.

None of them seemed out of the ordinary to me. They could be put in a few general categories: Tired of Being Married, Tired of Living Under My Parents' Rules, or Too Absentminded to Tell Anyone I'm Leaving Town for a While.

Vang came in with a cup of coffee around nine. "How was your time off?" he asked.

"It was all right," I said shortly. I hadn't told him I had gone to see Genevieve. She was living in a kind of departmental limbo, without a set date for her return. Our lieutenant was allowing it because she was a well-liked veteran. But I still didn't want to draw the department's attention to her absence and to the question of when she was coming back.

"What's the big news around here?" I asked.

"There's not a lot going on," Vang said. "I got all the paperwork on Mrs. Thorenson. Did you see the report? I left it on your desk."

"I read it," I said, moving it to the top of the pile.

Annette Thorenson had gone on a weekend trip upstate with a friend, to a resort south of St. Cloud. She hadn't come back. Nor had she told her friend anything to imply that she wasn't going straight home to where she lived in a Lake Harriet town house with a husband and no kids. Mr. Thorenson was beside himself.

"The gasoline card's been used," Vang said. "ATMs have been hit four times. Twice moving eastward to Wisconsin. Twice in Madison."

"And?" I said.

"His friends say the marriage is solid. Her friends all say it's not. One of them, who's recently divorced herself, said Annette asked a lot of questions in the key of: 'What's it like to get divorced and start over?' "

"See? Tired of Being Married," I said. I'd told him about my categories.

"So I asked if Annette knew anyone in Madison," Vang went on. "Turns out that's where she went to school. Lived there a year afterward, working."

"And she still has friends there?"

"I couldn't get any names. My guess is there's an old flame still in town. The problem is, it seems like she's keeping a low profile now that she's there. I gave the Madison cops her license number, hoping they'd pick her up and bring her into a station, have her call her husband and tell him flat out what's going on. But they haven't seen the car. And she hasn't used the ATM in the past few days."

" 'I'll buy, sweetheart,' " I said. The old flame was apparently picking up the checks.

"Yeah," Vang said. "But Mr. Thorenson doesn't believe any of it. He says someone must be forcing her to drive east and get money out of cash machines. I've tried to tell him that everything points to her taking a time-out from her life here, but he's not convinced. He calls here a lot and the word *negligence* keeps coming up. He wants to speak to my supervisor."

"I suspect you have a pink message slip for me."

"Several."

"I just need one."

I called Mr. Thorenson at his office and listened while he recounted his unsatisfying conversations with Vang. He was unhappy when I told him that Vang had done everything I would have.

"It might be time to bring in some private help," I said. "I can give you the phone numbers of several very competent investigators," I said.

"At this point, I'm thinking of contacting a lawyer, Miss Pribek," Thorenson responded, and hung up.

Too bad, I thought. I knew more lawyers than I did PIs; I could have made a referral there, too. *Miss Pribek.* If that pejorative courtesy title was his idea of subtle psychological warfare, I could see why his wife might have gotten tired of him.

The highlight of the day was a trip across town to examine the clean, empty apartment of a young man with a lot of gambling debts. Another person who'd left town of his own volition, I thought.

"Did you see the vacuum marks on the carpet?" I asked Vang on the way back. "Track-covering. Guilty conscience. People often clean when they're not planning on coming back."

"Yeah," he said. "My wife even cleans house before we go on vacation, so in case we're in a fatal on the highway, our families won't come here and see a dirty house. It's her version of wearing clean underwear."

We fell silent and I thought about the evening ahead.

If Genevieve had been on the job, she would have suggested we do something after work tonight, my first night without Shiloh around. She would have known that I'd gotten unused to living alone, but she wouldn't have made a big deal of it.

Maybe it was time for me to get to know my new partner a little better.

"You want to get a cup of coffee after work?" I asked, steering down the spiral ramp at the garage downtown.

Vang looked at me sidewise, maybe surprised. "Thanks," he said. "But I've got to get home for dinner. Some other time, okay?"

"You bet," I said, sounding old and Minnesotan to myself.

I stayed late at work, occupying myself with a motley assortment of small tasks that probably could have waited. When I ran out of those, I went to the courts where Hennepin County people regularly played pickup basketball, hoping to get recruited into a game. Shiloh and I had been among the regular players.

But nobody that I recognized was there. Instead, a group of rookies was playing two-on-two. They looked like they could have come straight from the U of M's women's team: all female, all tall, three-fourths blonde. They were also evenly matched; there wasn't room for an extra player, even had we known each other.

A small thing lifted my spirits when I returned home: there was a basket of tomatoes on the stoop. No note, but none was needed. Mrs. Muzio kept a prodigious garden all summer long, and vegetables turned up on our steps regularly. Standing on the kitchen doorstep at the back of the house, I looked over and saw the slow, wild demise of Mrs. Muzio's kitchen garden: a sunflower in death was half bowed under its own weight; the herbs had flowered and bolted. But the tomato plants were still heavy-laden with the last fruits of the season.

I doubted Mrs. Muzio knew Shiloh was gone. She left tomatoes more often than anything else, because she knew how much Shiloh liked them. Tomato sandwiches were his staple when he was too busy to cook. Often, when he came home on a quick break from work, he'd make one and eat it standing over the sink.

I pushed the strap of my shoulder bag onto a secure spot higher on my shoulder, held the basket in one arm against my ribs, and opened the door with my other hand.

Shiloh had said he'd call to give me a number where he could be reached at Quantico, but I didn't look at the answering machine right away. First, I put Mrs. Muzio's tomatoes away in the refrigerator, fixed myself a Coke over ice, went to change out of my work clothes. Only then did I go to the machine to find Shiloh's message.

There was none. The tiny red eye, often flashing when we'd both been out all day, was dim, unlit.

Well, okay, he's busy. He's been traveling, and then getting used to his new surroundings. The phone lines work both ways, you know. Call him instead.

That was going to pose a problem: I still didn't have a phone number for him.

There was probably a way to get through to the dormitory where the agents-in-training lived. Getting that number wouldn't be easy, though, at this hour. Dealing with the FBI often meant multiple calls and phone tag, even on official business. Even during office hours. This was only personal business, and it was after hours. In Virginia it was already eight.

I had the phone number of an FBI agent, the one who'd worked closely with Shiloh on the Annelise Eliot case. It might be helpful to call Agent Thompson first, explain the situation, and ask him to run interference for me with his peers.

It took several minutes of hunting around in the disorganized entries in our phone book, but I found Thompson's phone number. My hand was on the phone when something else came to mind.

Two months ago, Shiloh and I had watched a cable-channel documentary on the making of FBI agents. From it, I'd gotten an idea of what life at Quantico would be like for Shiloh. From the very first day there was a demanding round of training: baseline testing on physical conditioning, classroom instruction on procedure and law and ethics. At night, the agents-in-training lived like college students, studying at small desks with snapshots of spouses and children hanging over them, going to each other's rooms briefly to talk, decompressing after a hard day.

After years as an outsider, Shiloh was probably in his element at last, surrounded by people as single-minded and driven as he was. He was spending his small amount of free time getting to know others in his agent class, looking at the photos over the desks. Most likely many of them were doing that, getting to know each other, trading stories about the diverse career paths that had led them to Quantico. And I was about to make Shiloh the only one who had to go to the phone to take a call from his needy wife, who was worried because it had been *over twenty-four hours* and he hadn't called home.

I turned on ESPN and put it out of my mind.

"**. . . killed** two soldiers at a bus stop last year. No party has claimed responsibility for this year's bombing. . . . In Blue Earth, the search intensifies for 67-year-old Thomas Hall, the apparent victim of a single-vehicle accident. His truck was found early Sunday outside town, where it had crashed into a tree off the eastbound lane. Search-and-rescue teams are widening the scope of their hunt, but have not been successful in locating Hall. WMNN news time, six fifty-nine."

It was Tuesday morning, and the clock radio had awakened me, but I wasn't ready to get out of bed yet. When the phone rang several minutes later, I was still half asleep. I picked it up and had to clear my throat before speaking.

"I woke you up, sorry," the voice on the other end said.

"Shiloh?" He sounded strange.

Vang laughed. "I really did wake you," he said. He sounded very chipper. I sat up, a little embarrassed. He went on, "There's a grave out in Wayzata we've got to look at."

"Oh, yeah? What's the story?" I asked.

"They don't know yet. A woman called this morning. She lives in the same neighborhood—I mean, the same area—with a released sex offender, a child molester. Last night she saw him out with a flashlight, digging, his car parked nearby."

"And she knew it was a grave how?"

"Well, she said the hole looked about the right size to be a grave. She didn't see him put anything in it. He was filling it in, actually. I guess she lives on a hill, has a pretty good view of the area, so she could watch awhile."

"Is she part of a neighborhood watch?"

"Not officially, but this guy—his name's Bonney—makes everyone out there nervous. They all got the flyer about him being a released sex offender. This woman woke up at four A.M. worrying about what she'd seen and finally decided to call us. So now we're digging."

I sat up, feeling more awake. "We've really got a warrant to dig on his property? Probable cause seems pretty weak. Didn't anyone suggest we just talk to this guy first?"

"They sent a patrolman to do that," Vang said. "He's not home, and he's not at work, either, even though he's on the schedule. Nobody likes it. But here's the good part: He didn't actually dig on his own property. The lot on the other side of his back fence is undeveloped county land. That's where he was digging."

"Ah," I said.

"So, no warrant needed," Vang confirmed. "Should I pick you up? I'm at home right now, but I could come straight over."

I pushed the blanket off my legs with my free hand. "Yeah, that'd be good," I said. "I can be ready in fifteen minutes."

Thirty-five minutes later, Vang and I were standing on an acre of peaceful countryside near Wayzata Bay. Despite its proximity to the city, this was a place more rural than suburban in its flavor, with plenty of land between houses; I could see why Vang had called it an "area" rather than a "neighborhood" on the phone.

The crime-scene unit van was parked at the edge of the

road, and two officers were digging. Amateur graves are usually shallow, and exhuming them is work too delicate for a backhoe.

Marijuana farmers sometimes cultivate their crop deep in isolated public lands. The obvious advantage is that the growers have to be caught on-site for the crop to be linked to them, as opposed to having the incriminating plant on their own property. If Bonney had in fact killed someone, he had a similar incentive not to bury on his own property. He hadn't gone very far, but perhaps he'd felt it wiser not to travel with a body in his car.

Vang and I had just finished reading through the new missing-persons reports and be-on-the-lookouts for the last forty-eight hours; in addition, Vang had a printout of Bonney's criminal record.

"I don't get a vibe off any of these missing persons," I said. "All adults or late teens."

"They don't seem like Bonney's type, do they?" Vang agreed.

"No. Besides, you read his record, right? Sexual battery, child molestation. But he's never killed anyone, or even come close."

Vang listened but said nothing.

"Sometimes sexual predators progress to worse crimes, like homicide," I said. "But there just hasn't been a disappearance in the last forty-eight hours that seems to match up with this guy burying someone in a field near his house." I watched one of the officers pause and gingerly scrape aside some wet soil. Vang and I were keeping our distance for now, letting them do their work with a minimum of disturbance to the ground and surroundings. "Usually, you'll have a pretty good idea about these things. You'll get a call that someone's found a body and you'll know right away, 'We found Jane.' I don't get that feeling here." I sighed. "You know what I think? I think Bonney burned a damn casserole until the pot was beyond salvaging and took the whole mess out and buried it. His neighbor up the hill saw it, lay awake until a little hole became a yawning grave, and called us. Sometimes I think this whole sex-offender thing, with disclosure and flyers and neighborhood meetings, has gotten way out of hand."

I cut myself off. Shiloh had only been gone two days and already I was channeling him, spreading his unpopular liberal views to my new partner. "If they find something bad, maybe we'll ask for a warrant for the house," I said, backpedaling. "If not, let the parole officer make the surprise visits to look for a violation. It's his job."

"If I'd known it was going to take this long for them to disinter, I'd have stopped for coffee," Vang said.

"When they make you go out to the sticks at seven-thirty in the morning on a situation like this," I agreed, "coffee may be the highlight of the trip."

In truth, it wasn't coffee I wished I'd taken time for but a shower. There's something a shower provides that has very little to do with actual cleanliness. It's punctuation: without one, traces of yesterday and last night and bed cling to you, no matter how alert you feel, how you're dressed, or what you're doing.

The breeze picked up, coming from the direction of the lake. We couldn't quite see the water from where we were; it was obscured by bare, skinny trees that made up in number what they lacked in individual heft.

"Does my voice really sound like your husband's?" Vang asked, and I remembered how I'd answered the phone.

"Not really, the more I—"

"Hey, look at that," Vang interrupted.

I broke off and looked at the crime-scene officers. They were carefully lifting something wrapped in a green garbage bag out of the ground.

"It's definitely not a casserole dish," I admitted.

"But it looks kind of small to be a person," Vang said. We were already walking over. "Unless it's a kid."

"Or it's not a whole person," I said, and Vang winced.

The first officer, Penhall, took his camera and photographed the bagged form where it lay just next to the hole it had been lifted from.

Officer Malik took a penknife and, pulling the bag away from the object inside, slit the bag lengthwise without disturbing the knot at the top.

The first thing I saw as the blade slid through green plastic was tawny blond hair. But what was inside was blond all over: a golden retriever. Some dried blood matted the fur.

"Aw, shit," Malik said. It was hard to tell if he spoke as a dog lover or a technician who'd just wasted a lot of time.

"Well," Penhall said, "hold on. This guy killed a neighbor's dog, that's pretty serious." He looked at Vang and me for validation.

"Could you take the wrap all the way off?" I said.

Malik did. I looked at Vang and raised an eyebrow.

"It just looks like a dog that got hit by a car to me," Vang observed.

Malik was nodding agreement.

"Then why take the trouble to bury it?" Penhall asked.

"Because it's probably a family pet, belonging to someone around here. And Bonney's already very unpopular, because he's a child molester." I glanced up the hill to the neighbor's tall and graceful house. Morning sunlight glinted off the floor-to-ceiling windows of what was likely the living room. She and her family had a great view of the lake, as well as of the property of Mr. Bonney, released sex offender. "He doesn't want to make his reputation any worse than it already is."

Malik straightened up. "What are you gonna do now?"

"That's a good question," I said. "Dogs are property. I guess there's a property crime here. It's not missing persons. I think we're going to drop by the Wayzata police station and let them sort it out."

As Vang made a U-turn and pointed the car back toward town, he looked hard at Bonney's place, a single-story dwelling with a sagging porch roof.

"I wonder what we'd find in that house if we went in," he said.

"A civil suit," I said, "waiting to happen."

Vang drove us back to Minneapolis, but not to work. I needed to pick up my own car, and beyond that, I wanted a shower. There was time: our schedules and workdays have to be a little fluid, given the demands of the job. Vang and I had already put in nearly an hour before our day normally started.

"I forgot to mention it yesterday," Vang said, "but on Sunday night Fielding's girlfriend got one of those phone calls, like Mann and Juarez's wives got."

"Oh yeah?" I knew what he was talking about. Everyone did. Two wives of Hennepin County deputies had received anonymous phone calls lately.

The caller's voice, in both cases, sounded sincere and

regretful. He'd identified himself as ER staff and told Deputy Mann's wife that her husband had been critically injured in an accident in his squad car.

She'd been distraught, naturally, and wanted more details. The caller had hedged, providing a little more information couched in medical terms. Then he'd been "cut off" before he could say which hospital he was calling from.

Mrs. Mann had called downtown. It took dispatchers a few minutes to locate him, but before too long Mann had called home to reassure his wife that his watch had been completely without incident and he had no idea who would call her with a story like that.

Four weeks later the same thing happened to the wife of Deputy Juarez, except in her case, the caller regretfully said he'd been killed.

The coincidence was too great. A departmental memo was circulated, detailing the "sick joke" being perpetrated and telling officers to warn their families.

When the memo had gone around, a theory began to circulate right behind it, suggesting that the caller could be somebody with the county; somebody who'd gotten access somehow to a departmental phone list. Many cops had unlisted numbers, which helped to protect them from harassment or worse from people they'd arrested and helped build cases against.

"Is Fielding in the white pages?" I asked.

"I don't know," Vang said, "but they're saying it doesn't matter. Because of the Sunshine in Minneapolis site."

"Oh," I said, remembering.

The Sunshine site took its name loosely from "sunshine" laws, or freedom-of-information laws that provided access to information on public processes and officials. The site, started by husband-and-wife community activists, was something like a Drudge Report/Smoking Gun for the city. Among the information posted were phone numbers and sometimes home addresses for police officers and sheriff's deputies, all gleaned incidentally from various reports and court records that had been made public at one time or another. The theory, according to the site's creators, was that cops would think twice about harassing innocent citizens if they knew their home phone numbers and addresses were on the Web for anyone to retrieve.

"You're saying that both Mann and Juarez's numbers were on the site?" I asked. We were crossing under the railroad tracks in Northeast, approaching my place.

"Juarez is actually in the phone book," Vang said. "But yeah, all three are on the Web site, too. Nothing's written in stone, but that's one way this sicko could have gotten their numbers."

I shook my head. "That site seemed kind of funny to me at the time," I told him. "I looked myself up. It said, 'married to a Minneapolis cop' next to my name. Shiloh and I laughed about it."

"Yeah, well, nobody's laughing about it downtown. Some of the guys are saying this could help get the site shut down, if they can prove it's helping someone harass women anonymously."

"Good," I said as we pulled over to the curb.

"See you in about a half hour," Vang said.

I enjoyed the shower more for its being belated. I was starting to have a good feeling about today. There was probably just enough time to stop and pick up a bagel. I'd get one for Vang, too, although I didn't really know his tastes. Genevieve's I would have known: she almost always chose a sundried-tomato bagel, spreading it with a parsimoniously thin layer of lite cream cheese. Vang, much younger, rail-thin, and male, probably would rather start his day with a doughnut.

Wet-haired, dressed again, with my bag over my shoulder, I headed toward the back door. The sun was spilling through the east-facing kitchen window, and it was so bright that I almost missed the flashing of the message light on the machine. Almost.

"This message is for Michael Shiloh," an unfamiliar female voice said. "This is Kim in the training unit at Quantico. If you've had problems getting here or otherwise been delayed, we need to know. Your class was sworn in today. My number here is ..."

I replayed the message right away, as though that would make it make more sense. Kim's words revealed nothing new the second time and I felt the first rustlings of worry in my chest.

Come on, I told myself. *You know he's there. The message is just a bureaucratic mix-up. These are the feds; every ten years they do a census in which they lose several million of us. Just call her; she'll tell you it was a mistake.*

I picked up the phone.

"Good morning," I said when she answered. "My name is Sarah Pribek. You left a message on my machine, asking about Michael Shiloh, my husband. I guess he was delayed, and I just wanted to make sure he got there."

"He's not here," Kim said flatly.

"Oh," I said. "Are you sure you would know? I mean—"

"Oh, yes, I'm sure," she said. "It's my job to know. Are you saying he's not in Minneapolis?"

"He's not here," I said after a moment. I felt the muscles in my throat work emptily as I swallowed without realizing I was going to do it.

"Sometimes people do back out," she said. "Usually, they have second thoughts about the gun-carrying part of the job—"

"That wouldn't be it," I said. "I have to go." On that abrupt and artless goodbye, I hung up.

My first thought: he'd been in a serious car accident, maybe on the road from the airport to Quantico. But that wasn't right. If there'd been an accident, maybe Quantico and Kim wouldn't necessarily have been notified, but I should have been. Shiloh would have been carrying his Minnesota driver's license, and his home address was on it. They always notify family. But I'd heard from no one but Kim.

My next call was to Vang. "I'm not going to be in for an hour or so," I said. "There's something I need to run down. Sorry."

"Something on a case?" he asked.

"Something personal," I said, feeling evasive. "This probably won't take all that long," I said apologetically before hanging up.

Shiloh was not at Quantico. What did that mean?

If he'd changed his plans, if he'd decided to withdraw from the Academy, he'd have told me. And he'd have told *them*. But that didn't matter, I thought, because he wouldn't have changed his plans. Shiloh had wanted this. If he wasn't there, something had gone wrong.

Had he even gotten as far as Virginia?

Whether he was in Minnesota or Virginia seemed to be the first distinction I was going to have to make. If I couldn't narrow that down, I would waste crucial time, because I couldn't effectively deal with both places at once.

I reached for the phone book and looked up the number for Northwest Airlines.

"I'm going to need a passenger manifest for your two thirty-five flight to Reagan on Sunday," I told the ticket agent.

"What?" she said. "We don't—"

"Give that information out, I know. I'm a Hennepin County sheriff's detective. I know the drill." I shifted the phone to my other ear, already digging in my desk. "Tell your ticketing supervisor that my name is Detective Sarah Pribek and that I'm going to be down there in about twenty-five minutes with a signed request on stationery with our letterhead."

chapter **6**

The traffic wasn't too bad at midmorning. The brightest part of the morning was over and clouds were scudding in from the west. As I turned east on the 494, the familiar red-and-gray bodies of Northwest planes were launching themselves toward the sky ahead of me.

The ticketing supervisor at Northwest's offices—Marilyn, as her name tag identified her—led me to a small office not far from the main ticket counter.

I laid the request letter on her desk and she scanned it quickly, looking from the body of the text up to the letterhead.

"Can I see your identification?" she asked.

I took out the leather holder, flipped it open, and let her peer at it.

"Tell me again what you need?" she asked, sitting down behind her desk.

"I'm tracking down a passenger who was supposed to be on your two thirty-five P.M. flight to Reagan on Sunday. I'm not sure he was on it."

"Sunday?" she said. She rotated her office chair a little and sat forward to open a filing cabinet next to her desk.

"Name?" she asked, putting the printout on her desk.

"Michael Shiloh," I said. "Shiloh with an *h*."

I'd identified myself to her as Sarah Pribek, and now I opted not to mention that Shiloh was my husband. It seemed best to present myself as an impersonal agent of the law.

"Yup." Marilyn interrupted my thoughts. "Got him. Listed on the two thirty-five on Sunday, like you thought." She paused. "He did not check in for that flight."

"He wasn't on it?"

"No."

"What's the next flight after that?"

"Into Reagan or into Dulles? The absolute next flight was a two fifty-five into Dulles."

"Can you check that one?"

"There're a couple more flights into both airports; I can check all of them for you." She reached back into the filing cabinet; she'd left the drawer open, and now she walked her fingers over the edges of the documents. Licking her thumb, she culled several of them.

I leaned against the wall to wait, watching as she read. She shook her head slightly each time she finished with an individual manifest. When she was done she turned her desk chair slightly and faced me again. "He's not listed on any of them."

I nodded.

"Sometimes people fly into Baltimore," she said thoughtfully. I shook my head.

"No," I said. "I don't think so. But you've been really helpful."

I thanked her and took my leave, heading toward the escalator.

Shiloh could have flown into Baltimore, he could have chosen a different airline, but there was no reason for that. He'd *had* a ticket. More to the point, if he'd missed Northwest's 2:35 flight—and that in itself was very unlike him—and caught a later one, he'd have been at Quantico by now. Kim would have heard from him. No matter what had gone wrong with his travel plans, I couldn't imagine how he could be so late.

Had I completely ruled out the possibility Shiloh had gotten to Virginia? Not necessarily. It was possible that I was dealing with a situation where two things had gone wrong at once: Shiloh had missed his flight and taken a later one on a different carrier, and then something had happened to him in Virginia. If that was true, and I focused the search for him in Minnesota, that would be a disaster. It was essential that I narrow down from where Shiloh had disappeared.

Disappeared. I hadn't meant to think that, and doing so gave a little jolt to my nervous system, followed by a galvanic flush under my skin.

I sat on a bench for a moment and watched the travelers pass by.

Overhead, I saw a security camera discreetly peering down at passing travelers from a crossbeam. If worst came to worst here, I could always review security tapes. Maybe that would end up being the only thing to confirm Shiloh had been here.

Disappeared was fast becoming the operative term, whether I wanted to admit it or not.

About two years ago, an overprotective father from Edina,

a Minneapolis suburb, sent his bright eldest daughter off to school at Tulane University in Louisiana. He didn't want her to drive, he'd said, but she'd won a campus lottery for a parking space outside her dormitory and was thrilled about it. She was not about to be talked out of taking her little Honda.

Still, Dad was unhappy about her driving all the way by herself. He insisted that she call him both nights on the road as soon as she got a motel room, and she agreed to do so. For his peace of mind.

What Daughter didn't remember was that only a year earlier, her neighborhood had been gerrymandered out of the Cities' once all-inclusive 612 area code, something that was happening to suburbs of metropolitan areas nationwide as cell phones and the Internet gobbled up available phone numbers. The daughter hadn't taken notice. She hadn't spent the night outside the Cities for three years; therefore, she had never called home from far away.

When she tried to call home, her first night on the road, she got a recording saying her call couldn't be completed as dialed. Baffled, she'd tried again. Then a third time. She had no idea what was going on. She left a message on her father's voice mail at work, although it was a Saturday night and she knew he wouldn't get it anytime soon. Then, sensibly, she went out for a meal.

When her father didn't hear from her, he called us. Genevieve and I were skeptical. She'd been gone only twelve hours. She was 18 years old, off to college, getting her first taste of freedom. We were both certain about what happened: His daughter had forgotten to call.

"She wouldn't do that," he insisted. "She promised she'd call. She keeps her promises."

"I know you don't want to believe this," Genevieve had said, "but there's a perfectly logical explanation. We just don't know it yet."

"No," he'd said. "There isn't."

On Sunday afternoon his daughter called. Just outside the Louisiana state line she'd remembered the new area code and pulled over at a rest stop to try calling home again. This time she'd gotten through, embarrassed and laughing. Dad called us, just embarrassed.

There's a perfectly logical explanation. No, there isn't. Those two statements made up the yin and yang of most missing-persons cases. I said something like the former to people week in and week out, and they responded with the latter. Sometimes I told them the new-area-code story, as an example of the kinds of innocent things that sometimes kept people from coming home or checking in. Few relatives were comforted by it. They shook their heads, unconvinced. It was a good story, they thought, but it had nothing to do with their situation.

I understood for the first time how they felt. Driving north on the 35W, I kept telling myself that there was a logical explanation for why Shiloh hadn't turned up at Quantico or called me. And then from the back of my mind, another voice kept saying, *No, nothing can explain this.*

Around noon, Vang found me at the fax machine at work, sending a request for information to hospitals around the Quantico area. He did a mild take when he saw me.

"Where have you been?" he asked. "I thought you were going to be out for an hour or so."

"I was at the airport," I said. "And then at the hospitals."

I didn't tell him all of it. I'd also been calling and faxing cab companies, asking them to check their records to see if they'd sent a driver to our address. From Norwest, I asked for paperwork on our account, a record of recent activity; I'd requested phone records from Qwest.

I looked up at Vang. "I'm having a sort of personal emergency. I'm looking for my husband."

"I thought he was supposed to go work for the Bureau," Vang said. "Did he change his mind?"

"No," I said, watching my document inch out the other end of the fax machine. "But he never got there."

"Really?" Vang said, frowning. "You mean he didn't get to the Academy, or he didn't get to Virginia?" His words were measured, and his demeanor calm, but I could almost see a dozen questions jockeying for position in his mind. It was only natural. It's not every day a coworker tells you their spouse is missing.

"I'm not sure," I said. "He never got on the plane, but his things are gone." I considered Shiloh missing since two thirty-five on Sunday, the time of the flight he'd apparently planned to be on and wasn't. "I'm going to file a report, make it official."

Vang hesitated. "In terms of department regulations, I'm not sure you're supposed to be involved." He seemed to have moved on to points of procedure; those unspoken questions were apparently going to remain unspoken.

"I know," I said. "But with Genevieve gone, I'm the only one around here who regularly works major missing-persons cases," I said. Then I backtracked from my own dire words. "I'm not saying this is major. I'm saying that I can't come back to work until I've heard from him."

"I understand," Vang said. "Anything I can do?"

"I'm going to be getting some faxes, in response to my requests," I said. "You can call me and let me know what they say; that'd really help."

"Where will you be?" he asked.

"Home," I said. "A search of the house is where I'd start if this were any other case."

"...say analysts from Piper Jaffray. WMNN news time, twelve twenty-eight. More after this."

I turned the volume down on the radio and stuck the nose of the Nova out of the parking garage ramp, into the traffic.

It wasn't exactly true, what I'd told Vang. A search wasn't where I'd usually start. I'd start by talking to the people closest to him.

Like his wife. *Right.* I pulled out onto the road.

Other than me, who were those closest to Shiloh? His family was in Utah. He hadn't spoken to any of them in years.

He'd gotten along well with his old lieutenant, Radich, who still ran the interagency narcotics task force on which Shiloh had served. And then, of course, he'd known Genevieve longer than I had, but I knew they hadn't seen each other recently.

He'd had no partner, working alone on cold cases. Before that he'd worked mostly alone in narcotics, undercover, paired sporadically with MPD guys or Hennepin County deputies. Like me, he played basketball with a loose and ever-changing coalition of cops and courthouse people, but never seemed to forge serious friendships there. And Shiloh didn't drink, so he didn't go for beers with the guys.

Sometimes I forgot what a private man shared my bed.

As I parked the Nova where Shiloh's old Pontiac used to sit,

I thought what bad luck it was that Shiloh had sold his car last week. Until the day that we were all tattooed with clearly visible ID numbers on our skin—and I sometimes thought that day was coming—vehicle license plates served to identify us. Missing-persons reports went out with license numbers on them, and everywhere cops in patrol cars would be ready to spot the car and plates. It's a much more difficult task to find an adult who doesn't have a car.

Although the top of the driveway was much closer to the back door of the house, the one that led past the washing machine into the kitchen, this time I went into the house through the front door. I wanted to stand in the entryway where Shiloh's keys were missing from the hook.

Keys and jacket and boots. That's what had suggested to me on Sunday that Shiloh had simply left for the airport. And he had, hadn't he?

There was a simple sign I hadn't checked yet.

As a patrol officer, I'd occasionally collar people for minor crimes and then let them off, if I felt it was warranted. When I did, I had a standard line. "The next time I see you (working this street corner/with a spray-paint can in your hand/et cetera), have your toothbrush with you."

They knew what I meant: that they'd be spending a night in jail next time. Later, as a detective, I used the toothbrush as a litmus test for whether someone was missing voluntarily or against their will. It was a test that crossed boundaries of age, gender, and ethnicity. To a person, almost nobody left home knowing they'd be gone for more than twenty-four hours without grabbing their toothbrush on the way out. Even when they didn't have time to pack, they had time to retrieve it.

Thinking of this morning, I saw in my mind's eye my brush

hanging alone in the little rack of the inside door of the medicine chest. A quick trip to the bathroom confirmed this. His wasn't there. I went back into the bedroom and went to the closet door, opened it, looked up at the high shelf. His valise, too, was gone.

All signs were pointing toward his having gone to the airport.

Had he left me a note and I simply hadn't found it?

Shiloh had remarked once that our kitchen table was "a filing cabinet waiting to happen." It was always overloaded with bills, papers, mail, newspapers, newsletters, notes to each other. It was a mess I now needed to sift through.

The newspapers were local, the *Star Tribune* and St. Paul's *Pioneer Press*. Under that was the newsletter from the police union. A cadge letter from the Society for the Prevention of Cruelty to Animals: Shiloh gave them money from time to time. Here was the paperwork from the phone bill, with toll and long-distance calls itemized. A quick scan revealed all the numbers to be familiar, with none arousing my suspicions. A catalog from a gun dealer. A piece of cop junk mail: "... so revered, it's used by the Israeli police..." A wrinkled white paper bag from a delicatessen, flat and empty: I remembered it from when I'd brought home dinner late about three weeks ago. A slip of paper with a phone number on it, but this time it was one I recognized: the local FBI field office.

The last item, the deepest archaeological layer, was two sheets of scratch paper, one with red wax drippings on it. That was from the dinner we'd had on our wedding night, two months ago. Shiloh had dug up a boxy red candle and lit it, an ironically celebratory gesture, with the sheets of paper set underneath to catch the melting wax.

There was no note.

I walked back to the entryway, the better to start my search from scratch. Honestly, I did not believe that Shiloh had been injured or killed here. Even so, I had to look around.

There were no pry marks on the front door. The lock appeared untampered with, and I couldn't remember feeling anything wrong with it when I'd unlocked it.

I walked the perimeter of each room, looking at the windows for signs of a break-in. They showed none. The spaces behind the furniture showed nothing but dust bunnies. There was nothing valuable missing. Nothing cheap, either, from what I could tell. The shelves were as laden as ever with Shiloh's books. I would never be able to tell if any of them was missing. Shiloh's interests were extremely varied: fiction and nonfiction, Shakespeare, texts on investigation, a Bible, several slender volumes of poetry by authors I'd never heard of: Saunders Lewis, Sinclair Goldman.

There was nothing resembling dried blood or bloodstains anywhere.

The bedroom was tidy, although somewhat less so than Shiloh had left it—I hadn't made the bed this morning when Vang had called me.

When kids disappear, I look under their beds early on. Children tend to think under the bed is a sly hiding place. Often, the girl's diary is there. Adults use more care in hiding their valuables.

Even so, I sat on my heels and flipped up the blanket, which hung long from the rumpled surface of the mattress.

"Oh, no," I said.

It wasn't hidden, just sort of pushed out of the way for convenience's sake. If I'd been looking down last night I'd have seen the dull gleam of light on black leather, just under the bed frame.

I jerked Shiloh's timeworn hard-shell valise out. It was heavy. Obviously packed. I opened it. The shaving kit was inside the valise, the toothbrush in the kit. Shiloh had been efficient. He'd packed in advance, and then he'd put the valise where it would be out of his way, not underfoot in our narrow bedroom.

On top of the folded clothes was a paperback copy of a classic text on investigation, and inside that, like a bookmark, was a ticket for Northwest's 2:35 P.M. flight to Washington, D.C.

He'd never even left for the airport. Somehow, that made it real.

chapter **7**

I'm not sure how long I sat by the bed, not thinking but just internalizing. Some long moments passed and then I got up and walked back to the kitchen, to stand in the middle of Shiloh's vacated home and life in Minneapolis.

A missing adult male. What would Genevieve and I look at first?

Money, we'd say. How were his finances? Bad enough to skip town? How was the relationship with the wife? Did he have a girlfriend on the side? Did he have a problem with alcohol or drugs? Could he be involved in criminal activity? Did he have a record? Associate with criminals? Did he have serious enemies? Who would benefit from his murder? Did we have a good idea of the location from which he'd disappeared? If not, what's the house look like? And where's the car?

It was a fertile field of questions. The problem was, I could sort through them in about a minute's time.

Shiloh's finances were my finances, and I knew they were fine.

The state of our marriage? Interviewing spouses had taught me that no other question was so fraught with the possibility of self-deception.

But Shiloh and I were good. We'd only been married two months. We'd really have had to put a lot of effort into screwing things up in such a short time.

We kept two Heinekens in the refrigerator in case of guests. Those two green bottles were still in their place, untouched. Lapsed though he was from his childhood religion, there were parts of Shiloh's personality that approached the monastic. Though he drank when I first met him, he'd since completely quit, and as for drugs, I'd never seen him take anything stronger than aspirin.

A criminal record would have killed Shiloh's chances with the FBI, and he'd passed their rigorous screening. He associated with criminals only as a detective who had the usual relationships with informants.

Enemies? I suppose Annelise Eliot, whom he'd caught after thirteen years of life as a fugitive, had reason to hate him. But everything I'd heard about the case suggested she'd directed her hostility to larger and more political targets, like the lawyers in California building their careers on her prosecution, whom she denounced in the media while proclaiming her innocence.

No one, that I could see, would benefit from Shiloh's death.

The house wasn't a plausible site for some kind of violent event. I'd already searched it and it was in order.

I chewed the end of my pencil.

Maybe I was going at this the wrong way. I was thinking of Shiloh impersonally, as a case. But I knew him, maybe better than anyone. It was, in a perverse way, an ideal situation.

What had he done, the day and a half that I'd been gone? He was leaving for Virginia soon. He'd packed, to be sure. Maybe run a load of laundry beforehand. And he'd gone out to get food, probably, because we tended to restock the refrigerator on a basis closer to daily than to weekly.

Shiloh habitually ran every day, so he'd probably gone out for one of the long runs he liked when I wasn't at his side to quit after four miles. And what else? Maybe he'd read, maybe watched some basketball. He might have slept early, on a quiet Saturday night without his wife around.

It was a safe, sane, and boring course of events. None of those activities seemed to allow for Shiloh to simply disappear. Except . . .

A long-distance run had been, nominally, the most dangerous part of the routine I'd reconstructed for Saturday and Sunday. Mostly, people who ran never encountered more than an obnoxious dog, but there were exceptions. Runners took paths through quiet and dark places, away from city lights. Occasionally paramedics carried them from state parks and nature trails minus their cash, with head traumas or stab wounds. Shiloh, six-foot-two, young, and athletic, was the least likely of marks for a mugger, but it had been a theory that at least made some sense.

I went back to Shiloh's valise and opened it. Thumbing through the clothes, I saw the gray-green of his Kalispell Search and Rescue T-shirt, the one he favored for running and basketball games. Squashed against the frame, wrapped in a plastic grocery bag to keep the soles from rubbing against the clothes, were Shiloh's running shoes. He only had one pair.

Here were his running shoes; gone were his heavy-soled boots and his jacket. I felt a small twinge of satisfaction. This was progress.

Shiloh had gone somewhere on foot. Not running, not the airport, either. An errand. He'd gone out somewhere, casually dressed, and hadn't come back.

The phone rang.

"It's me," Vang said. "Some faxes came in for you from Virginia-area hospitals. No one fitting your husband's description has been admitted in the last seventy-two hours."

"I know," I said.

Genevieve, in my earliest days as a detective, told me: "When you've got a missing-persons case you think is really legit, one that you've got a bad feeling about, the first twenty-four to thirty-six hours are key. Work it hard and work it fast." Usually, cases like those were the disappearances of children. Other times the missing persons were women who turned up missing against a backdrop of suspicious circumstances: evidence of a break-in or a struggle, a chorus of friends witnessing to a creepy ex-boyfriend hanging around, a recently obtained restraining order.

No such events surrounded Shiloh's disappearance. In this case, I'd spent most of the thirty-six hours not realizing he was missing.

Even so, I was going to do now what I should have done

then: I was going to work all the angles I could think of in the next twenty-four hours.

I needed to talk to people in our neighborhood. Most of them were working people, though, and wouldn't be home in the middle of the afternoon. And some, our less immediate neighbors, would need a picture of Shiloh to prompt them.

There was one person, however, who knew Shiloh by sight and was almost always in.

The widow Muzio probably saw Shiloh more than any of our other neighbors. She thought the world of him, mostly because Shiloh looked after her. He did this because Nedda Muzio lived alone, and she was getting senile.

Mrs. Muzio had an aged, sweet-tempered dog with the rangy build and curly hair of a wolfhound, with maybe some shepherd in her blood, too.

This dog, who had the unlikely name of Snoopy, used to escape from Mrs. Muzio's backyard through a misaligned and unlockable gate. On a regular basis, Shiloh used to hear Mrs. Muzio yelling ineffectually for Snoopy. He'd track the dog down at whichever neighbor's trash can she was eating out of and bring her home.

Mrs. Muzio was always effusive in her joy at Snoopy's return, partly because she blamed Snoopy's disappearances on "rascals" who stole her. These same rascals stole her Social Security check from the mailbox, when Mrs. Muzio lost track of the date and didn't realize the first of the month wasn't coming for another week. They broke into her house and turned the faucet on, stole food from her cupboard, looked in the windows at night. Shiloh used to go over and patiently reason with her, but he never really made a dent in what he'd called her delusional structure. Fixing her broken gate, which he did one Saturday afternoon and which kept Snoopy inside, was a more concrete help.

When I'd first moved in with Shiloh, Mrs. Muzio had cast a forbidding eye on me. Her paranoia had marked me as an instant enemy. "Why you steal?" she'd yell when Snoopy went missing, or she'd shout *"Strega!"* when she saw me. *Witch,* she was saying; I looked it up in an Italian-English dictionary. Shiloh, amused, told me about the warnings she'd whisper to him about *that woman,* afraid for his well-being.

Then, for no reason that I could see, maybe just the wind blowing north-northwest, she stopped. Mrs. Muzio warmed to me. I was no longer *strega.* I wasn't even just Shiloh's girlfriend to her; I was *fidanzata,* his fiancée.

As I approached her house, I looked with worry at her front walk. It needed tending. The concrete was breaking up, tectonic plates rising and falling under the forces of Minnesota summers and winters. She could easily trip someday, coming or going. Maybe I'd mention this to Shiloh when I saw him again.

I knocked on the door, pounding with the side of my fist instead of my knuckles. It wasn't rudeness; Mrs. Muzio was hard-of-hearing.

"Hello, Mrs. Muzio, can I come in?" I asked when she appeared in the doorway.

Five-foot-two and stooped, she turned a benign, blank face up to me.

"You know who I am, right?" I prompted her.

"The *fidanzata,*" she said, her face creasing into a smile.

"Not anymore. We're married," I explained. She didn't respond.

"Can I come in?" I repeated, wiping my boots on her mat as an illustration and a cue.

I liked the inside of Mrs. Muzio's home. She cooked a lot, scratch meals with her garden vegetables, and as a result her home smelled of Italian cooking instead of the must of age that hung in the homes of many people in their eighties.

In the kitchen, she made coffee. I stood on her cracked, pale-pink linoleum and watched. She hadn't understood me when I'd told her that Shiloh and I had married. It didn't really matter, yet if I couldn't communicate that concept clearly to her, how well would this whole interview go? Could I make her understand anything?

I caught her eye. "I'm not Shiloh's *fidanzata* anymore. We're married." She looked at me with incomprehension. I held up my hand, showing her the ring. "Married. See?"

Understanding dawned and she smiled. "That's lovely," she said. Her accent made it *thatsa lovely,* the speech of a B-movie Italian widow. She poured the coffee and we settled at her kitchen table.

"How's Snoopy?" I asked.

"Snoopy?" she repeated. She nodded toward the back door, near which I saw gray-muzzled Snoopy sleeping near her empty food bowl. "Snoopy is-a . . ." she considered, "old. Like me." She laughed at herself, her eyes flashing.

Unexpectedly I saw a young girl six decades ago in Sicily, with dark eyes and a ready laugh and a strong body. I'd never seen her before in this widow's stooped form and that made me ashamed of myself.

"Listen, Mrs. Muzio," I said. "I need to talk to you. My husband, you know, Mike?" I paused.

"Mike?" she said.

"Right." I nodded affirmatively. "Have you seen him recently?"

"He fixed the gate," she said.

"That was months ago," I said. "Just this week, have you seen Mike? When was the last time you saw Mike?" I kept trying to hit the key words hard.

"I see him walking down the street," she said.

"What day?"

She squinted like she was making out Shiloh's form. "Yesterday?" she suggested.

"I don't think it was yesterday," I said. "Can you think of something else that happened on the same day that would narrow it down?"

"The governor was talking on the radio."

"About what?"

She shook her head. "He was talking on the radio. He sounded angry."

"That was the same day you saw Mike walking?" I asked.

"Yes. Mike is walking in the street. He looks angry. Very serious face."

"Okay," I said. "Have you seen anything strange lately? Especially around our house?" I knew I could be opening a Pandora's box, remembering the omnipresent "rascals," but Mrs. Muzio shook her head. If her memory was a bit fuzzy, she wasn't paranoid today.

I stayed another ten minutes to be polite, talking, winding the conversation back to neighborhood goings-on in hopes of jarring loose anything else that might help, but I learned nothing. I stood and set my empty coffee cup in the sink.

"You are leaving now?" she asked me.

"When Mike comes back we'll drop by for a visit," I promised.

Outside, a cool wind had picked up, rattling the dry-leaved branches.

Mrs. Muzio thought she had last seen Shiloh out walking and looking "angry." That was, by her account, the same day that she'd heard the governor talking on the radio and sounding "angry." Everyone seemed to be angry in Mrs. Muzio's world. I wondered how much faith I could put in her observations.

Then again, Shiloh, when he was deep in thought, often had a guarded, inward expression that some people might read as anger. Maybe old Mrs. Muzio was right.

She had said she'd seen Shiloh walking. Not out running, not in somebody's car. That squared with my theory that he'd gone out somewhere in the neighborhood on foot and not come back.

I'd done my hardest interview. It made sense to work from hardest to easiest. That made Darryl Hawkins next. I checked the time on my cell phone. Almost three o'clock; it was still too early. He and his wife wouldn't be home from work until around five. I needed an errand to take up the interim time.

I still lacked a good picture of my husband. I had only one, and I didn't think that Shiloh knew I had it.

Annelise Eliot had never really believed she was going to be identified and arrested after over a decade of peaceful life under an assumed name. When Shiloh finally came to her with an arrest warrant, she'd lost control. In an impulse that must have mirrored her thirteen-year-old crime, Annelise grabbed a letter opener off her desk and tried to stab him. He'd gotten a hand up in time, but she'd sliced a deep gash into his palm.

The local media hadn't been tipped to the arrest, but they were ready the next day for the arraignment at the US courthouse in St. Paul.

The *Star Tribune* and the *Pioneer Press* had run virtually the same photo: Shiloh among a small cadre of uniformed cops, bringing Annelise Eliot in for her first court appearance, a courteous but controlling hand on her arm. The bandage on his hand, from where she'd cut him, was clearly visible.

That image was the quintessential Shiloh to me, and I'd clipped it for that reason. But it wouldn't work to show to strangers. He'd turned his face away from the photographers, so that he was in profile.

When I got home, I picked up the phone and I dialed a number I'd come to know by heart.

When Deborah put Genevieve on the line, I said, "It's me. I need to ask you for a strange favor."

Silence on the other end.

"Are you there?" I asked.

"I'm here," she said.

"At your Christmas party, Kamareia had a camera." When the name Kamareia was hard to say, I realized I hadn't mentioned her directly all during my visit. "She was taking a lot of photos of people, including Shiloh. I need to go to your place and get one of those pictures."

There was another silence, but this time Genevieve broke it without prompting. "All right."

"I need to know where they might be," I added.

"Well," Genevieve said slowly, "there's a shoebox she keeps on the shelf in her closet. I've seen a lot of photos in there."

"All right," I said, "good. But your place is locked, right?"

"Mmm, yes," Genevieve said. "But the Evanses across the

street have my spare key right now." She seemed to think again. "I'll call and tell them you're coming."

"Thanks, Gen," I said. Then I asked: "Have you spoken to Shiloh recently?"

"No," she said. "Not for a long time."

Time and again, on the job, we'd asked loved ones for recent photos of missing persons. It was perhaps the most crucial item in a search.

Genevieve wasn't making the connection. She seemed to find nothing strange in the fact that I needed to go to her uninhabited, locked house in search of a recent picture of my husband.

"See you soon," I said, which probably wasn't true, and hung up.

chapter 8

The day Genevieve's only child died, the two of us had enjoyed a particularly good day at work, a productive day. I remember that we were both in good spirits.

I'd given her a ride to work that morning, since her car was in the shop, and I was taking her home as well. Since I had to drive her there, Genevieve had said, I might as well stay for dinner. And Shiloh, we reasoned, might as well come with us. Shiloh had been buried in the analysis of evidence that back then nobody had believed was the trail of Annelise Eliot. He was reluctant to stop and go with us, but Genevieve and I had worn him down. Genevieve had been particularly winning in her pleas. She was worried about him and how hard he'd been working.

It was February, one of those days in which the Cities were swaddled in a low-hanging layer of cloud that actually made for more warmth than a bright, clear day. Earlier, fresh snow had fallen, covering up the soot-stained ridges that lined the streets from the first weeks of winter onward.

Only the last of the day's business for Gen and me had been something of a waste of time: A missing-child report. We'd driven out to a small condominium complex in Edina to meet a young father whose six-year-old son had failed to come home on the big yellow bus.

The young man—"Call me Tom"—was a relative rarity, a divorced father who'd gotten custody of his child. "It's been tough," he said, leading us inside his condo, where boxes were stacked up in the living room.

"Did you just move here?" I asked him, but even as I did I sensed that these weren't moving boxes; they were all uniform in size and shape.

"Nah," he said. "Those are juicers. I sell them, and a herbal health and diet supplement, from here at home," he said. "And I just got my fitness-trainer credential, so I've been trying to build up a clientele base. Things have been pretty hectic."

It made sense. Tom had a compact but obviously well-built frame, and his brown gaze was intense but not personal, in the practiced way of a salesman.

Sometimes you just get the feeling, whatever the external circumstances of a disappearance, that nothing is seriously wrong. As Genevieve and I began our interviewing, I started getting that feeling right away.

Naturally, the ex-wife had been of most interest to us; abduction by noncustodial parents is far more common than stranger abduction. "Nah," Tom said, shaking his head emphatically. "I already talked to Denise at work. Kinda freaked her out, but I told her to stay put for now, that I'd already called you guys." He frowned. "She wouldn't just up and take him, believe me. She can hardly be persuaded to spend enough time with Jordy as it is," he said. "She's got a new boyfriend, and besides, she's an antiques freak. Half the time I pick Jordy up on Saturdays, he's spent his day walking around behind her in stores, looking at Tiffany lampshades and delft tiles. Is that how you entertain a six-year-old?"

I didn't know how to answer that, so I said, "What about other relatives?"

"What about them? You mean, would they take Jordy?" Tom looked puzzled. "I can't imagine it. My family's all in Wisconsin, and Denise's—" He broke off. "Oh, no."

Genevieve and I looked at each other. *Eureka.*

"What is it?" Gen said, cuing him.

"Oh, no," he said again, reddening. I suspected the heat in his face wasn't embarrassment but anger. "Hold on," he said, jumping up and going to the phone.

Tom dialed and spoke to an unknown party on the other end. It was clear within a minute that Jordy was safe and sound. "Is he there? He is?" Tom said. "I'll come get him."

I looked at Genevieve and spoke quietly. "What do you think?" I asked. "Wife's sister?"

She shook her head. "Mother-in-law. I'd almost guarantee it."

We got most of the story in overheard, and increasingly vitriolic, sound bites.

"Well, you didn't even tell me. God, I was worried as . . . No, I didn't. I said I didn't need you to take him for a haircut. No, I *did not agree,* I did not. . . . You're twisting what I said in order to . . . His hair is not . . . That's how they all wear . . . You're not listening!"

After a moment even unshakable Genevieve looked up at

the opposite corner of the room and rubbed the side of her nose with one finger, the embarrassed way people do when they're hearing a conversation they'd rather not. I stood up, in hopes of illustrating to Tom that Genevieve and I needed to leave, now that the situation had obviously resolved itself.

"Look, I gotta go," Tom said. "I'll come get him. *No, I'll come.* Just stay there."

He hung up and walked back to us, shaking his head darkly. "Denise's mother," he said. "I can't believe it. No, I *can* believe it. It just kills her that I got custody. She can't handle it."

He filled us in on the details: he and his mother-in-law had recently had a debate about young Jordy's hairstyle. From this debate, she had apparently incorrectly inferred that she had permission to drive up from Burnsville, where she lived, pick Jordy up after school, and take him to the barber. "I told her no, flat out, but of course she says I said yes," Tom said.

I say that Tom told both Genevieve and me this story, but his behavior was interesting to observe. He'd started out by directing his comments to me. Maybe it was because I was closer to his age, maybe it was because I was more visibly the regular visitor to a gym and therefore some kind of kindred spirit, maybe it was simply my ringless finger. But as I gave no encouragement to his airing of grievances, he correctly began identifying Genevieve as the more sympathetic pair of ears, probably because she was at least nodding in the right places. Gradually his attention and eye contact shifted. It was to Genevieve that he told the backstory: a history of meddling by the former mother-in-law, unwanted advice, veiled jabs at his child-rearing skills.

Finally, when his attention seemed solely on my partner, I drifted out of his line of sight and looked out the window at the parking lot, where a trio of warmly dressed kids were practicing free throws on one of those freestanding basketball hoops with a weighted base you can buy at sporting-goods stores. They were sure going to learn an unpleasant lesson, I thought, when they started playing on a court with a regulation-height hoop.

"Gen, we really should go," I said.

But Genevieve was a soft touch. "Listen," she told Tom kindly, "I know you wouldn't want to press any sort of charges, but it might be good if my partner and I had a talk with your mother-in-law about the seriousness of taking someone else's child without explicit prior permission."

Behind Tom's back, I scowled at Genevieve and shook my head. Genevieve ignored me, but fortunately, her offer wasn't accepted.

"Nah," Tom said, shaking his head. "It won't help. She'll just insist I gave her permission. She'll even tell you that she specified that she'd do it today and that I agreed. Thanks for the offer, though."

I was relieved, but Tom wasn't quite through with us yet. On our way out, he tried to sell Genevieve a home juice machine. Genevieve declined, but Tom pressed a card with his phone number on it into Gen's hand, "in case you change your mind."

As soon as Genevieve started the car, I said, "What did you think you were doing back there, volunteering the two of us to drive down to Burnsville to listen to the other end of that extremely tedious family squabble?"

Genevieve was unfazed. "It might have been interesting. Aren't you the least bit curious about whether the grandmother was an old battle-ax, as described? What if we found her to be gracious and reasonable and entirely in the right?" She accelerated slightly to merge with the traffic on the road.

"You mean, like the *gracious, reasonable* people we always deal with on the job?" I said. "Even if she was, I still don't think driving down to Burnsville would have been the best use of the county's time."

"It would have been proactive policing," Genevieve said, adopting a pedantic tone. "Would you rather have to straighten things out again, the next time *grand-mère* decides to borrow Jordy again without asking?"

I had no answer for that, and we fell silent for the rest of the trip.

But when we were back at our desks downtown, Genevieve said, "Hey, what were you laughing about back there?"

"At Tom's place? I didn't laugh," I said. "I thought I kept a very straight face when he finally realized where his kid was."

Genevieve rolled a leaking pen against a piece of scratch paper and then, dissatisfied, capped it and threw it in the trash. "Not then. A couple of minutes before that, when we were in his kitchen. I looked over at you and I could see you were trying really hard not to laugh at something. I had to distract the guy so he wouldn't see."

I thought. "Oh, *that*," I said. "You didn't see the sign on the refrigerator?"

"What sign?"

"He had a sign on his refrigerator, for those herbal weight-loss supplements, that said: 'I lost 60 pounds. Ask me how!' " I was almost laughing now, remembering it. "That cheery little sign was right in my line of sight, and I couldn't help it, I kept thinking of his kid."

Genevieve looked blank.

"A six-year-old weighs about that much. *I lost 60 pounds.*"

Understanding, Genevieve shook her head. "Your sympathy really bleeds sometimes. For all you knew, his son could have been picked up by a pedophile and—"

"Bullshit. You knew as well as I did from the moment we walked into his apartment that his son was fine. For a couple of minutes," I said, "I seriously suspected the kid was lost among all those boxes of juice machines in the living room."

Genevieve gave me her serene smile. "You're just upset that he didn't like you well enough to try to sell *you* a juice machine."

"Damn straight he didn't," I said. "And you know why? People know better than to try that shit with me. What is it with people and these home-sales things?"

"Oh, good," she said, "we're off on a rant now."

"Well, come on," I complained, "people actually believe the 'get-rich-working-from-home' ads in the back of magazines. But who do they end up trying to sell this stuff to? The people around them. Neighbors, family. I mean, is that really salesmanship? What happens when you run out of friends?"

Genevieve gave me a look. "That would take some of us less time than others."

It took me a moment to realize what she was saying. Then I winced. "Gen, sometimes you are so mean to me, I swear it almost feels good."

She was unapologetic. "I'm just saying, the home-sales work probably gives a single father like Tom more time to be home with his son," Genevieve said tolerantly. "Besides, it's the American dream. Everyone wants to be their own boss."

"Not me," I said. "I'm happy with my lot in life: working for you."

"Oh, *please,*" Genevieve said. "I do all the heavy lifting in this partnership. Like covering up for you when you're on the verge of cracking up in the middle of an interview situation in someone's kitchen." She turned away from me and typed steadily.

I wasn't ready to quit provoking her, though. "Genevieve?" I said.

"Yes?" But she didn't turn around to look at me. At least not right away. But in a moment the silence got to her and she swiveled her chair to look at me. "What?" she said.

"I lost sixty pounds."

Genevieve turned away again, but too late; her shoulders were shaking. She was laughing. I'd gotten her.

A lot of people would have frowned, I suppose, but cop humor is frequently dark. It doesn't affect the way you do your job.

"You just wait," Genevieve said. She was smiling, but she pointed a didactic, warning finger at me. "You wait until you've got a kid of your own. Then you'll understand. You'll want to go out to Edina and apologize on your hands and knees to that guy."

We worked awhile in silence. When I heard her roll open her desk drawer, I knew we were done for the day: she was taking out her purse. "You about ready?" she said. We didn't always leave at the same time, but today, of course, I was driving her home.

"Yeah," I said, shifting and stretching in my chair.

She closed her desk drawer with the heel of her hand. "As

long as you're driving me home, you want to stay for dinner?" she asked.

"That sounds good," I said, watching her stand and arrange her bright-red muffler over the nape of her neck, pulling the ends of her short, dark hair out over it. "I end up eating alone a lot these days. Shiloh's been working late almost every day." I stood, too.

"That's no good. Vincent was the same way when he was studying for the bar exam. I never saw him. Sometimes I was afraid Kam was going to start calling any tall black man she saw on the street 'Daddy,' " said Genevieve, pulling her jacket on over the red scarf. "Anyway, let's pick up Shiloh on the way."

"He won't come," I said as we headed for the elevators. "He's working on the Eliot thing."

"Let me handle him," Genevieve said.

"Oh, right. Amaze me with your Shiloh-handling skills. No"— I took her arm—"we're not going to the precinct."

Genevieve looked at me questioningly.

"At this hour, I'll bet you five bucks he's up in the law library," I told her.

And he was, by himself, deep in his work. He looked up at both of us when we came to stand at his side.

"Hey," I said, laying one hand on the table.

"Hey," Shiloh said in return. He touched the back of my fingers with his, a gesture no one else in the library could have seen unless they were looking right at table level. "I'll be home in about an hour and a half," he said quietly. "Hey, Genevieve, how have you been?"

"I'm good," she said. "Sarah and I are taking you to St. Paul for dinner at my house."

"Can't," Shiloh said, not elaborating.

"I already lost five dollars to your girlfriend, who bet me you'd be up here," Genevieve said, even though my offhand remark hadn't in any way been an actual wager. "So make it worth my while."

Shiloh glanced up at her, then took out his billfold and laid a five-dollar bill on the table. "Quit while you're even," he said, looking back down at his work, as if he expected her to go away.

"Kamareia has something she wants to give to you guys," Genevieve persisted.

"What?" he asked her.

"A photo, from the Christmas party, of the two of you," she said.

"Well, I'd hate for you to have to carry that in to work," Shiloh said. "I know how heavy a Polaroid is."

Genevieve was silent.

"This is important," Shiloh said. "And you know I can't work on it on my own time."

Genevieve sat on her heels so she could look up at him. "You're working too hard," she said softly. "You need to learn to throttle back, Shiloh."

When he still didn't respond, she said, "We miss you."

Shiloh ran a hand through his hair. Then he said, "Who's cooking, you or Kamareia?"

"Kamareia. It's your lucky night," Genevieve said. She knew she'd won.

It was around six-thirty when we pulled into her driveway. Downstairs, the interior of Gen's house was dim, although a little bit of electric light was falling down the staircase from upstairs, along with the sound of a radio playing.

Genevieve flipped on the lights, illuminating the empty, clean kitchen. Kamareia was nowhere to be seen. Genevieve frowned. "That's odd, she told me she was going to start dinner around six." She looked toward the staircase and the sound of the radio. "It *sounds* like she's here."

Her perplexity was understandable: Kamareia was responsible, and she genuinely liked to cook. "It's okay," I reassured Genevieve. "We're not starving. We'll live."

Genevieve was looking up the staircase. "Let me see what's going on," she said.

I leaned against the railing of the staircase, waiting, as Genevieve went up. I heard her knock on the door frame of her daughter's room and not find her inside. Her voice, as she went through the other upstairs rooms, took on an increasingly questioning sound, but not quite worried.

"Sarah." Shiloh's mild voice caught my attention. I turned to look at him, and he nodded toward the back of the house and the sliding glass door. The door was closed, but beyond that I saw footprints in the fresh snow.

Genevieve's house shared a kind of open backyard with the neighbors to the south, the Myers. There was no fence, so I could see straight across to the back of their house. And although I couldn't see their front driveway, the bushes that lined it to the side were visible. Red lights flickered on them in a familiar pattern.

Kamareia, I thought, and knew something was terribly wrong. It never occurred to me that it could have been one of the Myers who had been injured somehow, and Kam had gone over there to give assistance and call 911.

The Myers weren't at home. As in Genevieve's house, the entire first floor was darkened, and all the noise and light was coming from the top of the stairs. I went up two steps at a time.

On the landing was a two-foot-long section of pipe, splashed with blood. Streaks of blood on the floor, footprints of blood.

Unlike the rest of the house, the bedroom was brightly lit. Electric light immersed the two EMTs, the phone that was tangled on the floor, and Kamareia, naked from the waist down, her thighs and lower legs smeared with red. There was a lot of blood on the floor. Too much. I thought of the pipe outside and knew she'd been beaten with it.

I reversed so fast I nearly skidded on the hardwood floors and plunged back through the doorway. Genevieve was halfway up the stairs with Shiloh behind her. I met Shiloh's eyes and shook my head quickly, just once, *no*. He took my meaning right away and caught Genevieve from behind, stopping her.

I went back into the bedroom and knelt next to Kamareia. Her eyes, when I could bear to look at her face, were open, but I don't know how well she saw me.

"Stay back, please." The paramedic's voice was as clipped as her southern accent could allow.

"I'm a friend of the family. Her mother's here," I told her. "If you can, get her covered up a little."

Outside, I heard Genevieve screaming at Shiloh to let her go. She'd seen the pipe and the bloodstains.

"Maybe you should go take care of the mother," the other EMT, a young man, suggested.

Shiloh was having a hard time with her, to be sure. "Kamareia's been hurt. I don't know how bad," I said sharply from the top of the stairs. "She can hear you. If you want to help, shut up and stay calm."

Gen kept trying to look past me, through the doorway, but

she stopped yelling at Shiloh. He kept his grip on her shoulders anyway.

"That's good," I told Genevieve. "You've got to be tough for her like you would for anyone else on the job."

"What happened to her?" Genevieve's voice was high, foreign to me.

That was when they brought Kamareia out. She was covered with a blanket, but her face said it all anyway. Her nose and mouth, under the oxygen mask, was a delta of drying blood; she'd obviously been hit several times in the face. Her blood was visible on the clothes of the EMTs and it made bright streaks on the pale latex gloves on their hands.

Genevieve broke free of Shiloh's grasp and touched her daughter's face, then she put her hand to her own face like she was ready to pass out. Shiloh pulled her back and eased her down to the floor.

"Can you stay and take care of her?" I asked him.

Shiloh had a bit more medical training than I did, from his days in Montana where the small-town cops did all kinds of emergency work, and he nodded. His eyes weren't on me; they were on Kamareia, being carried away from us.

I caught up with the paramedics outside. "I'll go with you," I said abruptly. The young man was in the back with Kamareia already; the woman was just about to close the doors.

She gave me a sharp glance. Under her teased ash-blond hair and plucked eyebrows she had eyes as level and unshakable as any doctor's. She was entirely in charge here, and no one likes to be told how to do their job.

"I mean, I'd like to go with you," I amended. "Her mother's not functioning well enough to do it, but Kam needs someone with her." I stepped a little closer. "And if you didn't radio for a crime-scene unit already, you should do it on the way. We'll need one here."

She understood then that I was a cop. "I will," she said. "Get in."

The Evanses, the neighbors who had Genevieve's key, were working people. I was fortunate, though: they had a college-age daughter living at home, and she was there when I got to Genevieve's neighborhood, a peaceful street of tall, narrow homes. "This'll probably take me fifteen minutes, maybe twenty," I told the Evans girl.

I thought I might have to hunt around, if the shoebox wasn't in the spot Genevieve had suggested, or the photos weren't in the shoebox.

I stood for a moment on Genevieve's front porch, thinking of February, then I slipped the key in and shot the dead bolt back.

Inside, the house had the kind of clean stillness that greets you when you come home after a long absence. Gen had done a housecleaning before she'd left. I could see vacuum marks on the carpet, and a few fresh footprints. Those would be the tracks of the Evans girl, I thought. There were plants on the windowsill and the shelves, still green and full-leaved, and somebody had to be keeping them watered.

The room looked bigger and emptier than I remembered. The last occasion on which I'd spent a lot of time here, there'd been a fat, bushy fir tree in the corner laced with colored lights, a happy and slightly drunk crowd of cops and probation officers around, and Kamareia had been taking pictures.

Upstairs, I flipped on the lights in the room that used to be

Kamareia's. I'd never really been inside, but it was obvious that it was exactly as she'd kept it in life.

The room was done in light shades: a peach down comforter on the twin bed, a blond wood desk. It was Standard Schoolgirl from Dayton-Hudson, except for Tupac Shakur glowering down from the wall.

Kamareia had loved poetry, and unlike Shiloh she'd put thought into her bookshelf, organizing from the oldest, *The Canterbury Tales,* to the newest, a collection by poet Rita Dove. One volume, a collection of Maya Angelou's work, was vaguely familiar to me. Its cover design was a bright patchwork of color, and I had a vivid, isolated memory of seeing it in Shiloh's hands.

I sat on my heels and pulled the book off the low bookshelf. Shiloh's writing was on the inside front cover. *TO KAMAREIA THE WORDSMITH,* the simple inscription read.

Her backpack from school sat on the floor next to the desk, looking as if it were ready to be picked up and hauled to class. It wasn't what I had come for, but I sat on my heels next to it to see what was inside: a spiral notebook, a calculus text, *Conversations with Amiri Baraka.*

They were likely the very things she had carried home from school the day she died; the backpack's undisturbed contents testified to the abruptness with which Genevieve had closed the door on this room.

Genevieve had known her daughter well. The shoebox was on the top shelf, and inside were several envelopes from the photomat. Each was dated. I found the one marked 12/27.

Inside was a parade of candid shots, some of colleagues and friends of mine, some of strangers. Here was one of me, with

Shiloh's arm around my shoulder, his expression uncharacteristically unguarded.

I took the photo of the two of us, and another of Shiloh standing with Genevieve by the cheerful, squat Christmas tree. It was a good picture, well lit. You could see his face clearly, and almost his whole body; it gave a good impression of his height.

Replacing the photos, I put the shoebox back on its shelf, where Kamareia had kept it. Or as Genevieve had said, *keeps.* Keeps.

Goddammit, I thought.

I took the stairs two at a time on my way back down. I was ready to be gone.

Darryl Hawkins, his wife, Virginia, and their 11-year-old daughter, Tamara, were the newest additions to our Northeast neighborhood. Darryl, a mail carrier in his late thirties who looked about ten years younger than that, had come across the street early on to admire the Nova. He owned a Mercury Cougar he was fixing up; we'd talked cars for about twenty minutes.

Shiloh had noticed something else about our new neighbors: their dog. It looked like a black Lab/Rottweiler mix, and it lived on the end of a chain.

The Hawkinses' side gate was made of cyclone fencing. We could easily see through it to the backyard, and no matter what time of day or night, the dog was there at the end of its ten feet of chain. It got food and water and was brought inside in bad weather. But I'd never seen it walked, played with, or exercised.

It bothered me, but not as much as it did Shiloh.

"Well, at least he's not beating the damn dog," I pointed out. "And he doesn't beat his wife, like the last guy who lived there."

"That's not the way an animal's supposed to live," Shiloh said.

"Sometimes you can't help what other people do."

Shiloh had let it alone for a while. Then one afternoon I'd seen him sitting in the front windowsill, finishing an apple, watching something across the street. I followed his gaze and saw Darryl Hawkins waxing his dark-blue Cougar.

"You're thinking about the dog again, aren't you?" I said.

"He spends hours taking care of that damn car every weekend. The car's not even alive."

"Let it go," I advised.

Instead, Shiloh pitched the apple core into the bushes and swung his legs off the windowsill, jumping down to our front yard.

He was across the street for about fifteen minutes. Neither of them raised their voices; I would have heard it from where I was. But Darryl Hawkins's posture became rigid early on, and he came to stand very close to Shiloh, and Shiloh held his ground. I saw anger in the line of his back, too. When he came back his eyes were dark.

I didn't ask what the two of them said to each other, but it put a permanent end to warm relations between our two houses. Virginia Hawkins avoided my eyes, embarrassed, when we passed in the market.

When I returned from St. Paul, the blue Cougar was in the driveway.

Darryl answered the door, still in his USPS uniform.

"How have you been?" I asked.

"All right," he said. He didn't smile.

"I could use your help with something," I told him.

He didn't invite me in, but he opened the screen door between us so that we were face-to-face.

"You know my husband, Shiloh?" I said.

"Huh," Darryl said, almost a laugh, but without humor.

"Have you seen him in the last few days?"

"Seen him? What do you mean?"

"I mean, I'm looking for him," I said. "I haven't seen him or heard from him in four days, and to the best of my knowledge no one else has, either."

Darryl raised his eyebrows. "He gone? That's something. If it was you who wised up and left him, I could understand that."

"I didn't come here to get flattered at Shiloh's expense," I said evenly. "And he hasn't left me, he's *missing*. I'm trying to find out when was the last time you saw him, if you saw anything strange going on at our house or in the neighborhood."

"I ain't seen nothing in the neighborhood, except the usual." Darryl leaned against the doorjamb. "Your man? I see him running all the time. I don't even think about it anymore, so I can't remember the last time." He shrugged. "Now that you mention it, I ain't seen him running in about a week."

"Okay," I said. "Will you ask your wife and Tamara if they saw anything, and if they did, will you come over and let me know?"

"Yeah, all right." He half closed the screen door, then he said, "I didn't know you two was married."

"We got married two months ago," I said.

"Huh," he said. "Look, if I think of anything else I'll let you know. Really."

"I appreciate it," I said.

The rest of the interviews with our immediate neighbors

were as unfruitful. No one could remember specifics, except that they'd seen him running from time to time, and no one had seen him running in the past few days.

I showed the photograph around: to more neighbors, at businesses near our home, to kids on bikes, to adults walking home from work. "He looks familiar," a few people said, peering at the photo. But no one could remember having seen him specifically on Saturday or Sunday.

Ibrahim lifted a hand in greeting when I pushed open the swinging door to the Conoco. I waited for him to finish with a customer before I told him what I needed.

Ibrahim nodded, eyes narrowing. "Mike was in here a few days ago. Maybe more than a few." Ibrahim's English was perfect. Only his accent gave away his childhood home, Alexandria.

"Was it before last Sunday?" I asked.

He rubbed his balding head in thought.

"Try to remember something else that happened the same day, to set it apart," I suggested.

Recognition sparked in his eyes. "The fuel delivery was late that day. So it was Saturday."

"Did Shiloh come in before or after the delivery?" I asked.

"Oh, before," he said. "Maybe noon, one o'clock. I remember it now. He bought two sandwiches, an apple, and a bottle of water."

"Did he say anything that stands out to you?"

Ibrahim shook his head. "He asked how I was, I asked after him. That's all."

"When you asked him how he was, what did he say?"

Ibrahim frowned. "I'm sorry, I don't remember."

"That means he said he was fine, thanks," I said sourly.

Ibrahim smiled. "You're a clever woman, Sarah."

"Not lately," I said.

When I got in, the message machine light flashed in a single on-and-off pattern. One message.

"Sarah, Ainsley Carter wants you to call her when you get a chance," Vang's recorded voice said. *"It's an outstate number that she gave me, looks like she's back in Bemidji...."*

I picked up a pen and quickly copied down the number that he recited.

Ainsley picked up the phone on the fourth ring. "Oh, hi, thank you for calling, Detective Pribek," she said.

"How's Ellie?" I asked.

"Much better, it seems," she said, and I could tell from the lightness of her voice that she wasn't just trying to put a bright face on things. She sounded genuinely relieved. "The doctors at the crisis unit let her come home with us yesterday. Joe and I said we'd let her stay with us, and the psychiatric evaluation suggested she'd do okay under family supervision. And we're finding her a therapist in town."

"That's good," I said. "What do you need from me?"

"Nothing," Ainsley said immediately. "I just wanted to thank you. What you did that day ... I was too upset to realize it at the time, but what you did was extraordinary."

My leap into the river, the minor notoriety around the department it caused, my embarrassment...these seemed like events from a year ago.

"I'm just glad Ellie is getting better," I said.

"She's on her way," Ainsley said. "I really believe that she is. Detective Pribek?"

"I'm here," I said.

"When I tried to call you at your work number, your partner said you were on leave, and then he wouldn't say why."

"Well, I am on leave," I said.

"It wasn't because of Ellie, was it?"

"Of course not," I said. "Why would—"

"What you did was so extreme, I thought maybe you violated procedure and they put you on administrative leave because of it." Ainsley laughed a little. "At least, that's what I was afraid of."

"No, nothing like that," I said. "This is personal leave, not administrative."

"Oh, good. Well, I'm glad I got to talk to you. I just felt you should know what happened to Ellie, after what you did for her. You know, to give you a feeling of closure."

"Thank you," I said. It was true: on the job you deal with a lot of individuals who aren't criminals, just people with problems, under pressure they can't handle. You deliver a lot of people to crisis units for observation, and make referrals to domestic-abuse hotlines and sexual-assault counseling services, and then you never know what happens after that. "A lot of times I don't get that, you know, closure," I told her.

After we hung up, I tried to let the good news about Ellie lighten my mood. I felt nothing and instead drifted toward the television, thinking of the evening news, and turned on the TV in the middle of a news story I vaguely remembered from radio broadcasts in the morning.

Early Sunday the highway patrol had been called to investigate a Ford pickup wrapped around a tree outside Blue Earth, the apparent result of an unwitnessed single-vehicle crash. The owner, a man in his sixties, was nowhere to be found and the theory now was that he'd walked away from the wreck disoriented and gone off into the countryside. The story didn't really merit the time KSTP gave it, being set so far out of the Cities, but the visuals were good: a state police helicopter circling over the skinny trees of autumn, a tracking dog eager on its leash. KSTP showed earlier footage of the truck being towed off. The front-end damage was nasty, but otherwise the truck looked solid and powerful, well maintained in life, its paint still gleaming black where it wasn't marred by the crash.

KSTP cut to world news and the phone shrilled in the kitchen.

"Is this Sarah Shiloh?" It was a male voice I didn't recognize, using a name I barely thought of as my own.

"Speaking."

"This is Frank Rossella, down at the medical examiner's office? I'm sorry I didn't get in touch with you during business hours."

"What is it?" I said.

"There's a John Doe down here. We think you should take a look at him."

On my way out to the car, my little speech to Ainsley Carter came back to me: *A lot of times you don't get closure.*

As I slid behind the wheel, ready to drive to the medical examiner's building, a voice in my mind said, *Here's the closure you wanted, Sarah, here's your closure, here's your closure....*

I drowned it out with the noise of the Nova's engine.

chapter 9

Even when they aren't specifically assigned to Homicide, most cops get more opportunities than they would prefer to go to the morgue. Sometimes I went alone with a photograph in my hand. Other times I went with a relative of a missing person, to walk them through the identification procedure.

But I hadn't been down in a while, and I hadn't met forensic assistant Frank Rossella, who was new. The flat *a*'s in his accent suggested he'd come from Boston or New York.

He was perhaps five-foot-seven and in his thirties, his brown hair in a low pompadour. For a shorter guy, he walked quickly. I had to lengthen my stride to keep pace as we went down a hallway lined with stainless-steel doors, temporary housing for the dead.

I stopped in the doorway of the autopsy room. The tables were empty, but near one of them was a gurney with a corpse on it. The body was exposed from foot up to chin level, with the head draped. This was the opposite of procedure in many IDs, in which the body was tastefully draped except for the face and head when family members came down to see it.

Rossella saw where I was looking. "This guy took a shotgun blast to the face," he explained. "There're really no features to work with," he said. "Otherwise I'd just have had you ID using a Polaroid of the face, you probably know that we do that whenever we can. But that won't work here, and dental records aren't going to be of much use, either."

"Fingerprints?" I asked. I was having a little difficulty getting a whole sentence out.

"Not useful, either. Bad prints. We found this guy in the underbrush near the river, out of town a ways. He'd been out awhile, we don't know how long. He died a couple of days ago, that's as close as we can narrow it down."

Rossella looked at me, waiting. I moved to stand next to the gurney. There was a familiar scent on the body that I thought was the scent of the Mississippi.

I can still smell the river in your hair, I heard Shiloh say.

"Mrs. Shiloh?"

I didn't realize I'd closed my eyes until Rossella said my name and I opened them. "I'm sorry," I said.

You're working here, a voice said in my mind, not Shiloh's now but my own. *Do your job. Look at him.*

Despite having walked the survivors of murder victims through this, I now found I didn't know what to do. I felt like I was taking an important test and hadn't studied at all.

"I'm sorry," I said quietly. "Without facial features, I just don't know what I'm looking for. I mean, I'm not sure I can rule anything out with certainty."

The body was about Shiloh's height, but weight was hard to tell. He was clearly Caucasian, and I didn't think he'd been heavy in life.

"How tall is he?" I asked.

"Seventy-two inches long."

"Long?" I said with distaste, before I could stop myself.

"Tall," Rossella said.

"Shiloh was six-foot-two."

"Sometimes measurements taken after death are imprecise," he said. "The limbs aren't usually straight when rigor mortis sets in. It makes measuring tough." He paused. "In fact, I had to break some of the fingers to get prints."

"What?" I said. Even though I didn't want to, my gaze immediately went to the hands, looking for the bent and distorted fingers. I'd heard people crack their knuckles before, and that was loud enough. How much louder, I wondered, was the sound of breaking bone?

I looked up to see Rossella's eyes on me.

"It happens," he said, calmly meeting my gaze. "I thought you'd have heard about it before."

"No," I said, trying to regain my mental footing. I looked at the hands again. Both were bare.

"He doesn't have a wedding ring," I said.

"It could have been taken, if this was part of a robbery," Rossella suggested. I stepped in closer to the right hand.

"What is it?" Rossella asked.

The right arm was stiff, of course, and resisted my attempts to turn it over. I ended up sitting on my heels instead, holding up the hand a little so I could see it clearly. When I saw the palm, I drew in a deep breath, relieved.

"It's not him," I said.

"You see something?"

"Shiloh has a scar on his palm," I said, pointing. "This guy doesn't have it."

"I see," Rossella said.

He pulled the sheet down, over the body.

"Thank you for coming in, Mrs. Shiloh," Rossella said. "I can't tell you how sorry I am to have put you through this." Then he smiled.

On the way to the elevator my knees were shaking, just a little.

When I got home, there was a strange car parked outside the house, a dark late-model sedan of a make I didn't recognize. A man stood at the door, made a silhouette by the brightness of the motion-sensor floodlight his approach had switched on.

I pulled the car up short, halfway up the driveway, and jumped out.

He turned and stepped down, onto the sidewalk, and his features became clear to me. It was Lieutenant Radich, supervising detective on the interagency narcotics task force.

"Lieutenant Radich? What's going on?" I asked. I slammed the car door and started across the lawn, not going around to the front walk like I usually would have.

I must have spoken more sharply than I realized, because he shook his head and lifted the white bag in his hand like a flag of surrender.

"Just a visit," he said. "I was picking up some food after working late and thought you might be hungry."

When had I last eaten? I'd made coffee when I'd gotten up in the morning. Down at the station, more coffee. I had no memory of a meal.

"I am," I said. "Come on in."

I'd met Shiloh during his undercover narcotics days, and Radich had been his lieutenant back then. But I knew him best from pickup basketball games. He wasn't as frequent a player as Shiloh or I, but very competitive. At 50, he had a perpetually tired face and Mediterranean coloring, a streak of gray in his black hair.

"I got your message," he said as I turned on lights in the living room and the kitchen. "I left word on your voice mail at work, but I guess I should have tried you here instead. I haven't seen Mike. Haven't talked to him in, maybe, three weeks."

"That's what I would have guessed," I said.

"Sorry," he said.

"Do you want a beer?" I asked.

"Sure," he said.

I took one of the two Heinekens out of its place in the refrigerator door and opened it. I went to the cupboard to find Radich a glass.

"No need," he said. He took the cold bottle from my hand and took two deep swallows. Pleasure registered on his tired face, and I was suddenly glad for hospitality beer in the kitchen of two people who no longer drank. "Long day?" I said.

"Not as long as yours, I imagine," he said. He set the bottle down on the kitchen table and started unpacking his deli bag. "Sit down and eat."

He'd brought two sandwiches and a container of potato salad. I brought plates and spoons over, poured myself a glass of milk. I was afraid if I had Coke at this hour, as tired as I was, my hands would start shaking.

We ate in near-silence. When I picked up the sandwich he'd bought for me, the bread was warm, and the cheese on the edges was melted. Radich had brought me a hot meal. My hands quivered, and I realized for the first time why religious people gave thanks before eating.

Radich probably wasn't ravenous, like me, but he settled down to the business of eating as wordlessly as I did. I was almost through with my sandwich before he spoke.

"What do you know?" he asked, looking levelly at me over his beer.

"Nearly nothing," I told him. "I don't know where he is, I don't know why he's there. I don't know of anybody who would know anything. If Shiloh weren't my husband, and I were investigating this case, I'd be hammering away at me, interviewing and reinterviewing. Because I'm the one who lived with him, I'm the one who knew him best, and ... and ..."

A strange thing happened then. I just heard myself say *knew him best,* and suddenly the rest of the sentence got away from me. I had no idea what I was supposed to say next.

Radich put his hand on my shoulder.

"I'm okay," I said. I swallowed a little milk. "And no one else seems to know anything." I was relieved finally to have remembered what I was going to say.

"Enemies?" Radich asked.

I shrugged. "Well, every cop has to worry a little bit about retribution," I said. "But we're both careful. Unlisted and unpublished. He gave informants his cell-phone number only."

Radich nodded slowly, thinking. "What have you done so far?"

"Less than I thought I'd get done in one day," I said. "I'm putting together the paper trail. Interviewing neighbors. And"—I disliked even saying it—"I just went to the morgue."

On the other side of the kitchen wall, a noise like earth-bound thunder boomed, a sequential reverberation. Radich looked up.

"What the hell was that?" he said.

"A train," I said. "They're putting a freight together up at the yards. When they hook cars up, you can hear the impact travel down the rest of the train. Like vertebrae of a spine."

"You get used to that?"

"It doesn't happen all that often," I said. "But the trains run right past our backyard several times a day. More than several. I'm used to it, and Shiloh even likes it, he says."

"Were you in the morgue looking at an unidentified body?" he asked, returning to the subject at hand.

"Yeah," I said. "It wasn't him."

Radich drank the last of the Heineken before he spoke again. "Why'd they call you? They couldn't fingerprint?"

"I guess not," I said. "This forensic assistant said the fingerprints were—" I stopped to retrieve the exact word from my memory. "He said something about the fingerprints not being useful."

"Why not?"

"I . . . I don't know." It had seemed reasonable at the time. I hadn't questioned Rossella, I suppose, because I'd been so damn afraid that this was it, the end, that I hadn't been thinking logically. "He said something about exposure or the body being outside."

Radich shook his head, slowly. "I know forensics isn't your line, it's not mine, either, but I do know that they can almost always print. Sometimes in real hot, dry conditions the skin gets unprintable, I've heard of that."

"Well, that wasn't the case here," I said slowly, seeing the right hand again as I checked for the scar Annelise Eliot had left there.

"Tough on you, to have to go down there for nothing," Radich said, dismissing the issue. He started packing up the trash into the deli bag.

"I'll clean up," I said, waving him off. "I really appreciate the dinner."

Radich stood. "I know you've got my phone number down-town," he said, taking a pen from his jacket, "but I don't think you've got my home number." He cast a glance around the table, saw the pale peach take-out menu of the deli he'd gotten the sandwiches from, and wrote on the margin of it. When he handed the menu to me, there were two numbers on it. "Home and cell," he said. "If you need anything, any help... or more food"—his mouth quirked slightly at the corner, not quite smiling, like he was worried even a small joke wasn't right given the circumstances—"you call me."

"Thanks," I said. "Really, thanks." I didn't know what else to say.

"Hang in there, kid."

"I'm trying," I said.

"We all feel for you."

His black eyes were warm with compassion. Radich had been a cop too long to suggest that everything was going to be all right.

chapter 10

I went by work the following morning. Vang was already in.

"Any news, Pribek?" he asked.

I shook my head. "Nothing," I said. "It's making me kind of crazy. Nobody knows anything. Nobody's seen him."

It was true. I'd collected faxes from Qwest and the bank, which I was looking over. The only number on our phone bill that I hadn't identified right away I'd called, and it had turned out to be the prosecutor's office in San Diego. The lead lawyer on the Eliot case, Coverdell, had explained that Shiloh had answered a few questions about the investigation.

"When did you speak with him last?" I'd asked Coverdell.

"Over a week ago. I don't remember the day," he had said.

Vang picked up his phone, dialed, and listened with the receiver held against his shoulder. He said nothing, only wrote on a pad. Checking his messages.

When he hung up, he said, "Prewitt wants to see you."

"He does?" I glanced up, searching Vang's face for implications. Prewitt was our lieutenant. "Did he say why?"

"It's about your husband, I figure. What he said was 'When you see her, ask her to come see me.' It didn't sound urgent. If I were you, though, I'd catch him now, while he's in." He paused. "Bonney turned up, by the way."

I must have looked blank, because Vang said, "You know, the Wayzata sex offender? Turned out he'd switched shifts with a coworker who'd needed a day off later in the week, so his absence from work was totally innocent."

"Yeah?" I said without interest.

"Admitted to hitting and burying the dog, too. Cried when he told us about it—um, you want to be left alone, don't you?"

"Sorry," I said, looking up. The faxes had recaptured my attention. "I'm kind of distracted right now."

Vang nodded. "Well," he said. "I should go, then. The missing-child task force is meeting."

"Oh, yeah." Were I not on leave, I'd be going, too, as Genevieve would have.

But Vang's voice told me he wasn't finished, and again I looked up from my paperwork. "What?"

"Look, Prewitt got in touch with the medical examiner," he said. "He told him about the situation. You might be getting a call if they've got a likely John Doe in the morgue."

"I already did."

"Really?" Vang said. "That was fast. I should have called you last night and warned you."

"Don't worry about it," I said.

But it was too late. I'd managed to put Rossella out of my mind, but suddenly he was a figure on my mental landscape again. I thought about the way he'd called me *Mrs. Shiloh* when we were in the morgue, not *Detective Pribek,* and his private smile after he'd thanked me for coming in.

The sergeants to whom I'd answered in my career generally had to move stuff off their spare chair before someone could sit down: manila folders, papers.

Lieutenant Prewitt had a real office, although a small one, and his guest chair was vacant. He had audiences often. Genevieve had reported to him; I did now, in her absence. But since taking over her responsibilities, I hadn't really had the opportunity or need to talk to Prewitt.

"You wanted to see me?" I said, standing in his open door.

Prewitt looked up from his work. He was a young 55, with all his hair yet. It was salt-and-paprika now, instead of the carroty red I'd seen in pictures of him in his uniformed days.

"Please," he said. "Come in and sit down."

I did as he asked.

"I saw your report," he said. "Tell me what's going on."

I ran a hand through my hair, a gesture I thought I'd outgrown, and summarized.

"Shiloh was supposed to leave for Quantico on Sunday on a two-thirty flight," I said. "He never made it. His things are still at the house. He hasn't called, he left no note. I've checked the usual sources—hospitals, the highway patrol—and haven't found any suggestion of an accident."

Prewitt nodded. "Have you talked to his friends?"

"I've spoken to Genevieve recently—I mean Detective Brown—and I'm sure she hasn't talked to him. And Shiloh was kind of tight with Lieutenant Radich, but he hasn't heard anything, either."

"Those are the only people you asked?"

"Well, no," I said. "I spoke to the FBI agent he worked with on the Eliot case, and neighbors, of course." It didn't sound like a whole lot of people, now that I thought about it. I chewed a bit of dry skin on my lower lip. "Shiloh wasn't ..."

"He wasn't what you'd call real sociable, was he, Detective Pribek?" Prewitt said.

"No, sir," I said.

"Family?"

"Shiloh and them really didn't talk."

Prewitt lifted his eyebrows and nodded to himself. I'd said nothing untrue, but felt angry with myself, as though I were exposing the most dirty corners of Shiloh's life to Prewitt, who wasn't even his superior. Shiloh was MPD, not Hennepin County.

"How was your relationship?"

"It was good."

"Was Shiloh drinking?"

It doesn't matter how high you go. Cops are blunt.

"He doesn't drink," I said.

Prewitt sighed, like a doctor who couldn't find anything wrong with the patient before him and had six more in his waiting room. "So," he said, "what are we going to do about you." He said it flatly, not like a question at all.

"I'm going to keep investigating."

"That's a conflict of interest. I thought we were granting you personal leave."

"You are. And I know it's a conflict," I said. "But it's not the kind of conflict of interest we usually see. It's not as if I'm investigating a case in which a family member of mine is a suspect, or being sent to arrest someone who committed a crime against someone close to me." I paused to collect my thoughts. I wasn't used to speaking this plainly to superiors. "Shiloh is missing. I can't just let other people look for him."

Prewitt nodded and tapped his desk with a pen. He looked back up at me. "Believe me, Detective Pribek, I'm not insensitive to your ... to your situation."

I wondered what unspoken word or words he had tripped over.

"But if you want to be involved unofficially, it has to be just that. Unofficially." Then he tapped a pen against a folder. "I'm not naive. I realize that your shield may aid you in your search for answers. I can't expect that you won't use your status with this department. For that reason, you need to consider yourself, personal leave or not, a representative of the Sheriff's Department. Your comportment must reflect that."

"I understand," I said.

"Another thing, I'm not sure how much support we can give you."

I didn't know what to say, and Prewitt, fortunately, went on.

"Shiloh lived—lives—in Minneapolis," Prewitt said. "It's MPD's case to investigate. Generally, we don't get involved in cases like this, a single missing adult male, when it's in their jurisdiction." He didn't elaborate. "Moreover, unfortunately, we're down two people now in our investigation division. You and Brown."

"I know," I said.

"We'd like to offer you more help, but in light of that, we really can't."

"I know," I repeated.

"Of course, his report's gone out. Everyone knows he's one of ours. I'm sure there's more than the usual concern out there." He paused. "Did he really not own a car?"

"He used to," I said. "He'd just sold it a week ago."

"I see," he said.

I heard dismissal in his tone and knew I should stand, but there was something else I wanted to say.

Prewitt must have seen it on my face. "What is it, Detective Pribek?"

"It's something that..." I was trying to step carefully, "...something that I would bring up to you if it happened in our department. In-house. But it's not, so I'm not sure I should pursue it."

Prewitt's eyebrows dipped slightly. "That really doesn't tell me very much." His words were a little sardonic, but there was curiosity in them, too. I'd said too much to call the whole thing off; now I had to move on.

"I was in the morgue last night," I said. "A forensic assistant called me in. He wanted me to make a visual ident on a body he thought was Shiloh. It wasn't."

"I'm sorry about that," Prewitt said. "It happens."

"Maybe," I said. "But Shiloh had a scar on his right palm. It was part of the description in the missing-persons report. Clearly that wasn't checked. I'm wondering if I should go over there and bring it up with someone." *Over there* was the medical examiner's office. I could see that Prewitt understood, but his face said he didn't agree.

"It sounds like simple negligence to me. It's unfortunate that you had to go through that, but mistakes do happen."

I sat silent, once again missing my cue to take my leave. I

wanted to tell him something that had only recently coalesced in my mind: Rossella had said he was sorry I'd had to come in, but now I had the opposite impression, that he was secretly glad. But I couldn't tell Prewitt that. Feelings were just feelings; I couldn't expect anyone else to use them as a basis for action.

"Is there something else you're not saying?" he asked.

I touched the copper wedding ring on my hand. "He said he'd broken some fingers to take prints."

Finally I had Prewitt's attention; his eyebrows rose. "He told you that? That's a little unusual," he said.

"It's very unusual," I said. "As far as he knew, he was talking about my husband. I've never heard a pathologist or a forensic assistant say anything like that in the presence of a relative."

"He may have felt he could speak that openly to you because of what you do for a living. Sometimes people who work closely with police officers overestimate the thickness of their skin; they may even feel the need to speak in raw terms to cops, to impress them," Prewitt said slowly. "I think it very likely that he meant no offense. Relatives of the dead are sometimes too quick to see innocent behavior as inappropriate." He paused, and then said, "I don't think it's something you should pursue ... although that's up to you, of course."

"No," I said. "I'm sure you're right."

Well done, Sarah, I thought, angry with myself. *Your husband is missing. What would make you feel better? I know! Screwing up the career of a forensic assistant.* At least I hadn't mentioned Rossella by name.

I stood up, to take my leave. But now it was Prewitt's turn to prolong our meeting.

"Detective Pribek," he said, catching my attention as I was at the door. "I'm really not impervious to your pain." It was what he'd meant to say earlier.

"Thank you, sir," I said.

Alone in the stairwell, I reviewed the conversation in my mind.

Prewitt had been concerned with how I was going to comport myself while I looked for Shiloh; he was preoccupied with the personnel problem that my absence posed for him. He'd made a small effort to sympathize. *I'm not impervious to your pain.* Vang hadn't even said that much when he'd heard.

I appreciated Prewitt's words. But he had also asked the pertinent questions, made the relevant points. *Was Shiloh drinking?* he'd asked. *How were you getting along?* he'd wanted to know. I knew what he was really getting at.

Grown men rarely go missing, as a rule, Genevieve had taught me. I knew from experience that was true. They disappear on purpose, leaving town to escape debts and romantic entanglements gone wrong.

That was the unhappy truth behind Vang's embarrassed silence, Prewitt's questions. They both believed Shiloh had left me.

chapter **11**

I spent the afternoon in more routine procedures. Looking at paperwork first, sitting on the couch with documents spread out on the low, scuffed coffee table.

Shiloh's credit-card statement showed only one charge to an airline: $325 to Northwest Airlines. That was accounted for. In the absence of a charge to Amtrak or Greyhound, I went to those terminals in person. No ticket agents recognized the photo of Shiloh.

An investigation, when it is fruitless, makes increasingly wide circles. What cops don't like to admit is that the outer circle of an investigation can be like the uppermost layer of the earth's atmosphere. It's thin and unrewarding. There's not much out there to run across. Usually. But you ignore it at your peril.

For me, that outer layer was going to be our neighborhood,

which I would walk once again. Looking, thinking, retracing the steps Shiloh might have taken. I sensed it was useless even as I took a hooded jacket off the peg in the front hallway and went out the door.

After Shiloh's sixteen weeks of FBI training, when he'd received his first assignment to a field office, I was going to pack up and join him. It was nearly impossible that he'd be assigned back to Minneapolis. Shiloh had been almost apologetic when he'd told me this.

"Hey," I'd said, half kidding, "I'm a lowly cop. Who am I to stand in the way of the important work you'll be doing: catching fugitives, hunting down terrorists—"

"Pretending to be a thirteen-year-old girl on the Internet," Shiloh had interjected. "I'm serious. New agents rarely get desirable assignments. It's likely that we're going to live in an economically depressed second city. You'll be on a drug or gang task force somewhere, if the local cops are hiring at all."

"I'll find something," I'd said.

"Life there is going to be a lot different than it is here," he'd insisted. "And you've lived in Minnesota a long time."

"Then it's time I saw someplace else," I'd said.

Shiloh had painted a dark, if vague, picture of the city we'd live in after he got his first assignment. But had it been this neighborhood, the one he'd called home for years, that had somehow turned on him? Shiloh had owned no car at the time of his disappearance; Mrs. Muzio had seen him out on foot during the time I'd been downstate. The evidence suggested that whatever had happened to Shiloh had happened here.

The course I was following had taken me across University Avenue, one of the main roads through Northeast. Now I paused and looked down a wide, paved back alley that ran behind a Laundromat and a liquor store. A girl rode past me on a pink bicycle with high handlebars and a banana seat, wobbling slightly as she stood in the pedals to get more speed out of her efforts, taking a shortcut home.

The alleyway, like everywhere else I'd walked, looked wide-open and safe in the light of day. I had difficulty seeing it—or anywhere nearby—as the scene of a violent crime, even at night. Ours was a neighborhood with streetlights and foot traffic. It never got truly dark, truly isolated.

But that was a fallacy a lot of civilians bought into. They believed that total seclusion and darkness were necessary for crimes to be committed. It wasn't true. Smash-and-grab robberies, assaults, even murders, took place in semipublic places, with people not so far away.

A robbery gone wrong was perhaps the most likely scenario.

Had Shiloh been carrying a serious amount of money with him when he disappeared? It seemed unlikely, and it probably didn't matter. Money was only a risk when people had reason to believe you had it on you. Shiloh didn't dress like money, and he knew better than to let people see large bills when he had them. But people got jacked every day, rich or not.

What would Shiloh do then? I couldn't honestly say. I could imagine a calm and practical Shiloh who'd hand over his money and appease a nervous teenager with a gun or a knife. But I could also imagine a contrary Shiloh who'd resist, the same one who'd refused for months to give up on his theory that Aileen Lennox was Annelise Eliot, the one who'd picked a fruitless argument with Darryl Hawkins.

Either way, he could have gotten killed for his efforts, his

ID disappearing along with his money into a stranger's bloody hands.

So where was the body? I could visualize the rest of it, but I couldn't see a mugger disposing of the body. He'd just gotten away with robbery and murder. The worst thing he could do was stay with the body a moment longer than he had to. The smartest thing would be to run.

" 'Disappeared without a trace' is a cliché," Genevieve told me early in my training. " 'Nobody disappears without a trace' is my anti-cliché. It's the golden rule in Missing Persons."

The one case that seemed to be proving Genevieve's saying wrong was the one I was personally involved in. That in itself was suspicious. Maybe I was doing something wrong. Maybe I was too close to it. Was that what another cop would say? What Gen would say?

There were another seven hours left in my thirty-six-hour window, but it didn't matter to me anymore. There was something I wanted to do, and I didn't want to wait.

At five Wednesday evening I was at the Lowes' farm again, outside Mankato.

I could have called Genevieve. Technology has changed a lot of things. You can't turn on the TV anymore without a wireless company selling you the idea that you can trade stocks and give presentations from the top of a mountain in Tibet. Cops are among the few people who still understand the need for face-to-face communications. I'd strongly felt that this conversation with my partner wasn't something I could do over the phone.

I needed Genevieve. She'd taught me. I had to believe she could help when I didn't know what else to do. Eating up Highway 169 at 71 miles per hour, a borderline safe speed in case of patrol cars in the bushes, I'd rehearsed how I would explain things to her.

In the back of my mind was the idea that this would help Genevieve as much as me. She needed to be doing something other than hiding in a century-old farmhouse, grieving for her daughter. She was good at this work; surely it would help.

When Genevieve came to the door, she looked unsurprised, like I lived across town.

"Come in," she said, and I followed her inside. But once inside, she didn't seem to know what we should be doing.

"Where's Deborah and Doug?" I asked.

"Doug will be home soon," she said. "He sometimes stays at school to grade exams. Deb's gone to Le Sueur. She coaches the girls' basketball team and they've got an away game."

When she stopped speaking, Genevieve simply stood and waited for me to take the lead again.

"I need to talk to you," I said.

"All right."

I glanced to the side, into the living room. It seemed like the place Genevieve would take a guest who'd come to talk, if she had been thinking like a host. It seemed she wasn't.

"Do you want to make some coffee or something?" I said, awkwardly taking her role.

We went into the kitchen, Genevieve trailing me. When I started looking for coffee and filters, she took the initiative of reaching up to a cabinet over the refrigerator and bringing down what I needed. The sleeves of her T-shirt fell away, revealing the smooth muscles of triceps and deltoids. She hadn't lost all her work in the gym, not yet.

I took the cream from the refrigerator. There were eggs in the door of the refrigerator, smooth and brown, and I remembered the Lowes' henhouse outside.

"The eggs are from the chickens outside, aren't they?" I said.

"Yes," she said.

"They must really be fresh, they must—" *For God's sake, Sarah, this is not a social call.* I turned to make eye contact with Genevieve. "Shiloh's disappeared," I said.

Her eyes were on me, a sober brown gaze. Yet she said nothing.

"Did you hear what I said?" I asked her.

"Yes." Her voice was flat. "I don't understand."

We never got back to the living room. I told her the whole story in the kitchen, first as the coffee brewed, then as we drank it. She sat down at the kitchen table. I remained standing, restless from the drive.

As little as I knew about how and why Shiloh had gone missing, it took a long time to tell. I wanted to make clear to her that I'd pursued all the angles I knew, that every one had been a dead end. She had to understand that this was serious.

"Will you help me?" I asked finally.

Genevieve looked out the window, at the fallow fields of the neighbor's lands, the stubble lit by the last rays of the setting sun.

"I know where Shiloh is," Genevieve said dully.

It was too good to be true, but my heart leapt anyway.

"He's in the river," Genevieve said. "He's dead."

It was like a verdict, so calmly absolute was her voice. Genevieve was my teacher. Her voice was the voice of truth and fact to me. *Get a grip, Sarah,* I told myself. *She can't know that; she can't know that.*

Genevieve wasn't looking at me, so she couldn't see the hostile stare I was giving her. "Could you try to be a little more helpful?" I said thinly.

She turned and looked at me, and now there was a little more light, something alive in her dark eyes. "I am," she said. "I was listening to everything you said. It's the only thing that makes sense."

Her voice was very matter-of-fact, as though Shiloh were someone she'd never met. "You used to tell me yourself, he'd get depressed. He had his dark periods—"

"But not now. He was getting ready to go to Quantico—"

"Maybe he was afraid of that. He might have thought he wouldn't make it in the FBI. Shiloh was hard on himself. The prospect of failure would have scared him."

"Not that much." I felt warm in the generous heat of the farmhouse's furnace system and shed my jacket, hanging it across the back of a chair.

"Or maybe he was afraid of your marriage not working out," she said.

"We've only been married for two months."

"And already the two of you were going to be living in different parts of the country. Just the day before his trip, you went out of town without him."

"For godsakes, I asked him to come along," I told her. "He didn't want to come."

"Maybe not," she said. "But then he was home alone.

Asking himself how much longer he was going to have you, whether he'd ever measure up to his impossible expectations for himself. Shiloh knew how easily plans for the future can go wrong. At some point he walked out to the bridge—it's only blocks from your house, right?—and jumped."

I understood something then. Genevieve had moved down here from the Cities because the Mississippi River and its many bridges were too great a temptation. Asked to theorize about what could have happened to Shiloh, Genevieve had plotted a course like the one she'd so often wanted to take.

"He wasn't suicidal," I pointed out. "He wasn't even depressed."

"She was happy in her marriage," Genevieve said.

"*Who* was?" I demanded, baffled. The conversation seemed to have taken a completely unforeseen turn.

"She was happy in her marriage," Genevieve repeated. "He wasn't gay. She wasn't depressed. If he was cheating on me, I'd have known. She wasn't the kind of kid to stay out all night without calling." It was an unemotional litany. "You've heard those lines a thousand times. So have I. All detectives do. Wives, husbands, parents . . . sometimes they're the last to know the important stuff."

What she had said was true.

"Sometimes depression is just biological. There doesn't have to be an obvious trigger," she went on. "And people with depression get good at hiding it from the people around them. It wasn't your fault."

I shook my head. "He didn't kill himself."

One of the things that made Genevieve a master interrogator was her voice. It was low and soft, no matter how awful the things were she had to ask. She'd never sounded more dispassionate than she did now. Deep in her own despair, she was oblivious to the pain she was causing me.

"If it wasn't suicide, then it could have been another woman. You said he didn't seem to take anything much with him when he left the house. He went somewhere in the neighborhood. Maybe a bar."

"Gen," I said, my voice higher and more strained than normal, but she didn't seem to hear me.

"Shiloh was a healthy young guy whose wife was out of town. He went looking for some strange pussy and found the wrong woman. She stabbed him or shot him and got help getting rid of the body."

"Fine," I said, forcing my voice back into its normal low register. "You're welcome to your theories. But at least come back to the Cities with me and try to prove them. Will you do that much?"

When she didn't speak right away, I thought I'd won.

Then she said, "Back when I was a cop—"

"You're still a cop," I said.

She ignored me. "Back then, I assumed I was jaded. Just because of what I did for a living," Genevieve said reflectively. "But the world is a much worse place than I ever imagined." She paused. "I don't really think I want to know what's happened to Shiloh."

Silence fell in the darkening kitchen and I couldn't think of anything else to say.

"Well," I said finally. "Thanks for the coffee." I picked up my jacket.

At last I'd startled her. "You're staying, aren't you?" she said. The chair scraped as she got up to follow me.

"I can't," I said. "I've got things to do."

"You're going to drive back to the Cities? Now?"

"It's not late," I said at the front door. "You can always come with me. That's what I intended."

She followed me onto the porch. At the bottom of the steps I turned back. I was looking up at her. It was a rare circumstance, given the difference in our heights.

"Help me, Gen. Help me find him. I've gotten as far as I can on my own."

She shook her head. "I'm sorry."

I walked three steps toward my car and then turned around again.

"If this was Kamareia," I said, "I'd never stop helping you look for her."

I expected anger, expected her to accuse me of cheap tactics in drawing her daughter's memory into the argument. But instead she said "I'm sorry" again. The terrible thing was, I could hear genuine regret in her voice.

The mud in the yard sucked at my boots like it wanted to keep me there. The Nova slung a few pounds of it at the apple tree in the yard before finding purchase and rocketing toward the road.

chapter **12**

I knew what came next: Utah. If you don't know where someone is, look into where they've been. It's a truism in Missing Persons, although police rarely have the luxury of following up on it. But I was working for no one but myself, and I was going to Utah.

Shiloh had grown up in Ogden, north of Salt Lake City, in the middle of a pack of six children. He'd left home young. His parents had since died, and he didn't keep in touch with any of his brothers and sisters except for an annual Christmas card with his youngest sister, Naomi. With his older brothers, and Naomi's twin sister, Bethany, he didn't even have that much contact. Of course, I'd asked him why.

"Religion," he'd said simply. "To them I'm like somebody chronically ill who refuses treatment. I can't live around that."

"I know a couple of people who were raised in strict

Christian homes—Catholic or Mormon—and aren't religious anymore. Their families deal with it okay," I'd pointed out.

"Some families do," Shiloh had said.

He'd left home at 17, before finishing high school, and of course I'd asked him about that, too.

"It was logical at the time," he'd said. "I knew I wanted a different life than the one I was headed for, and I knew it wasn't going to happen if I stayed there."

Years after he'd left Utah, his family, and their faith, he'd gotten a letter from his younger sister Naomi. Shiloh had answered it, and they'd kept writing to each other for, as he told me, "a couple of months before things cooled off."

"Why'd you stop writing?" I'd asked Shiloh.

"She was starting to look at me as a project," Shiloh had said. "I could tell she was working toward getting me to come home. A reconciliation first with my family, then with God."

It seemed Shiloh had succeeded in introducing a touch of frost into their relationship, because since then they'd only exchanged Christmas cards.

Back at home in Minneapolis, it took me several minutes of sorting through the box of addresses on torn scratch paper before I found the one I needed. Naomi and Robert Wilson. The address was in Salt Lake City, and I felt certain they'd be listed in directory assistance.

There was no reason to believe Shiloh had been in contact with any of his family lately, but I needed to check it out. The ground I'd covered here, at any rate, had been stony to start with, and wasn't going to get any more fertile. And if there were no fresh leads in Utah to help me find Shiloh, there might be old ones that would help me understand him better.

Over a dinner of shredded wheat, I collected "Robert

Wilson" or "R. Wilson" numbers for the Salt Lake City area and began making the calls.

"Hello?"

A young woman answered at the second number I tried. She sounded the right age.

"Is this Naomi Wilson?" I asked.

"Speaking," she said politely.

"Naomi, this is Sarah Shiloh." I paused for a second to think how to proceed.

"Who?" she said. "Did you say your name was Sarah Shiloh?"

"Right," I said. "Your brother Michael is my husband."

"Michael? You're Mike's wife? Ohh!" she said, and laughed, sounding flustered. "Let's start over. Yes, this is Naomi Wilson, you've reached me." She laughed again. "You confused me because... well, never mind. Listen, can I talk to Mike? We haven't spoken in a long, long time."

Something in my chest felt a little colder, leaden, at her words.

"I wish you could," I said. "I'm looking for him. Nobody, me included, has seen him in several days."

There was a brief silence on the line, then Naomi Wilson said, "What are you saying?"

"Your brother is missing," I said. "That's why I'm calling."

"My goodness," she said. The words seemed inadequate, but belatedly I realized that of course a good Christian wouldn't say *Oh, Christ*. But Naomi's voice was somber as she said, "Where are you, in Minneapolis? Is that where he still lives?"

"That's where we live. But he was supposed to go to Virginia, and he never got there," I told her.

"He's missing? And you think he's out here? He's not here,"

she said, answering her own question. Then she corrected herself. "Well, not that I know of. But is that what you think, that he's somewhere out West?"

"I don't know. I need to come out and talk to you in person, maybe the rest of your family also."

"All right," she said. "When are you coming?"

"Tomorrow," I said. "A morning flight. With the time difference I'm pretty sure I could be there by midmorning. What time is good for you?"

"I work at a day-care center," Naomi said. "There are two of us there until noon, then I'm on my own until three-thirty. If you can come anytime in the morning, I can get away to talk. I'm going to have a few questions for you, too—about Mike, and how the two of you met and so on. It's been a long time since I actually spoke to him."

She gave me the address of her preschool and day-care center on the outskirts of Salt Lake City. Then she added, "You'll recognize me right away. I look like I'm ten months' pregnant."

I called Northwest and made the arrangements with my credit card, then packed. Shiloh's valise was on the floor, right where I'd left it after I'd pulled it out from under the bed and realized what finding it meant. As an afterthought to my packing, I retrieved Shiloh's old Search and Rescue T-shirt from the suitcase and threw it into my bag.

A freight train rumbled northward on the other side of the bedroom wall. I was sitting on the bedroom floor, cross-legged. I needed sleep but had reached that state where the effort of just getting undressed and brushing your teeth seems like a very sizable obstacle between yourself and your bed.

Instead I reached for the book in Shiloh's valise, pulled the Northwest ticket out. It was a broken promise, an unfulfilled contract, and the last known signpost on the sane, reasonable course of Shiloh's life before some unknown wrong turn.

I turned the ticket over, looking at the terms and conditions printed in palest green type on the back.

My heart did a gentle double thump. There was writing across the back, seven numbers in light pencil, the barest of spaces between the third and fourth number.

Shiloh was careful and he was reliable, but the only things I knew him to organize thoroughly were the notes and papers related to his investigations. Otherwise, he kept things in a state of manageable disorder. He stacked the bills on the kitchen table, wrote addresses down on scratch paper, and stored them in a box of letter-size envelopes, where he also kept the stamps. He wrote phone numbers down inside the city phone book, and on one occasion, in pencil on the wall over the phone. Numbers he needed over the short run he'd write on anything handy. Like the back of an airline ticket.

I drummed my fingers hard several times on the cover of the book. He'd written on his ticket. Did they take tickets from you at the gate? Or would Shiloh have this on landing in D.C., where he knew he'd need it? Or was it a Minneapolis number he'd copied down for immediate use?

I carried it to the phone and dialed the straight seven digits, no area code.

"Hello?"

It was a woman's voice, apparently at a private residence. She sounded older—60 to 70. In the background a TV was turned up loud enough that I could recognize the voices from a syndicated situation comedy.

"Hello, ma'am?" I said.

"Hello?" she repeated.

"Do you need to turn the TV set down?" I suggested. "I can hold the phone."

"Yes, wait a minute."

The television noise died; still, I was careful to speak loudly when she returned. "Hello, ma'am? What's your name?"

"Are you selling something? It's kind of late."

"No, I'm not. I'm trying to find a man called Michael Shiloh. Is that name familiar?"

"Who?"

"Michael Shiloh."

"I don't know anyone named that," she said.

"Is there anyone else there you could ask?" I suggested.

"Well," she said, sounding baffled and mildly put out, "there's no one here but me, and I don't know anyone by that name."

I believed her. Her cigarette-rasp voice, the TV set turned loud for a watcher deafened by old age . . . she sounded like a retired widow.

"Thanks," I said. "Sorry to bother you."

I knew the Cities' other area codes by heart. When I tried them, one phone rang endlessly. The other number had been disconnected, no longer in service.

With one hand on the phone's plastic tongue to break the connection, I held the receiver against my shoulder. D.C., then, I thought. Maybe this was somebody who lived near Quantico.

With a 202 area code, and the new area codes that had sprung up in the vicinity of D.C., I had two more brief and fruitless conversations and heard one more prerecorded, no-longer-in-service message.

In Salt Lake City, those seven digits connected me to the automated customer-service line of a ski- and mountaineering-goods company. ("Your call is important to us....")

Trying the area codes of outstate Minnesota wouldn't hurt, I thought.

In northern Minnesota, up in the Iron Range, the number couldn't be completed as dialed. But in southern Minnesota, it rang.

"Sportsman."

"Hey," I said. "Who's this?"

"This is Bruce, who's this?"

He sounded like he was in his early twenties, and his tone was professionally flirtatious, like a bartender's. There was crowd noise in the background.

"Is this a bar?" I asked. "You're not a sporting-goods store or anything?"

"We're a bar all right." The bartender laughed. "You need directions?"

Airball, I thought. Just some saloon down in the sticks.

"No," I said. "Actually, I'm trying to find out if anyone there knows a man named Michael Shiloh."

"Ummm," Bruce said. "I know a lot of the guys who come in here—and of course everyone who works here—and I don't know him."

"Okay," I said, and gave him my name and work number anyway. "In case you make a connection later," I explained.

"Area code 612," he said, commenting on my phone number. "Sounds like you're in the Cities. I guess you're not gonna drop by." There was a sudden burst of enthusiastic noise in the background, the cheers of people following a televised sporting event. "Too bad, you sound like a fun gal."

I was sure that was the last thing in the world I sounded like.

"Thanks for the thought," I said. "Just have someone give me a call if that name's familiar to them, okay?"

"I sure will," Bruce said.

After I had brushed my teeth and washed my face and done everything I normally did before I slept, I sat above the covers of the bed with my legs curled underneath me, afraid to actually go to sleep.

I was afraid of what my mind would bring me in the dark. In the late watches, all troubles seem darker and past mistakes more inescapably destructive.

When the charges against Royce Stewart, Kamareia's murderer, were dismissed, the full impact of it didn't really hit me until one sleepless night a few days after the judge released his ruling. I'd had to slip out of bed and into the living room, where the sound of my grief wouldn't disturb Shiloh.

Something woke him, though, and he came out into the unlighted room and held me with my wet face against his bare chest and stroked my hair, and in the dark he told me about a dream he'd been having.

I dream about Kamareia's blood on my hands, he'd said.

The words startled me. None of what happened was your fault, I told him.

No, he said, *I mean literally. That afternoon when we found her, I got her blood on my hands. After you went to the hospital with her, I was trying to calm Gen, and I put my hand on her cheek. I got her daughter's blood on her face. I didn't want her to see, I wanted to take her into the kitchen to wash it off, but there was a mirror at the foot of the stairs. I knew she was going to see it. And she did. I keep dreaming about that, about looking down* and seeing Kamareia's blood on my skin. I dream about washing it off. Horror novelists tell you that small amounts of blood give water a pink tinge, but it's not true. It's just a fainter and fainter red until finally the water runs clear.

The dissociative, faraway sound in his voice made me uneasy. Grasping at anything comforting to say, I repeated, "It wasn't your fault." I could think of nothing else to tell him.

No, he said. *It's his fault.*

I knew who he meant. Shiloh's arms tightened around me, and he said, *He should have died for what he did to Genevieve alone.*

Sometimes I thought about Shiloh's dream of blood when people who didn't know him well called him remote and detached.

When I finally did get in bed and turn out the bedside lamp, I directed my thoughts to something positive, to tomorrow. Tomorrow I would be in Utah, meeting Shiloh's family at last.

Shiloh's sister Naomi had always been, by his account, the sibling most interested in him. She had said on the phone that she was interested in how we'd met.

If Naomi Wilson was still as devoutly Christian as Shiloh had made his whole family out to be, I thought, she might not be ready to hear all the details of that story.

chapter **13**

Several years ago, my father's last girlfriend—whose name I learned and forgot in the span of a week—called to tell me my father was dead. She (Sandy? Was that it?) barely tracked me down in time for me to make the service. I'd had just enough time to call my sergeant and explain, and then buy a black dress and a pair of heels at Carson Pirie Scott before catching a flight west on a bargain regional carrier.

After spending most of his adult life in New Mexico, my father had tired of the cold winters and isolation of the high country and moved to Nevada, where his money would stretch even further than it had in the Southwest. In the desert sun of Nevada, his life savings bought him a condominium and some good times with a new girlfriend. The girlfriend (Shelly?) was a full ten years younger than him. That didn't surprise me. My father had always been a very handsome man, and he had remained that way until the heart attack claimed him. Or so people in Nevada told me.

Sandy or Shelly had arranged for him to be buried in Nevada. There was no reason to take the body back to New Mexico. My mother wasn't there; she was buried in Minnesota with her people. My brother, killed while serving in the army, had merited burial in a military cemetery with honors.

So my father was buried in a modern memorial garden on the outskirts of town, one of those where flowers too uniformly bright to be real decorate acres of sameness, and the grave markers, also alike, lie flush in the ground, hidden by green grass until you are nearly on top of them. As the nonsectarian chaplain said his few words under the canopy that shaded the coffin and mourners, I let my mind wander until one of my high heels pierced the overwatered turf and began to sink in, bringing me back to reality with a jolt.

One paper plate of food, forty-five minutes of small talk with my father's friends and neighbors, and one long rental car drive later, and I was on my way back to Minneapolis again.

There wasn't a spare seat in the coach section of the flight back. My fellow travelers seemed mostly to be retirees who'd been on gambling vacations, taking a break from Minnesota in January in the warmth of the West. As soon as we were in the air, the pilot got on the overhead and cautioned us, smooth-voiced, that the flights ahead of us were experiencing some "chop" from storms over the plains. The other pilots weren't kidding. Fifteen minutes after his initial announcement, the pilot got back on the mike and told the two flight attendants to take their seats.

The plane bounced like a sled being pulled too fast over old snowpack that had turned to hard, uneven ice. The whole airframe made crunching, shuddering noises, bouncing hard enough to shake the wattle of the blue-haired old woman sleeping next to me.

I'm not afraid of flying, but that night I had a very odd feeling, one I've never had since. I felt completely adrift and out of control. I was surrounded by human beings, but they were strangers. I felt lost, as if up in this black stratum between clouds and stars not even God could know where I was. I looked hard out the window, hoping for city lights, anything that could give me a point of reference. There was none.

I hadn't bought a real drink while I had the chance, and now I wanted one. For me it was always a physical craving that had two locations: I felt it under my tongue, and deep in my chest. I chewed the last cubes of ice from my Coke and felt a pang of regret when they ran out.

Had my mother lived, I was sure, we would have been close. She died when I was nine. My brother Buddy had been a bully, full of a sense of entitlement to whatever he wanted. Physical strength was the only thing he'd respected; at five years younger, I'd never had enough. My father, a long-distance truck driver, had slept in the main room of our trailer when he'd been at home, just so Buddy and I could have separate rooms. He never knew it, but he really needn't have bothered.

It had been a great relief to me when Buddy, at 18, had joined the army and left home. My father saw it differently. He spent long stretches on the road, and felt that no 13-year-old girl could be ready to spend those days and nights alone, without the supervision of at least an older brother. He'd put me on a Greyhound for Minnesota, where my mother's aunt still lived.

It was in Minnesota that I discovered basketball, or rather the coach discovered me, because at 14 I was head and shoulders above most of the girls in my class. I nearly lived at the gym after that, both in regularly scheduled team workouts and afterward, working to perfect free throws, striving for an absurd three-quarter-court shot. Just as a song can get stuck in your head, I sometimes heard a repeating loop of gym noise as I tried to fall asleep at night: the kinetic slamming of the ball against the hardwood floor, the shudder of the backboard, the squeaks of athletic shoes.

Everyone needs a place, and that was mine. Our team won a state championship in my senior year. There was a photo in our high-school yearbook from that night, one reprinted from one of the newspapers. It was taken just after the final buzzer, when in the midst of the celebration my co-captain, Garnet Pike, had literally picked me up in her arms, both of us laughing. Garnet was a little taller than me, and we'd all been hitting the gym hard that year. Even so, a second after the picture was snapped, we both fell, and I hit the court so hard the coach was afraid I might have fractured my tailbone. At the time I hadn't felt a thing. Immortality ran in my veins that night; we were all untouchable.

UNLV came calling, and I went to play for them, but it was never the same. College didn't suit me, and while I saw some action in games, it wasn't much, not nearly enough to make me feel needed. I'd said nothing—to do otherwise would have looked like whining—but what ate at me was the feeling that I was at UNLV under false pretenses, that I wasn't earning my place. Certainly my grades didn't justify my presence on campus.

In the media guide for that season, I look unhappy, and you can see the ridiculous sheen I put in my hair as if to underscore the distance I felt from my clean-cut, ponytailed, or cornrowed teammates. The next year I let registration slide by without signing up for any classes, then wrote a letter to the coach, packed up, and went to find a series of dead-end jobs, my last, restless detour on the road to being a cop.

Buddy had died in a helicopter accident over Tennessee, the one that took the lives of thirteen servicemen. My father hadn't believed me when I'd said I wasn't leaving my police academy training to come home for the funeral. In his world, Buddy had been a noble hero; in his world, I'd loved and admired my brother as much as he did. He had continued to expect me until the very day of the service.

The night of Buddy's funeral, I'd gotten home to find an eight-minute message on my answering machine. Outrage was my father's main theme, some disappointment, some melancholy, but always returning to anger.

He had raised me single-handedly after my mother died, he said. He had never been drunk in front of me. And later, he'd never begrudged the checks he'd sent east for my support, while I'd never written him and rarely called. Finally, he'd segued into a paean to Buddy, the fallen hero, and that was when the tape ran out and cut him off.

It was too bad that the conversation was one-sided, because it was the last substantive one we'd ever had. I thought of picking up the phone and calling him. But I knew that he wouldn't and couldn't hear what I had to tell him about Buddy, the noble warrior. So in the end I hadn't responded, and a long twilight had fallen on our relationship. Ultimately, if his girlfriend hadn't gotten my address off an old Christmas card, I wouldn't even have known about his death, nor been on a crowded bargain-carrier flight back from his funeral.

Landing at MSP, I felt relief at being on solid ground again, weariness from adrenaline letdown, and a desire for Seagram's that had suddenly doubled. I had to take a cab home anyway, so there was no reason not to stop at the airport bar.

I was almost the only person in there. A bartender sliced up lemon wedges, her face faraway. A tall, lanky man with auburn hair nearly to his shoulders and two days' growth of beard was drinking at the bar.

Instead of sitting at the bar as well, I'd taken a table against the wall, giving that man his privacy. Despite that, we kept looking at each other. Accidentally, it seemed. The TV turned a blank green face down at the bar, and there was no one else around, and it seemed like we didn't really know where to put our eyes except on each other. Maybe we sensed in each other an equality of misery.

The man leaned forward and spoke to the bartender. She mixed up another whiskey and water like mine, more vodka for him. He paid and carried both drinks over to my table.

He was kind of good-looking; maybe a little too lean. I would have described his face as Eurasian, or maybe Siberian. His eyes had just a bit of slant to them, like the eyes of a lynx.

"I don't want to intrude, but that dress looks like a funeral to me," he'd said.

We introduced ourselves without last names. I was Sarah, just back from a family funeral; he was Mike, recently out of a "very brief, very wrong" affair. We didn't expand on those circumstances. We didn't talk about what we did for a living. Within twenty minutes he'd asked me how I was getting home.

He drove me to my place, a cheap studio in Seven Corners. Inside, I left my sober black funeral dress and stockings on the floor with his weather-beaten clothes and work boots.

These were my careless days, and I hadn't been a stranger to the one-night stand. I always awoke just enough to hear the men get up to leave, but never opened my eyes, always feeling a sneaking, sorry sense of gratitude that they wouldn't be there in the morning.

This one seemed to dematerialize from my bed; I never heard a thing. I would have felt my usual relief, but for one memory.

At the airport, we'd walked in silence to the short-term parking and he'd led me to his car, an old green Catalina.

"This is nice," I'd said. "It's got character."

He didn't say anything, and I turned around to look. He'd stopped and leaned up against a concrete pillar. His eyes were closed, his face lifted into the wind that came off the airfield, frigid January air scented with aviation fuel.

"Is something wrong?" I asked.

"Nope," he'd said, his eyes still closed. "Just sobering up, so I don't cash in our chips on the 494."

I'd crossed to where he was, looking out at a Northwest plane climbing an invisible ramp of air into the night sky. And then I'd said something I didn't even remember thinking first.

"I've outlived my whole family," I said.

"God, I wish I had," he said, and I was just drunk enough that it made me laugh, a surprised, giddy sound. He opened his eyes to look at me, and then he pulled me into his arms and held me, hard, his beard scratching my cheek.

It should have been all wrong in the etiquette of a one-night stand, way too intimate for the rules of hooking up without intimacy. But it didn't bother me. It didn't even surprise me. It eased a tight feeling in my chest that even Seagram's hadn't touched.

Genevieve and I worked out together, as was our custom, later that week. On this occasion our trip to the weight room was interrupted. We were walking near the basketball courts when a voice rang out.

"Hey, Brown!"

Genevieve stopped and turned, and I followed her example.

The man who'd yelled stood on the free-throw line, flanked by three other men, all younger than him. "Why don't you introduce us to your friend!" he called.

"Those are all narcotics guys for the city-county task force," Genevieve said, "except the really tall guy. That's Kilander, a county prosecutor."

She raised her voice. "You mean my *very tall* friend?" she yelled back. Then, to me again, "You want to meet them? They're probably recruiting for some kind of team."

Clearly, I saw, she was friendly with their ringleader, Radich, who up close resolved into a Mediterranean-looking man of Gen's age with a rough-edged face and tired-looking dark eyes. Kilander was about six-five, with blond hair and blue eyes, polished and sincere-looking like an ex–farm boy turned news anchor. The other two were a lithe mid-height black man of my age, Hadley, and an ex-military–looking Scandinavian with a painfully short buzz cut and flat blue eyes, Nelson.

"This is Sarah Pribek. She's a patrolwoman," Genevieve said. "And more important, a state champion point guard in her high school days."

The men exchanged smiles.

"So," Genevieve continued, "why don't you consider me her agent in negotiations for whatever crappy interagency team you're putting together?"

"Putting together?" Radich said innocently. "We need someone right now, to sub in. Nelson's leaving. And you can play, too, naturally, Detective Brown."

"Naturally my ass," Gen said.

"Wait," I interjected. "One guy's leaving and two of us sub in?"

"I count as half a person or something," Genevieve explained.

"No," Radich said. "We were already playing three-on-two. Where the hell is Shiloh?"

"I'm here," a new voice said.

Watching Genevieve joust with Radich, I didn't even see him approach, returning from somewhere on the sidelines. I turned to look at the newcomer, and my throat worked involuntarily.

There wasn't even a ripple of surprise in those lynx eyes, but I knew he recognized me. He was clean-shaven this day. I wanted to take my eyes away from his face and couldn't.

Radich carried on with introductions. "Mike Shiloh, Narcotics, this is Genevieve Brown from the Investigations Division—"

"I know Genevieve."

"—and Sarah Pribek, Patrol."

"Hey," he said.

"They're going to play with us for a little while. Kilander got first pick last time, so you call it this time. Brown or Pribek."

Genevieve looked at me and rolled her eyes at the foregone conclusion.

Shiloh's gaze passed over both of us, then he looked at Genevieve and jerked his head in the direction of his teammate, Hadley. "Come here, Brown," he said.

"Mike!" Hadley sounded disgusted. Radich flashed a mildly surprised look at Genevieve, who lifted both shoulders in a *search-me* fashion.

In all the confusion, I hoped nobody saw the shock of the insult register on my face. Kilander, the prosecutor, was the only unperturbed one; he flashed me a smile as though we had a great and sexy secret.

So that was how it stacked up. Genevieve darted gamely among us, with slow-footed Radich guarding her. Hadley did a pretty good job of covering Kilander, his speed counterbalancing Kilander's height and skill. But really the game was all Shiloh and me.

He was very good, I had to admit, pressing me on my weak low-post moves, not letting me get out where I could sink my three-pointers. I managed, though, to keep his scoring down. Our teams were tied for much of the game. Shiloh crowded me, but was careful not to foul me. Finally my temper snapped and I body-slammed him.

Shiloh marked this victory by not commenting on my loss of control as he stood and accepted the ball from Hadley. Genevieve, though, as we all moved aside to let Shiloh take his free throws, hissed gleefully in my ear: "You just cost your team the game." She was teasing, but I was annoyed with myself.

"Maybe he'll miss."

"He doesn't miss," Genevieve whispered back.

Shiloh accepted the ball from Radich, bounced it in the judicious, time-killing way of basketball players everywhere, shot, and whanged it off the rim.

I laughed in relief that my teammates took for triumph. Shiloh ignored me. It didn't matter in the end. His team ended up winning the game by a narrow margin.

As Genevieve was saying goodbye to Radich, Shiloh turned to me from about six feet away, stopping in the middle of following Hadley off the court. Sweat made his faded green

Kalispell Search and Rescue T-shirt stick to his ribs, reminding me of the flanks of a cooling racehorse.

"Kilander was a forward at Princeton," he said.

"Yeah?"

"Yeah. Maybe you should work on your passing game."

Out of earshot, on our way to the locker room, Genevieve was less diplomatic. "What the hell was that?" she demanded.

"What?"

"I've never *seen* two people so competitive in my life. Do you know Shiloh from somewhere?"

"Why is it my fault?" I complained evasively.

"You fouled him," she said.

"It serves him right for not picking me for his team. What the hell was that, by the way?"

Genevieve turned thoughtful. "I don't know," she admitted. "I don't know him that well. I'm not sure that anybody does. He's not real well liked around the department."

"Why not?"

Genevieve shrugged. "He does things like what he just did with you. He probably didn't even realize that he was snubbing you." She bent over to lace up her boots, one foot propped on a bench. "He's competent, from what Radich says, but not real good with people. Radich is his lieutenant, you know."

I turned that over in my mind.

"He and Kilander have a little history. An unfriendly one." Then, just as the conversation was getting really interesting, Genevieve changed the subject. "Are you on midwatch tonight?"

"Nope," I said. "Got the whole day off. Why?"

"I told you that you should come over for dinner sometime;

tonight's as good a night as any. My daughter's fixing it. She's already a better cook than I am."

I reflected that I would have to get Genevieve to talk about Kilander and Shiloh some other time, but in the following days the opportunity never came up. The next thing I heard about him was that I was being taken off the street for a night to work with Det. Mike Shiloh on some kind of stakeout.

Wear street clothes. That was about the extent of my instructions when I went to meet Shiloh at the motor pool. He was dressed only marginally better than the night I'd first met him, and just nodded for me to accompany him as he signed out an unmarked car, a dark-green Vega.

"Where are we going?" I asked when we were on the road.

"Outside the city," Shiloh said. "Meth country."

A minute after I decided we were going to drive in silence, he went on. "This is actually going to be pretty dull," he said. "In a small town, it's harder to blend in. Hard to park for a while without attracting too much attention. With a female partner you can pass for a couple out parking after a date."

"And you thought of me."

"No," Shiloh said flatly. "Radich did."

I wondered if he couldn't forgive me for seeing him weak and needing someone. I wondered if it had crossed his mind that I could be pissed that he, too, saw me weak and needing someone. Maybe we were going to carefully avoid mentioning having slept together for the rest of the time we knew each other. Damned if I was going to bring it up.

"Well, I'll have to thank Radich," I said.

"I wouldn't," he said. "This is a no-brainer. Like I said, dull."

"What did you do to your arm?"

"What?" Shiloh followed my gaze to the crook of his elbow, to the round Band-Aid there. "I gave blood. I'm O negative, a universal donor. They call me a couple of times a year, asking me to come in and donate." He pulled off the Band-Aid, revealing unmarked skin.

That was the end of the conversation until we got to our destination, parking across the street from a dispirited-looking working-class bar.

Shiloh switched off the ignition.

"Why here?" I asked.

"Both the guys hang out here, the ones we think are running a lab out of a house down the road from here. This place is like their de facto office." He paused. "Which is good, because it's very hard to surveil a farmhouse without being noticed. There's no pretext for us to be parked out there."

"What are we looking for?"

"Something to prove they're not just two underemployed guys who spend too much time at the bar. I'm hoping if I spend some time out here watching, they'll have guests. Someone we're familiar with, someone with priors. A lot of these guys, they have long rap sheets. They get out of prison and go right back to cooking." Shiloh turned slightly to face me, his posture, if not his face, telegraphing interest. He was, I realized, getting into character. It was Date Night. "I need to see them associating with people like that. It's not enough for a warrant, but it'll contribute." He laid a hand gently on my shoulder and I disciplined myself not to let the touch show on my face.

"Genevieve tells me you're from Utah," I said, just to make conversation.

"Genevieve told you right," he said.

"You're Mormon, then?"

"No, not at all." Shiloh looked almost amused.

"Why is that funny?" I asked him.

"My father was the minister of a small nondenominational church. He didn't even consider Mormons to be Christian."

"He was fundamentalist?"

Shiloh lifted a shoulder negligently. "People like to hang labels. But to my father there were just two kinds of people in the world: sheep and goats."

"Those are the choices?" Neither sounded very flattering to me. I hadn't heard the gospel story of the final judgment.

"Sorry," he said wryly, and if I'd known him better, I might have laughed.

"So how'd you get from Utah to the Twin Cities?" I asked, changing the subject.

"It wasn't particularly a destination," he said.

For a little while, he told me about his training and his first patrol work in Montana, then about coming east to work in Narcotics, his nomadic years of buy-and-bust operations and more complicated undercover work. His eyes flicked away from me frequently, out at the street. I didn't try to help him surveil; I wouldn't have known who I was looking for. He occasionally ran a finger along my neck and collarbone in a possessive, affectionate way. Staying in character.

Then he tired of talking about himself. "Where are you from?" he asked me.

"Up north," I said. "The Iron Range."

It was my standard answer for people I'd just met. I don't know why, but I rarely mentioned New Mexico to people unless I thought we were going to get to know each other well. Mike Shiloh didn't belong in that category, I thought.

But his very next words required me to break my own rule. "So you're a native Minnesotan?" he said.

"Okay, no," I said. "I lived in New Mexico until I was thirteen."

"And then what?"

"And then I came here." It wasn't that I was trying to kill the conversation; I knew we had to do something to pass the time. But my feeling was that your childhood is like the weather: you can talk about it all you want, but there's nothing you can do about it.

"Why?" Shiloh asked me. He wasn't prying. Asking questions is just a cop's instinct. They do it even with people who aren't criminals or suspects, the way Border collies will try to herd little kids when no farm animals are around.

"I had a great-aunt who lived here. My father sent me to live with her. He drove a truck, so he was away from home a lot, on the road." I paused. "My mother died when I was nine. Cancer."

"I'm sorry," he said.

"It was a long time ago," I said. "Anyway, my father worried about me when he was on the road. He arranged with my aunt—great-aunt, I mean—for me to live here. He thought I needed a maternal influence in my teenage years, too, I guess. It wasn't like I was incorrigible or did something wrong."

Goddammit. I didn't know where that last part had come from. Maybe in some way I'd been afraid that this was the conclusion to be drawn from my story.

But Mike Shiloh either didn't notice my embarrassment or didn't want to draw attention to it. "Do you ever go back there, to New Mexico?" he said.

"No," I said. "I don't have family there anymore. And the years I spent there seem like so long ago. It's like..." I tried to find the right words. "...everything in New Mexico seems like something that happened to somebody else. Almost like a past life. It's weird, but—"

What am I doing? I thought, stopping short. "Sorry," I said. "I was rambling. I just meant," I was quick to explain, "those years weren't that eventful. Nothing really happened to me in New Mexico." I could feel heat rising under my skin.

But once again Mike Shiloh chose to overlook my consternation. "I know the feeling," he said, and smiled. "Nothing much ever happened to me in Utah."

His words were light and casual, but he was looking at me seriously. No, that wasn't it. He was looking at me in an assessing way and yet a kind way, also, a look that made me feel—

"Come here, come here," Shiloh said quickly, startling me out of my thoughts. He gestured me forward. "I need to look over your shoulder and not get seen, okay?"

At his direction I slid onto his lap; for the next moment we were a couple making out across the street from the bar. His hands laced on my lower back, his face buried against my neck and shoulder.

"That's good," he told me.

I was distracted from the intimacy of it by worrying about what I was doing. I tried to move just a little, to look natural, without getting in his way.

"Be casual about it," he said quietly into my neck, "but turn around and look at the guy in the dark jacket, walking in from the parking lot."

I turned slightly, tucking my chin down against my shoulder. "I see him." The man disappeared through the bar's windowless double doors as I spoke.

"He's someone I know from Madison," Shiloh said. "And when I say I know him, I mean I busted him once. So I can't go in there."

"But I can?"

"Right," Shiloh said. "You'll go in and sit where you can see him. Check out who he's sitting with. Get a thorough description. But not yet. We'll give him a couple of minutes to get settled."

"All right," I said, pleased at the prospect of being in action.

"But you can get off my lap now," he said.

I pulled away hastily. If it hadn't been so dark, I would have worried about reddening.

The bar, when I was inside, was nearly as dark inside as the street outside. The man I'd followed in was close enough to the bar that I could sit there and surveil him, but the two men he was with had their backs to me.

After one sip, I left the draft beer I'd ordered on the bar and went to the cigarette machine. I rooted in my purse, acting frustrated.

I crossed to the table where the three men sat. "Excuse me? Could any of you give me four quarters for a dollar?"

"Sorry, babe," Madison said coolly.

"No, I got it," said one of his companions. He was, I saw, a very tall man. His exact height was hard to gauge, but his legs stretched a long, long way under the table.

"Thanks," I said, laying a weathered single on the little round table and taking the quarters from his hand.

I went back to the cigarette machine, bought a pack of Old Golds, and headed toward the ladies' room. But instead of going into the bathroom, I went out the side door, which was hidden from view of the bar.

I stood at the driver's-side window of the Vega and Shiloh rolled it down.

"Two blond guys," I said. "One's really, really tall and has long hair, clean-shaven otherwise, blue eyes. The other guy is average height, I think. Looks a lot like his friend, except the hair's a little paler and cut short. He's got a tattoo on his left forearm."

"A barbed-wire pattern?"

"Yeah," I said, pleased. "Both guys are clean-shaven. The tall guy was wearing—"

"Good," Shiloh said, waving me off. "I don't need to know what they were wearing."

"Now what?"

Shiloh jerked his head toward the passenger side of the car. "Now we go back to Minneapolis."

"Really?" I was disappointed. It didn't seem like a whole night's work.

"Really," he said. "You did good."

Genevieve and I worked out together about a week later. In the locker room, she wanted to know how I had liked my first stakeout.

"How'd you hear about that?" I asked her.

"I ran into Radich again. You know how it goes: You don't see someone for months, then you see them twice in a week."

"It was okay. Dull," I said. I hadn't thought it was, but that had been Shiloh's assessment, and I wanted to sound sufficiently jaded.

"Oh. I thought you might want to work in Narcotics, since you're getting your foot in the door," she said.

"I wouldn't call one stakeout a 'foot in the door.' "

"What about the raid?"

"What raid?"

Genevieve studied my face. "They're going to raid the lab. Radich said he was going to talk to your sergeant about borrowing you again to go along. I guess he hasn't yet."

"Lundquist didn't mention it to me."

"I shouldn't have said anything—"

"In case Lundquist says no? Don't worry, I can deal with that."

"Radich probably hasn't asked him yet, is all. Lundquist won't say no. They'll have enough people anyway; this is just something nice for you, so you can learn. Because you helped them out."

"What help? I sat on Shiloh's lap and pretended to be his girlfriend."

"Did it bother you they asked you to do that? Nelson couldn't have done it."

"I was okay with it."

"Shiloh was okay?"

"Yeah, he was fine. What were you going to say about him and Kilander the other night?" I asked.

"Kilander?"

"About their, what, 'history of unfriendliness'?"

"Oh, that. Nothing serious," she said. "I don't remember all the details, but when Shiloh had just got here from Madison, he went in on some kind of raid on a club in north Minneapolis. The whole case was kind of shaky. It ended up being Kilander's to prosecute. And I guess he needed Shiloh to . . ." I could see her mentally reviewing her list of mild, noninflammatory words. ". . . to be *cooperative* in his testimony. Don't ask me what about, I don't remember.

"Shiloh didn't like the whole case, thought it was flimsy. He wasn't about to color his story in any way." Genevieve yanked open her combination lock. "Kilander would have had a very unhelpful witness on the stand. Instead he decided not to call Shiloh at all. And lost the case."

"What did the MPD guys think?" A cop's opinion was more important than a prosecutor's, at least to me.

"Well, obviously the story got around—that's how I heard it. And someone sent away for some ACLU membership stuff and had it sent to the station in Shiloh's name, like that's supposed to be really embarrassing. I doubt it was Kilander. Not his style." Genevieve laced up her boots. "Why do you ask?"

"It's always good to know the department gossip," I said lightly.

When I got to the squad room, there was a message waiting from my sergeant, Lundquist. *See Lt. Radich.*

If it's hard to surveil a farmhouse, it's also hard to sneak up on one, for the same reasons. In fact, Radich had explained, we weren't going to be subtle. Instead, this would be a dawn raid. We'd come through the door on a no-knock warrant and catch everyone sleepy and unprepared.

It was five twenty-five in the morning, and I was riding out toward Anoka in the same green Vega that Shiloh and I had used before. This time I was sitting next to Nelson.

We rode mostly in silence. I felt more comfortable with Nelson than with Shiloh. He was the kind of cop I was used to, with a buzz cut and a blunt way of speaking. He related to me like another cop would. He hadn't seen me naked forty-five minutes after we'd met in an airport bar.

I'd been working on the street until 1 A.M. and hadn't even tried to get a few hours of sleep. The fact that I was going to stay up all night had worried both Radich and Lundquist. But they must have read in my face how badly I'd wanted to come along, because in the end they had let me go. At the moment I didn't feel sleepy at all. I felt like I had washed down several dozen wasps with too much black coffee.

As I was checking my weapon by the side of the car, Shiloh came over to me.

"I guess I should thank Radich for thinking of me again," I said.

"No, this was my idea," he said mildly. "Look, I came over to tell you something—"

"He explained everything," I interrupted. "I'm going to stay behind Nelson and just cover him; you and Hadley are going in the front and he and I will take the back."

"That's not it," Shiloh said. "This is something I learned from a psychologist. If you ever get scared, not that people like us ever do," and he paused to let me know that was a joke, "you can put your hands on a doorway—car door, anything—and imagine that you're leaving your fear there."

I put my weapon in its holster.

"It's something you can do and not be obvious about when there're people around," he said.

"Thanks," I said shortly.

He wasn't deceived by the surface politeness of my response.

"I didn't mean I think you're scared."

"I know."

He looked away, toward the house. "Just do it like we talked about it. This one isn't going to give us any problems."

Radich had said much the same thing earlier; now Shiloh had said it. I guess something had to go wrong under that much karmic prodding.

Two of them were sleeping on a couch in the first-floor living room. Shiloh and Hadley went directly upstairs, hearing the muffled sound of running feet above. Nelson got the tall man from the bar up against the wall—seeing him standing, I could now gauge him at an impressive six-foot-six or -seven—and started handcuffing him. The couch's other occupant, a skinny blond woman in her early twenties, made a bolt for the nearest exit, a window.

Even before Nelson jerked his forehead in the woman's direction, I went after her. The woman was pretty quick; she had jerked the sash window up and gotten her head and shoulders out by the time I reached her. When I did, she hung on to the windowsill so hard that its edge sliced her palm. She shrieked.

"Look what you did, bitch!" she yelled, seeing her own blood, spreading her hand so I could see it.

"Please put your hands behind your back," I instructed her.

"Get your hands off me! Look what you fucking did! Get your hands off me, you fucking bitch!"

"Trace," Nelson's suspect said, tiredly. He knew a lost cause when he saw one. Trace—or Tracy, more likely—didn't seem to hear him. She wasn't listening to anyone. She kept yelling at me while I tried to read her the Miranda rights. It was making me nervous. If she couldn't hear herself being Mirandized, I wondered, did she have a possible loophole in court?

Out of the corner of my eye I saw Hadley and Shiloh coming back downstairs with a third suspect. I had successfully gotten Tracy handcuffed but wished she'd shut up. I was starting to feel self-conscious about being the only one who couldn't keep my suspect under control.

Just then something very strange happened. The staircase had a traditional open railing, supported by carved wooden posts. A bronze blur, like part of the wood framework come to life, dropped from between two of the posts, landing almost directly in front of Nelson. Nelson made a remarkably controlled jump but didn't go anywhere, his pale blue eyes showing white at the edges.

I didn't even have to look down to know what it was. The percussive sound of a rattlesnake's warning was familiar from my childhood out West.

For a split second everybody was frozen, even the snake coiled to strike.

I stepped forward, caught the snake behind its triangular head, and broke its neck.

Its rattle, persisting after death, filled the house. Hadley and Nelson were looking at me like I'd just split the atom. Tracy had stopped in mid-scream to stare at me with her mouth open. Only Shiloh seemed unsurprised, though he was looking at me with a glimmer of some unreadable thought in his eyes.

"Maybe we should move everyone outside," he suggested.

We did, but someone had to go back in and make sure the house was safe. Nelson and Hadley showed no interest whatsoever. Their eyes went to me.

"You're the dragon slayer," Hadley said, only half joking.

"Sure," I said. "I'm game."

"I'll go with you," Shiloh said.

There were no more loose snakes. Upstairs, we found the terrarium.

At one end, a heat lamp shone down on a broad basking rock. At the other end was a cool retreat box. Two adult snakes seemed to sleep on the sand, coiled against each other.

"God save me from drug dealers and their goddamn affectations," Shiloh said wearily.

"Are we going to have to call Animal Control?" I was sitting on my heels, looking into a little half-size refrigerator, which held not only dead mice but little bottles of antivenin.

"The pound, are you kidding? They won't touch this," Shiloh said. "I think we're going to have to get Fish and Wildlife out here, or someone from the zoo, which means one of us is going to have to stay here."

"I could do that," I told him.

"No, Nelson and I need to get everything into evidence. Go on back, process the suspects in, write up your paperwork. Hadley will enjoy riding back with you. I think he's in love."

It was a joke, but I saw him realize what he'd said. He'd accidentally evoked what we were both trying hard to forget. We'd been walking on a thin layer of ice, and he'd broken through with an innocent remark. We both felt the cold water it splashed on our newfound rapport.

Shiloh was right about one thing, though. Hadley called me. We dated for six companionable weeks, something we kept a secret from other officers.

One night I was on patrol alone. Crossing the Hennepin

Bridge, I'd seen a cardboard box sitting on the pedestrian walkway, by itself, no one around. That struck me as mildly strange and I wanted to see what was in it.

I approached the cardboard box with caution that turned out to be unnecessary. The box was open at the top. Two kittens slept inside on pages of newspaper.

Someone had felt a spasm of compassion at the last minute and couldn't throw them over the railing into the river. Now they and their box would go to the squad room until Animal Control was open in the morning.

I was in no hurry to go back to my car, looking out over the Mississippi and the riverbank instead. There was still no traffic on the bridge, no cars moving below in my line of sight. It was like being on an empty movie set. Downtown, windows in the high-rise buildings glowed with light, and in the distance I could hear the rushing sound of the 35W, like blood heard through a stethoscope. Those were the only signs of life. It wasn't normal, even for two-thirty on a weekday morning. But it wasn't disturbing. It was mystic.

Motion below caught my eye, a lone figure in the distance.

It was a runner, making long strides like a cross-country athlete close to the finish, down the middle of an empty street whose wet black surface gleamed in the night.

Just by watching I knew several things about him: that he'd been at this pace for a little while and was capable of keeping it up for a good time. That he was feeling the energy of running down the center of a street that was almost never empty. That he was the kind of runner I wished I could be, the kind who could let his mind go and just run, without keeping track of distance and thinking about when he could stop.

When he drew nearer I realized I knew him. It was Shiloh.

He passed right under me, and as he did there was engine noise behind me all of a sudden, two cars going eastbound, and the moment of stillness was over.

A few days later I met Hadley for lunch and we discussed our relationship. We agreed that it wasn't ultimately going to work out. I don't know who actually used the phrase *the long run,* but I suspect it was me.

I did not call Mike Shiloh or contrive to cross his path downtown.

Neither was I asked to help the narcotics task force again, although Radich stopped by to thank me for my help. The rattlesnake incident had made me briefly famous in the department, but now that had mercifully died down. I was an unassuming patrol officer again, working my midwatch and dogwatch shifts, which were uneventful.

An early warm spell settled over the Cities. Genevieve took a week off during Kamareia's spring break, and without a workout partner for the weight room, I took to running in the afternoons along the river. I told myself that I wasn't avoiding the pickup basketball games in which the Narcotics guys sometimes played; I was simply cross-training, and besides, the warm weather was too pleasant to waste by exercising indoors.

I always walked my last quarter mile to cool down. That's what I was doing one evening a little after five, walking and enjoying the scent of a pizza restaurant nearby, when I turned onto my own street and saw a pair of long legs on my front steps. The rest of my visitor was out of sight, sitting on the top step within the entry alcove, but the scuffed boots were vaguely familiar, as was, I suddenly realized, the green Catalina parked on the street.

I was glad to have recognized who it was in advance; it allowed me to not look surprised when I came face-to-face with Mike Shiloh for the first time in two months.

It had been about that long since our cluster of encounters, and seeing him gave me that little shock, the one of both recognition and of realization that your memory hasn't painted someone quite true. I registered everything anew: the slightly Eurasian features, the longish, curling hair, which clearly hadn't been cut in the interim, and most of all, the direct, unapologetic gaze. Given his place on the highest of the steps, he was almost on a level with me, even seated.

"I figured if you were working midwatch you'd be there by now," he said by way of greeting. "Have you eaten?"

"Did you think of calling first?" I asked.

"I'm sorry," he said. "Is Hadley here right now?"

He kept a completely straight face, but I sensed amusement. He was pleased at having guessed something Hadley and I had worked hard to keep off the grapevine.

"I am no longer seeing Detective Hadley socially," I said, using the most formal phrasing I could think of, and the coolest tone.

"I'm glad to hear that," Shiloh said. "Last Friday evening I saw Detective Hadley in the Lynlake district with a young woman. She was dressed like she might be 'seeing him socially.' "

"Good for him."

"You didn't answer my question. Are you hungry?" He

tilted his head slightly, interrogatively. "I was thinking of a Korean place in St. Paul, but that's negotiable," he said. "It all depends on what you want."

I realized that for a while now I'd been trying to decide who this man was, and if I liked him, and still I couldn't come to a conclusion.

"Before I go anywhere," I said stiffly, "I want to ask you a question."

"Go ahead," he said.

"Why drink in an airport bar?"

If nothing else, I'd surprised him; I saw that in his face. He rubbed the back of his neck a minute, then looked up at me and said, "Airports have their own police. I wanted to go somewhere that I wouldn't run into any cops I knew."

I heard the truth in his words. Truth, and none of the easy cynicism that would have allowed me to send this man away and stop thinking about him once and for all.

"Come in for a minute," I said. "I need to change."

chapter 14

Naomi Wilson, formerly Naomi Shiloh, hadn't exaggerated about her size. She wore a loose yellow dress and a coral-colored sweater that was left open to accommodate her huge belly. She was standing at the edge of the well-tended play yard of the day-care center, watching the children.

When she saw me coming, I saw her take my measure: my height, the black leather jacket I'd thought would be best against autumn out West.

"You must be Sarah," she said. "Call me Naomi."

Her hair was darker than Shiloh's, and I didn't see much of his features in her open, sweet face. But demeanor, of course, is part of appearance. The older we get, the more our faces reflect our lives and our thoughts. And already it was clear that Naomi and Shiloh were worlds apart on that count.

"Do you mind talking out here?" Naomi gestured at a picnic

table nearby. Obviously she was comfortable in her sweater, used to being outside with the kids. "I can have Marie come out, if you'd rather go inside."

"Outside is all right," I said.

"Can I get you something first? Some tea or water? Apple juice? Graham crackers?" She smiled at her joke.

"Coffee would be good," I said.

"We don't actually have any," she said apologetically.

Too late I remembered Shiloh telling me that in Utah, where 75 percent of the population is Mormon, even the soda fountains served caffeine-free cola.

"Right," I said. "I'm okay, really."

At the table, it took a moment for her to comfortably adjust herself.

"Is this your ninth month?" I asked.

"Seventh."

"Twins?"

She nodded. "It runs in the family."

"Where does your twin sister live?"

"She's still in school," Naomi said. "Bethany didn't go straight through college in four years like I did."

I was about to get to the point at hand, but Naomi focused thoughtfully on me as though I'd suddenly materialized. "So Mike is married," she said. "I don't know why, but that surprises me."

"Yeah?"

"He was always kind of a loner," she said.

"He still is, in a way. Before he went missing, he was supposed to be going to the FBI Academy in Virginia. That would have kept him away from home for four months, but I understood."

"He was going to be an FBI agent?"

"Yeah."

"Wow," she said. "That's amazing." Naomi even laughed. "Mike, an agent of the FBI."

"Why does that surprise you? You knew he was a cop."

"True," she said. "I know, it's just . . ."

"Was he wild as a kid?"

"You know . . ." She glanced upward slightly, the way people do when accessing memories. "I don't really know. That was kind of the impression I got, growing up."

"From your folks?"

"Yeah, and from Adam and Bill. But now that I'm thinking about it, I can't remember anything specific that they said. Maybe I just assumed anyone who left home so young was a rule-breaker."

"An outlaw," I said.

"Yes," she said. "How did you two meet?"

Naomi seemed more interested in Shiloh's life in Minnesota than in his disappearance. Maybe that was only natural. To her and her family, Shiloh had already disappeared, in a sense.

"Through work," I said. "I'm a cop."

"I should have guessed," she said. "You look kind of like a police officer, I mean, you're—"

"Tall, I know," I said, smiling at her. "When was the last time you spoke to Mike?" I asked. It was time to get down to business. If I knew what my business in Utah was at all.

"I don't talk to him at all," Naomi said, mildly surprised. "I get Christmas cards from him."

"But you were the one in your family who tracked him down," I said. "The two of you seem to have the closest relationship."

"I wouldn't say close," she said. "He left home when I was only eight years old."

"Why'd you start looking for him?" I asked.

She considered. "In our family, I was kind of the record-keeper. Family's important to me. Well, it was to all of us. But I've always been the one who took pictures at family gatherings and put the albums together. I guess that's why, when I was a senior in high school, I started to think about Mike and whether it might be possible to find him."

"Did you use one of those Internet people-finder services?"

Naomi shook her head. "That was too expensive, with the money I had then. I just did what I could. I had a lot of friends, and whenever they'd go out of town, I'd ask them to look in city phone books. It's not a common name, Shiloh. Eventually, my friend Diana called from Minneapolis and said she'd seen a Michael Shiloh in the white pages, just a number, no address.

"I was too shy to call the phone number, so I called directory assistance. I said, 'I know you can't give me an address, but is this the M. Shiloh on Fifth Street?' I picked that street name at random. And the operator said, 'No, I'm showing an address on 28th Avenue.' So I was really excited then. It was like a project. I had Diana ask her cousin back there to look through voter-registration records, and his whole address was there."

"I wish everyone I worked with on the job had your initiative," I told her. I wasn't just flattering her; her dedication was impressive.

Naomi looked pleased. "I was a freshman in college by then. I wrote him a letter, although I was trying not to get my hopes up. Then, three weeks later, I got a letter.

"It wasn't a long letter, but I must have reread it four times. I just couldn't believe I'd found him. He hadn't been a real person to me up until that moment. He had this funny writing, all caps, kind of spiky."

"I know," I said. "What did he say?"

"He mostly answered the questions I'd written to him. He said that yes, it was him, and he wrote a little about his 'lost years.' The time he'd spent working around Montana and Illinois and Indiana and, what? Wisconsin, I think.

"He said that he'd gotten a GED instead of finishing high school, and that now he was on the police force. He told me he liked Minneapolis but wasn't sure he was going to settle there permanently. And 'I'm not, nor have I ever been married.' I thought that was a funny way to put it, like he was up in front of a Senate panel." Naomi paused, thinking. "He said that I shouldn't rush into marriage and motherhood. He thought I should take some time off from school and see the world, or at least America. Get some perspective on things. And then he told me to 'study hard.' " Her eyes narrowed, looking at something over my shoulder. "Sorry, I'll be right back."

I turned and put one leg back over the bench, watching as Naomi went to referee a dispute over a piece of playground equipment. It took a few minutes for her to sort things out and soothe the hurt feelings, and then she walked back to me.

"Where was I?" she said.

"You'd just gotten your first letter from him."

"Right," she said. "Well, it seemed like a promising start to me. So I wrote him back, and he wrote me. And back and forth, a couple of times. I wrote him almost immediately after I'd get one of his letters, but usually there was a wait for his answers to my letters.

"Finally I wrote to ask him if, since he wasn't sure he was going to put down roots in Minnesota, did he think he might ever come home to Utah? I asked him why he'd stayed away so long and said that everyone would probably be happy if he came back, at least for a visit. He never answered that letter. Six weeks later, I decided to call him." She smiled, but with a slightly wry look. "So I did. He picked up, and I said, Hi, this is Naomi.

"He said something like 'Yes, Naomi?' and I thought he didn't know who I was. I said, Your sister Naomi, and he said, 'I know.'

"I was starting to feel uncomfortable. He was totally different on the phone than in his letters. I said something to the effect that I'd just called to talk and he said, 'About what?' "

I felt embarrassed on her behalf, because I could so easily hear Shiloh's cool voice saying it.

"I don't remember exactly what I said, but I was really embarrassed. I managed to get off the phone without hanging up on him outright, but it wasn't smooth. I never did that again." Naomi laughed a little, as if still embarrassed.

"I didn't contact him again until Dad died. The awful thing was, Mom had died a year earlier, and I hadn't called him. It's so awful to say it slipped my mind, but I was really broken up and I just didn't think about Mike at all. The next year, when Dad died, I'd been through it before, so in a way it was easier. And I had Rob. We were engaged then, and he was really supportive.

"Mike had moved by then, and he was unlisted, but I left a message with him at the police department and he called me." She paused, remembering. "It was very different from the other time I'd called him. He was really kind." She smiled. "When I told him the news, he asked me how I was doing and how I was feeling, about Bethany, and so forth. I told him about the funeral arrangements, and"—she looked rueful—"I guess I just assumed he was coming. Looking back, I can't remember that he ever said he was. So the day of the funeral came, and he wasn't there. He just sent a flower arrangement. I've got to admit, I was hurt. Not on my behalf, but on the whole family's."

I remembered the flowers. The florist had called the house with a question about the order, and if it hadn't been for that, I wouldn't have known his father had died at all. I'd asked him why he wasn't going back to the funeral, and offered to go with him. Shiloh had refused and had brushed off further questions.

On the day of the funeral, Shiloh had more or less stayed drunk, and for weeks afterward he'd been such intolerable company that I took to volunteering for extra shifts at work and spending free time with Genevieve and Kamareia.

"Naomi," I said, "your father's death hit him a lot harder than you might have realized."

Naomi glanced up at me. In retelling the family history, she'd forgotten that I was someone who lived with Shiloh and was a witness to his daily life.

"Well," she said, "anyway, two months later, when Rob and I got married, he sent us a gift. I'd forgotten that I'd even mentioned the wedding to him when we'd talked on the phone." A breeze ruffled Naomi's dark hair and she brushed it back into place. "It was a beautiful leather-bound photo album. It was like he knew I liked to make up family albums, even though I'd never mentioned it. It was a perfect gift. But no note. After that we started exchanging Christmas cards again, but his are just signed. There's nothing personal about them." Her voice dropped a little lower. "I guess I don't really understand him at all."

"He can be hard to understand," I agreed. "Or, to be honest, he can be a—" *Don't say prick* "—a heel."

Naomi giggled. "But you married him!" she said, a little shocked at my spousal disloyalty. Then the laughter dried up and she was serious.

"Is he really missing?" she asked, as if I hadn't made that patently clear.

"Yeah, he is," I said.

A squall rose from the playground and this time we both turned. A little blond boy sat, legs akimbo, in the gravel. Blood was springing up from a fresh scrape on his elbow. Scratched elbows and knees: the common colds of childhood.

This time I followed Naomi. She took a travel-size package of tissues out of her sweater and pressed them to the boy's blood-smeared skin.

Around him, other children had formed a semicircle to look on, miniature versions of the people I saw on the job, the ones who stopped everything to watch at accident and crime scenes.

"This might take a little while. I've got to take him inside to the bathroom." Naomi made her voice higher and brighter. "What're all those tears for, Bobby? Everything is just fine."

"I understand," I told her over the sound of Bobby's subsiding whimpers.

"Maybe you could come over tonight, for dinner, and we could talk some more."

That was exactly what I'd been planning to suggest after our meeting here was finished, and now I didn't have to. "That'd be good," I said. "If you have pictures of Shiloh, anything of his, high-school yearbooks, I'd like to see them."

"Sure. I have lots of family pictures." She lifted Bobby by the arm.

"Before I go," I said, "I need something to do with the rest of the day, and I was hoping to talk to your older brothers and

Bethany, ask them a few basic questions. I need to know when they saw him last, or spoke to him last. Do you have their daytime phone numbers available?"

Naomi, half bent to hold Bobby's arm, shot me a harried but thoughtful glance. "I think I can tell you the answer to those questions. They haven't spoken to him for years, since before I tracked Mike down. I know I'm the only one in the family who was persistent about finding him."

"That was pretty clear from what you've said today," I told her. "But I have to make sure. I'm just being thorough."

"Come with me," Naomi said, starting to lead the boy toward the building. "I know all their numbers by heart. I can write them down for you."

A cab picked me up outside the day-care center about a half hour later. Asked for a recommendation, the driver took me to a family-run two-story motel in downtown Salt Lake City. "I don't need to be near Temple Square," I told her. "I'm not a tourist."

"Still, it's worth seeing while you're here," she said.

"Maybe next time," I said.

I knew what the afternoon held. Whenever you really need to reach people, it seems that invariably you only reach answering machines.

I prepared for this by getting a vending-machine sandwich and a Coke and some ice from the hallway dispensers, fortifying myself for a long wait. Then, in the room, I dialed the work numbers of Shiloh's siblings, reached a grand total of none of them, and left messages. Then I ate lunch and dozed off waiting for return calls.

I must have slept deeply, because when the phone woke me and a man's voice responded to mine, I said "Shiloh?" just as I had with Vang.

"This is Adam Shiloh, yes," the voice said, sounding a little bemused at the familiarity of my address. "Is this Sarah Pribek?"

"Sorry," I said, sitting up on the edge of the bed. "You sound like . . . like your brother."

"Mike? I wouldn't know. It's been years, literally years, since I've spoken to him." I heard the noise of an office intercom behind; he'd called me from work. "I suppose that's a regrettable thing," he went on.

We talked briefly about Shiloh, but it was clear to me early on that Adam, who'd lived in Washington State for the last six years, knew nothing about his brother's adult life. I heard a woman's voice in the background, rising above generic office noise. The words were indistinct to me except for the last: *coming?*

"I've got a meeting to go to," Adam Shiloh told me. "But if there's anything I can do for you, please let me know," he said.

"Thanks, I'll remember that," I said.

An hour later Bethany Shiloh called from her dormitory in Southern Utah. We traveled the same territory, even more briefly, that I had with Adam. No, she hadn't seen or spoken to Shiloh since he'd left home. She didn't know any old friends of his. She wished to meet me, someday, after "all this is over."

I hung up and took out my legal pad, then realized I had nothing to write. Talking to both Adam and Bethany was progress only in the sense that those conversations had been necessary to my investigation, not in the sense that they'd given me information that had helped.

Shiloh's siblings had one thing in common. They all seemed very calm about his disappearance. But then, they hadn't seen him in years; maybe that was to be expected. I couldn't judge them. I probably seemed to be taking things a little too calmly, too. From the outside.

Naomi and her husband, Robert, lived on the outskirts of the city in a single-level house. I turned up at the predetermined hour, and Naomi greeted me at the door in the same dress I'd seen her wearing earlier.

"I looked around for things of Shiloh's, like you mentioned, but I really only have my albums," she said. "We could look at them after dinner, if you can wait."

"I thought I heard someone at the door." A young man came into the entryway. He was tall and lean, with blond hair and green eyes; an extraordinarily handsome man, I thought. "Is this your sister-in-law?"

"Right, this is Sarah," Naomi said. "Sarah, this is my husband, Robert."

"Call me Rob," he said. He held a slotted fork: Rob was doing the cooking tonight.

Over dinner, Rob asked me a number of questions about being a sheriff's detective. Eventually, Naomi asked specifically about Shiloh's case.

I told them how Shiloh had disappeared, or rather, how I'd discovered him to be missing without finding the usual indicators of what had happened to him. I tried not to paint the situation as black as it probably was, whether to comfort her or me, I didn't know.

"Leave the dishes," Naomi told her husband after dinner.

"I'm going to show Sarah some things, and we'll probably need to talk, but I'll get them later."

I followed her down a hallway into the house's spare bedroom, newly converted into a nursery. There was a rocking chair in it already; the other chair looked as though it had been conscripted into service from the living room for my visit.

"This was our storage room," Naomi explained. "There's still a lot of stuff in the closet." However, she'd taken several albums out of the closet. Now she scooped them up from the chair they were resting on and set them on an ottoman between us.

"The first one is probably the one of most interest to you," she said. "There's a lot of stuff from when the six of us were growing up."

I sat in the rocking chair and started looking.

The album told a time-honored story for which no words were needed. It began with pictures from a courtship: the yet-unmarried Shilohs at a lake together, in a larger group of young people, at a church event.

Then came marriage, a bridal party outside a church. A bride with her proud mother and sister. A nervous groom with his men; you could almost hear the jocular laughter. The first home. Babies. Children. Shiloh, his reddish hair in a child's impersonal buzz cut. Shiloh with his older brothers, outdoors quite a bit. The appearance of the twin girls, Naomi and Bethany. I watched Shiloh growing from a skinny child to a lanky teen, his face shifting from a child's characterless openness to that pensive, guarded expression characteristic of the man I knew. If I'd been alone I might have studied those photos all night, but they were teaching me nothing helpful and I turned the pages faster.

Then I flipped back a page. "Who's that?"

Naomi leaned closer to look at the photo I was pointing at. The whole family stood against an unnatural blue backdrop, in a traditional studio portrait. In it, the teenage Shiloh stood next to a girl nearly as tall as he was. If Shiloh's hair was the color of old copper, hers was bright new copper, worn loose and long. She wore a white scoop-neck dress and didn't smile.

"Sinclair. She's two years older than Mike, four years younger than Adam."

Six kids, I thought. I'd heard about the two older brothers, and of Naomi and her twin, Bethany. And then Shiloh made five. I'd never quite realized that didn't add up. "Where is she in all the other pictures?"

"Well, she is in some of them, but for most of her life she didn't live with us," Naomi said. "She was deaf from birth, so she was away at school." She flipped backwards in the album. "Here, she's in the background, see."

Naomi was looking at a Christmas-dinner photo, a hectic kitchen scene. I had taken the little girl with bright red curls for a visiting relative.

"I never knew Shiloh had a sister who was deaf," I said.

"Really?" she said. "That's funny, because they were close."

"I'm sure that he didn't mention her."

"We didn't have her around for all that long. She came home to live at seventeen and left at eighteen. Kind of abruptly."

"Tell me about it," I prompted.

Naomi sat back. "Well, Bethany and I never knew her much at all. We only got to know Mike a little better." She placed a hand on her gravid belly. "While we were growing up, Sinclair was at a school for the deaf. I guess she used to come home summers at first, but that was before my time. Later, when she got used to living with deaf people, and had friends at school, she started staying away over the summer, and just came home at winter break. Bethany and I would have to get reintroduced to her; we were five, six. Mom would say, 'This is your sister, remember?' and we'd be like 'Okay, hi!' It was like she was some visiting cousin.

"When Bethany and I were six, Sinclair was seventeen. In a year or two she'd be in college or married, and Mom wanted to bring her home for a while before that.

"We've always been a close-knit family; I guess I said that earlier today, didn't I?" Naomi asked. "It was hard on Mom to have Sinclair living away from home most of the year. She and my dad decided she could make it in a public school with the help of a translator from the district, and so they brought her home.

"Anyway, I guess things didn't go as hoped. None of us were that good at sign language. Except Mike. He was the family translator. But Sinclair wasn't too happy to be home, she was ... well, I don't really know the details. But within a year she left."

"She ran away?"

"Sort of. She was eighteen, but it was in the middle of the school year, I think. She didn't waste any time." Naomi was still looking at the photo. "When Mike left, they blamed it on her."

"He left when he was seventeen, so that would have been a year later."

"Yeah. But it was partly because of her. Mike got in trouble for letting her back into the house. She needed a place to stay, and he sneaked her inside without anyone knowing."

"And your folks kicked him out? Just for that?" I hadn't realized Shiloh's parents were so authoritarian.

"I don't think they made him leave," she said uncertainly. But she wasn't sure. To her, these were like events that had happened to a previous generation, nothing to do with her. "I think he left on his own."

"Why?"

"There was this big scene late at night. I don't really remember it. Bethany went out of our bedroom to see what was going on, and they told her to go back into her room. She came back and told me she'd seen Sinclair going down the stairs with a gym bag over her shoulder. I guess Mike got caught sneaking her in," Naomi said. Her voice took on more certainty, like she was convincing herself. "My father was really angry. Sinclair left right away, and Mike was gone a day later."

"Really," I said.

Naomi turned two pages ahead in the photo album. "There," she said. "That's the last picture we have of Mike. Taken five days before he left."

It was a candid spur-of-the-moment shot, slightly dark with underexposure. Shiloh, long-legged and seated on a couch, was holding a hand half over his face against the bright surprise of a flash, as if he were looking into the headlights of an approaching car. There were a few tiny lights in the background, like fireflies indoors.

"Maybe it's hypocritical of me," Naomi said, "but I never tried to get in touch with Sinclair the way I did with Mike. She was always completely foreign to me. She was somebody I couldn't talk to, and she couldn't talk to me."

"Can I have this picture?" I said.

"That one?" Naomi looked startled. "All right."

I peeled back the protective cellophane and took the simple Polaroid out. "Who in the family would know more about Sinclair?" I asked.

"Mike," Naomi said. "The six of us were paired off pretty

neatly, like mini-generations: Adam and Bill, Mike and Sinclair, Bethany and me. Mike and Sinclair didn't spend nearly as much time together as Bethany and I, or Adam and Bill, but they were close when she lived at home. Not just because of age but because of Mike's good sign-language skills."

"Who else?" I asked. "I need someone I can talk to."

"Bill, I guess. He was the second-closest to Mike in age. And he was here the night our father caught Mike sneaking Sinclair into the house." She seemed to remember something. "Oh, but Bill won't call her Sinclair. That's our grandmother's maiden name; Sinclair adopted it around the time she left. Bill calls her Sara," Naomi explained. "That's why I was so startled when you called me last night. You said you were Sarah Shiloh, and I was thinking 'This can't be happening!' "

"Yeah," I said. "I can see where that would throw you."

We spent the rest of the time in simple questions. I asked the names of schools Shiloh had gone to in Ogden and if Naomi remembered the names of any close friends from his school years. Did anything he'd written in his letters or on Christmas cards seem important now? Nothing came to Naomi's mind. "I'm sorry," she said. "Is there anything else I can do?"

"Could I use your phone?" I asked. "I didn't get in touch with your brother Bill today, and I'd like to call him and ask if I can see him in person, tomorrow if possible. I don't want to call too late, it'd be rude."

Naomi nodded. "That's fine. There's a phone in our bedroom, where it'll be quieter." She set the photo album back on the ottoman with the others.

I stood and stretched, waiting for Naomi to rise as well.

"You know, I am worried about Mike," she said. "If I sounded like I wasn't, well, he and Sinclair were the family's black sheep. It's hard to think of a rebel as somebody vulnerable."

She looked up at me from her seated position, and instead of standing, Naomi touched my arm. "Will you pray with me?" she asked. "For Michael?"

chapter **15**

The next morning, Friday, I rented a dark blue Nissan and headed up the I-15 to Ogden. Ogden wasn't just where the Shiloh family had lived for many years; it was where Bill Shiloh had settled and begun raising his own family. The traffic thinned as soon as I was fifteen minutes out of the city.

In my shoulder bag, along with the clutter of my daily needs, rode the photo I'd taken from Naomi Wilson. It was wrapped in a Ziploc bag to keep it from getting scratched up. Naomi might ask for it back someday.

It was commonplace for detectives to ask for photographs of missing persons, which was probably why Naomi hadn't questioned my taking it. If she'd thought about it, she might have wondered why I didn't have a photo of Shiloh myself, and why I needed one that was over a decade out of date. That

Polaroid was going to be useless in my hunt for Shiloh, but I'd wanted it anyway.

It was hardly a profound character study—just a young man, surprised by someone who wanted to take his picture, looking not into the lens but past it, trying to see who the photographer was.

But Shiloh had grown into his adult face quickly, and this Shiloh looked an awful lot like the one I knew. His hand raised to shield his eyes, Shiloh looked oddly vulnerable, like somebody looking into the bright heart of a mystery, someone about to disappear. Which he had been.

In a way, Shiloh had disappeared twice. He'd left his family so abruptly he might as well have been missing, except that they had known he'd left them deliberately. They'd known the reason why.

Actually, I wasn't really clear on the reason, when I reflected on it. He'd told me he'd left home over religious differences with his family. He'd neglected to tell me that those religious disagreements were exacerbated by a family crisis involving a black-sheep sister who'd been banned from the house.

Bill Shiloh wanted to meet at his office, not his home. Shiloh had said his brothers were in "office supplies, I think," but Bill's directions led to a paper mill.

"Sorry about the noise when you're coming back here," he said when we were both in his office. "But it's pretty quiet inside here. It has to be, I spend a lot of time on the phone." He closed the door behind us.

The mill was, in fact, in full swing behind us, but the noise was almost entirely blocked out by the door. The room was narrow and windowless save for the plate glass that looked out onto the mill floor. There were several metal filing cabinets behind the desk, and three grade-school art projects on the wall, each announcing "Dad" in colorful ways. Each child represented, I thought, seeing a picture of a family of five on the desk.

"So you're Michael's wife," Bill said, virtually the same words Naomi had gotten down to business with. "He's settled down?"

"Yes," I said, like Shiloh had led a wild previous life.

"How long have you been married?" he asked.

"Two months."

Bill Shiloh raised his eyebrows. "That's not long." He made it sound like a judgment. "And you're with the Minneapolis police?"

"The Hennepin County Sheriff's Department," I said.

"So are you here in that capacity, as an investigator?" he asked.

"My husband is missing. He has been for five days," I said sharply. "That's why I'm here."

"I didn't mean to offend you," he said mildly.

Since coming to Utah, I had somehow become Shiloh's proxy to his family, and now I was getting angry on his behalf, reading judgment into innocuous remarks. I swallowed.

"You didn't," I said.

"How can I help you?" Bill asked. He seemed warmer now, and looked a little tired, like I felt. "I mean, why do you think Mike's in Utah?"

"I don't," I said. "I came here to find out more about his life before I met him. It might help, it might not." I realized I hadn't asked the obvious. "You haven't heard from Mike, have you?"

"No," he said.

"When was the last time you did?"

Like his sister, Bill was taken aback by my question. "I haven't spoken to him since he left home."

I nodded. Now seemed as good a time as any to get into that. "Naomi told me that you were a witness to some sort of scene that resulted in his leaving home shortly thereafter. Is that true?"

"Yeah. Does this have anything to do with him being missing now?"

"I don't know," I said. "It's the only part of his life that I don't know much about. He told me he left home because he was growing away from the religion you all had been raised in."

Bill raised his eyebrows. "He said that?" He shook his head, emphatically. "No. That's not what I remember."

"What was it, then?"

"Drugs," he said.

"Are you serious?" I saw that he was. "He was using habitually?"

"Habitually? I don't know," he said. "My father caught him, though. In our home."

"Naomi didn't mention that," I said.

"Naomi probably doesn't know," Bill said. "She and Bethany were really young, and our parents shielded them from a lot of what was going on. But I was right in the middle of it. Do you want to hear the whole story?"

I nodded assent.

"It happened on Christmas Eve."

Not fireflies in that photo, but Christmas lights.

"We were going to have a full house the next day. I was home from school, and Adam was coming the next afternoon, after he and Pam, that's his wife, and the baby spent Christmas morning with her folks in Provo. So for one night I had a room to myself,

Mike had Sara's old room, and the girls were where they always slept. The next night I was going to room with Mike, while Adam and his wife were going to take the other bedroom.

"Anyway, back then I was going steady with this girl, Christy. I promised her I would call her at midnight her time, because it was Christmas Eve. Christy had gone home to her folks' in Sacramento, so I had to call at one in the morning. I got up to do it, really quietly, because everyone else had gone to bed. I called her and I was going back upstairs on tiptoe when I saw the bathroom door open and this girl walks across the hall and goes into the room where Mike is and closes the door. Just like that."

"You didn't recognize her as your sister?"

"No. It was sort of dark and she'd cut her hair so that she had a short, stubby ponytail instead of long hair. I could see that she was wearing one of Mike's T-shirts. I stood there thinking, *I can't believe it.* I always knew Mike had a lot of ... I guess you'd say sangfroid, but bringing a girl over on Christmas Eve, that was really something.

"At this point, my father's heard people moving around and gotten up. He opens the door and asks me what's going on." Bill stopped at this point, fell silent for just a beat. Then he said, "I've thought about that night a lot since then. If I'd known then what I know now, I think I would have said, 'Nothing's going on. Go back to bed.'

"But I thought Mike had brought a girlfriend into the house. I mean, a *girl* in his *room,* and on Christmas Eve, with all of us there. And all I could do was call my girl on the phone: 'I miss you, honey, see you soon.' I was sort of annoyed about it. So instead I say, 'Mike's got a girl in his room.' " Bill lowered his voice, imitatively, on the last part. "My dad looks at me like he doesn't believe me but puts on his robe and comes out. He goes to the door and looks back at me like I'm going to be in trouble if there's no one in there, and then he knocks, opens the door, and flips on the light.

"That was it for being quiet. He yelled, 'What the hell is this?' It was the only time I'd heard him use that kind of language. I tried to get a look at what was going on, but he went in and slammed the door.

"I could still hear him yelling inside. My mom came out and so did Bethany from her room. I don't know how Naomi slept through it. But in a minute or two, the girl came out of Mike's room and in the light I saw that she was Sara.

"She had on Mike's shirt still and a pair of sweatpants, and her shoes in her hand and a bag over one shoulder. She ran down the stairs and out without even putting on her shoes. I looked into the room and saw Mike sitting on the edge of the bed with his head in his hands, and then my dad told Bethany and me to go to bed, and I could see he meant business.

"I couldn't believe he was so mad at Mike just for giving Sara a place to stay. But obviously something was really wrong. Mike left in the middle of the night Christmas night. The next day my dad got us all together and told us that he'd caught Sara and Michael doing drugs together."

"What kind of drugs?"

"Dad didn't say. It must've been something worse than a little marijuana, not to say that marijuana wouldn't have been bad enough." He straightened. "I'm going to have a cup of coffee. You want one?"

"Yeah, that'd be nice," I said.

When Bill returned with two cups of coffee, I said, "Naomi said Sara left on her own, but you make it sound like she was banned from the house."

Bill considered. "She did leave on her own. But I guess that our parents told her, 'If you go, don't come back until you're ready to live under our rules. Don't come around for a cash handout or a hot meal or to do laundry.'" He surveyed me, to see how I was taking it. "Tough love, you know?"

"Mmm," I said noncommittally. I wasn't here to editorialize about parenting methods. "Before that Christmas, did you know that your sister used drugs?"

"I didn't. My parents might have," Bill said, stirring his creamer in.

"Have you heard from her since she left?"

"No, none of us have. I know she's a published poet, but she uses a totally different name. Her first name, Sinclair, was our grandmother's maiden name, and then her husband's last name is . . . it escapes me right now."

"Goldman," I said. A mind's-eye view of our living-room shelves in Minneapolis had supplied the name, *Sinclair Goldman,* to me. It was the name on one of the slender books of poetry that Shiloh owned.

"Yeah," he said. "Goldman. I used to know her husband's first name, too. Something with a *D*. He was a Jewish guy." He paused, then let go of that train of thought. "It's funny, if a friend of a friend hadn't told me about her poetry, I could've walked past her book in a store and never guessed it was my sister who wrote it."

"Other than the drug issue, do you remember your sister as being wild?" I asked.

"Wild?" Bill repeated. "Not really. But she was ... immovable. If she wanted to see friends, she'd do it, even if it meant sneaking out of the house. I think it scared my folks as much as it made them angry. She was deaf. That made her vulnerable, even though she didn't want to acknowledge it. And then there was the signing-or-speaking thing."

"Meaning what?"

"Sara was working on her vocal skills at school, and then she just stopped. It frustrated my folks, because it would have made things much easier if she could speak. But she decided she didn't want to speak, so she didn't. That was just the way she was. It was nothing personal, but she'd made up her mind and that was it."

I nodded. "Was your father a strict disciplinarian?" The coffee was watery and joyless, worse than any I'd had at any rural sheriff's substation. I set it aside.

Bill shook his head. "No," he said. "When we'd done something wrong, we got talks. Very *long* talks, about God's will for our lives. With plenty of quotation from the Bible." He smiled, fondly. "If there were actual punishments to be handed out, particularly when we were younger, my mother had to do that part. Why?"

I tried to think of the right way to say what came next. "It just seems extreme to me, that such a long estrangement would grow out of adolescent drug use."

Bill lifted a shoulder. "Well," he said, "I don't think it was so much drugs as it was ..." He trailed off.

I raised my eyebrows.

"You've got to understand my father to get it," he explained.

"Tell me," I said.

Bill hesitated. "I'm not the most articulate person in the world."

"Neither am I," I said, smiling a little. "Relax, you're not addressing the UN General Assembly."

"Okay." Bill tapped a pen against the desk, composing himself. "My father was a winner of souls. I know that phrase may sound extreme, but if you knew my father, you'd know it wasn't. Before he became a pastor, he used to travel to do his evangelical work. All around the country. Those were the best days of my father's life."

A light flashed on Bill Shiloh's phone, and he glanced down at it, but the phone didn't ring. He'd set it to go automatically into voice mail.

"When he and my mother got married, she went on the road with him. She was a part of that life. But when they had Adam, and then me, they realized they had to settle down somewhere. I don't think it was easy for my father to make the change from evangelist to pastor. A congregation has more complex needs than simply salvation."

"Marryings and buryings," I said.

"And ongoing spiritual nourishment, and annual budgeting, and committee meetings. All but the smallest of churches have those things. My father gave himself to that kind of role, but he made it as much of a challenge as possible. Or God did. My father felt a calling to come to northern Utah, right to the heart of Mormon country. He didn't want to go anywhere where he'd be 'preaching to the choir.' My father liked uphill battles."

That sounded familiar.

"He used to go into Salt Lake City and preach on street corners. He'd hand out tracts near the Temple. He bought an old school bus for the church. When he was finished overhauling it, there was a cross bolted to the front grille, 'New Life Church' painted on the sides, and 'I am the Resurrection and the Life' on the back." Bill laughed. "Oh, yeah. You definitely saw *us* coming down the road.

"The thing is, my dad bought that bus when our own family car needed eight hundred dollars' worth of transmission work." Bill smiled. "Mom just put up with it. She understood what evangelism meant to him. It wasn't just a job. It was his life. He got a phone call once, in the middle of the night, from an unsaved friend. This guy, Whitey, had been stiff-arming him for months, brushing off invitations to come to church. Then he called up in the middle of the night, wanting to talk about Jesus. My dad dressed and put on his jacket, picked up his Bible and car keys, and drove across town. Like an ER surgeon. He came home and said Whitey had found Christ at four-thirty in the morning." He shook his head, looking fond again.

"None of us kids have really followed in his footsteps. We're all Christian, of course. My wife and I go to a Presbyterian church now, and take my kids every Sunday, pray with them. But I didn't feel any calling to lead a church or be an evangelist. And neither did Adam. Maybe that disappointed my father, too, but I think he knew from fairly early on it was going to turn out that way. I think he felt if any of us were going to follow him into the ministry, it would be Mike."

"Are you serious?" I said.

"Yeah," Bill said. "Mike used to read the Bible for hours on end. He knew the word of God backward and forward." He paused. "You know what snake-handling is?"

"I've heard about it," I said, thrown off by the shift in the conversation.

"It comes from the Gospel of Mark, where Christ says his apostles will handle poisonous serpents and not be harmed. When Mike was fourteen, a couple of families joined the church who'd moved up from north Florida. They were into snake-handling; they had prayer meetings where they'd pass poisonous snakes between them. We didn't realize it right away, but Mike was doing that with them."

"Shiloh did *that*?"

Bill looked amused. "Yup. He never told you?"

I shook my head.

"Well, he did. When my mother found out, she just about had a heart attack. She and Dad had a hard time talking him out of it. I think he finally gave it up just so our mother wouldn't worry." Bill lifted a shoulder. "What I'm trying to say is this: My father recognized in Mike a part of himself that his other kids didn't seem to inherit, and I think that's why it hurt him so much when he lost Mike." He paused. "For years, my father just never mentioned him."

"What about Sinclair?" I asked.

"Sara? I think she was different," Bill said. "She went to a secular school—for the deaf, I mean—and from the time she came home we all realized she wasn't a believer. Right from the beginning she started ... acting out, I guess you'd say. Wearing makeup, sneaking out to see boys, coming home smelling of alcohol. It wasn't easy on my folks, but it did give them time to adjust to losing her. It was like— Do you know the parable of the sower?"

I shook my head.

"It's about different kinds of seeds. How some never sprout, others spring up right away and look promising but ultimately die, and then others start slow but eventually become healthy and fruitful plants. It's a metaphor."

"For evangelism," I said.

"Yeah, a metaphor for the different kinds of people who turn to Christ, or don't. Sara was like the seed that lands on rocky soil and never sprouts at all, but Michael was the one who looks promising but fails in the end to fulfill that promise. Mike was there, and then all of a sudden he wasn't. It would have been less painful if he had never lived in Christ at all. I think that's why my father never talked about him. Afterward."

"After what?" I said. His words sounded so stark, drawing an absolute line.

"After Mike left," Bill said simply. "Maybe my parents sound harsh to you, not worrying about where Mike and Sara were and how they were living. But my father didn't worry about physical well-being, just the health of the soul. When he'd talk about Michael and Sara at all, he would say that they couldn't go anywhere that God didn't know where they were, and that was the most important thing. Likewise, he said, it didn't matter if they lived in the house across the street if they had turned their backs on God. If they were lost to God, they were lost to my father as well." Bill looked at me closely, as if to see whether his words were reaching me. "My father told us God could forgive anything, but not until He is asked."

A silence fell between us. It wasn't exactly uncomfortable, but within a minute I broke it, changing the subject. "And you?"

"What about me?" he asked.

"Did you like your brother?"

"Mike? Yeah, I guess so." Bill was surprised at the question, but he was thinking about it. "When he was a kid, he used to want to tag along with Adam and me. We used to jump freight trains to get across town when we didn't want to walk somewhere, and Mike could always keep up with us. We never had to slow down for him. We'd swim at this lake up in the hills, with steep bluffs on one side, and Mike used to jump from the heights, totally fearless. Even I only did that once, but he did it all the time.

"And he knew all this stuff, even as a kid. It was cool to talk to him. When he was older, it started to get under my skin. It wasn't that he showed off his IQ." Bill wrestled with a thought. "But he was just real smart, and you could tell that he knew, even though he didn't say anything. He knew he was different.

"I guess that's why I was angry when I thought he had a girl in his room on Christmas Eve. Like he felt it was okay for him to do that, because he was Mike. Since then, I've wished I'd covered for him." Bill shook his head. "I didn't know then he was going to up and leave home because of what happened."

After a moment of silence, I realized Bill Shiloh was done. There was no moral to the story, no coda, other than his expression of mild regret.

I had one last question, but I thought I already knew the answer. "I don't think Mike's in trouble," I said. "But if he were, do you know of a friend he'd go to?"

"To Sara," Bill said. "He'd go to her."

chapter **16**

After two open-ended interviews, casting with a broad net
for anything that might be useful, I finally had a very specific
task: finding Sinclair Goldman.

That task led me to the public library at midday. None of
Shiloh's brothers or sisters seemed to have a current or even an
old phone number or address for her. Sinclair, of course, was
deaf, but I was working on the assumption she'd have a TTY
phone, one adapted for use for the hearing-impaired.

Normally, a phone number would make things easy. Vang,
back in Minneapolis, could run any name I gave him through
the national phone disc and come up with a number. It was de-
ciding what name to give him that would be the problem.
Sinclair's last name could be Goldman, or she could have split
up with her husband and gone back to Shiloh. Her first name

could be Sinclair, if she'd had it legally changed, or it could still be Sara.

Sitting at a broad table in the library's reading room, I mixed and matched the possibilities on a piece of scratch paper. Sinclair Goldman. Sara Goldman. Sinclair Shiloh. Sara Shiloh. Four possible names. No, six, I realized. Naomi told me that Sara spelled her first name without the *h*. But one thing I'd learned in doing routine investigative work was to always account for clerical errors, especially common misspellings of variant names. Michele and Michelle. Jon and John. If I asked Vang for this favor, I'd have to include Sarah Goldman and Sarah Shiloh as possible names. Vang's list might stretch into the hundreds of listings. Even a thousand.

Some of those women I'd actually reach the first time. But I'd also end up leaving dozens of messages on machines and in voice mailboxes, then I'd be stuck by a phone in a cheap motel room somewhere, waiting for return calls.

There was even a possibility that Sinclair's phone wasn't listed under her name but her husband's, whose first name I didn't even know. *Something with a* D, Bill Shiloh had said.

There had to be a better way than going through official data banks.

When people aren't crooks, and aren't hiding, there are a couple of easy ways to find them. Through their profession is one way.

Sinclair was a poet. She didn't seem to be well known, if there was such a thing as a well-known poet other than the rare few called on to read at presidential inaugurations. But even so, she was a semipublic person. Her name, Sinclair Goldman, was her brand. She wasn't likely to have changed it, even if she'd broken up with her husband.

Through an entryway off to my left I could see into another room, full of computers. They were Web stations. I picked up my piece of scratch paper and crossed to the doorway.

Every station was occupied. Nearby, a sign advised, *Please sign up for Internet time. Half hour while others are waiting.* A clipboard hung below.

Almost all the users seemed to be high-school students. Did the schools release them to do library research on their own? Did they cut school to go on the Internet? I'd been no stranger to cutting school as a kid, but never to go to a library.

The youngest user was perhaps 15. He was looking at pictures of muscle cars.

"Excuse me," I said. I held up my Hennepin County badge. "This is police business."

His eyes widened a little and he got up, reaching for a backpack next to the seat.

"Don't move your stuff," I said. "This probably won't take long."

I slid into the warm seat and typed the address of a metasearch engine Shiloh favored into the window of the browser. When the portal came up, I typed "Sinclair Goldman" into the search field.

It drew two hits. One was the site for Last Light Press; that was promising. The other one was of more interest. It was the site of Bale College.

Clicking through, I learned that Sinclair Goldman was on the Bale faculty for the current semester. Sinclair Goldman was a lecturer, Creative Writing 230. Practice of Poetry. My heart felt a little lighter, like it always did when a trail was getting warmer.

Further mouse-clicking told me her class met today, but too

late for me to catch her there unless Bale was somewhere in northern Utah. It wasn't. The 'Getting Here' page showed a star on a map a bit south of Santa Fe, New Mexico.

"Just another minute," I told the waiting kid as I clicked on "Contact Us" and reached for the library's supply of scratch paper and a little half pencil.

I called from a quiet phone near the library's rest rooms, and the operator switched me through to the literature department.

"This is Detective Sarah Pribek," I told the young man who answered the phone. "I'm trying to get in touch with Sinclair Goldman. I know she's deaf," I put in quickly. Already I'd heard him draw in his breath to explain that to me. "But I have to get in touch with her today. It's police business."

"She's on campus right now. She has a poetry seminar from two to four." He had a pale, hollow voice and a student's accent. Apropos of very little, I imagined him. About 20, with very short hair dyed white-blond from some more mundane color.

"I'm in Utah," I said. "I'm coming to Santa Fe, but not that fast."

"We're not in Santa Fe. We're—"

"I don't need directions. I just need to know where I can get in touch with Sinclair Goldman after she leaves campus. A phone number or an address."

Predictably, he balked. "We can't give addresses out."

I'd expected as much, and I couldn't press the issue. I was on the phone. He was right not to give out her information on my word that I was a police officer.

"A phone number, then," I said.

He sounded incredulous. "I really don't think she has a phone. Ms. Goldman is hearing-impaired."

"I know that, but—"

"I *can* tell you she has office hours here on Tuesday from—"

Goddammit. "Look, I'm a sheriff's detective from Minnesota. I'm not coming to New Mexico to talk to her about a *term paper*, and I can't wait until Tuesday. Will you please check for a phone number?"

A beat of silence. "Please hold."

He came back a minute later. "I have a number," he said, sounding surprised. He read it. "The thing is, there's a name in parentheses next to it. Ligieia Moore. Does that mean anything to you?"

"Thanks," I said. "I appreciate your help."

Ignoring his question, I broke the connection with my index finger and waited before dialing again.

Sinclair was in class right now, so was anyone even at home? Maybe D. Goldman, husband. Or Ligieia Moore, whoever she was. Maybe this number was some kind of contact. An assistant? Her editor, even?

The phone rang four times and someone picked up. "Hello?" It was a light, feminine voice.

"My name is Detective Sarah Pribek, and I'm trying to reach Sinclair Goldman. Who am I talking to?"

"This is Ligieia," she said. "Sinclair isn't here. Did you say you were a police officer?"

"I'm a sheriff's detective from Hennepin County, Minnesota," I said. "I need to talk to Ms. Goldman as part of an investigation. I called Bale College, and this is the number they gave me for her. Is there a better one I should have called?"

"No," Ligieia said. "This is the right number. Do you sign?"

"No," I said. "I'm afraid I don't. You're saying if I want to talk to her, I'll need a translator."

"Yes. I translate for Sinclair, usually. In her classes, and I read her poetry at the slams. If you want to set something up, a meeting, it'd be easiest to do it through me. I'll talk to her when she gets home."

"Might her husband be able to translate for us?" I suggested.

"Sinclair isn't married," Ligieia said.

"She got divorced, then," I said.

Ligieia paused, processing the fact that I knew a little bit, at least, about Sinclair. "Yes," she said. "I'm going to need to tell her what this is about." Her voice lifted a little, prompting me.

I wished hard that I knew sign language. Already, it was unpleasant going through an intermediary I didn't even know, and it would probably be more intrusive when I was face-to-face with Sinclair. "Like I said, I'm a detective with the Hennepin County Sheriff's Department. But my married name is Shiloh," I said.

"Oh," Ligieia said, surprised. She recognized the name.

"I'm also Sinclair's sister-in-law. Her brother Michael, my husband, is missing. So it's police business and it's family business, too."

"Oh, wow," Ligieia said. The phrase made her voice sound yet younger. "Okay. Are you in town? Or up in Santa Fe?"

"I will be, as soon as I can get a flight. I'd like to talk to Sinclair tonight," I said.

"Well," Ligieia said, "I'll have to talk to her before we can set anything up. Can I give you a call back?"

"I don't have a number where I can be reached," I said. "It'll really be better if we can set something up now, and you can tell me how to get to her place." I was pushing.

"Really, I can't do that," Ligieia said. "I'm her housemate, and I translate for her sometimes, but that's all. She's completely independent. I'm not like an aide for the disabled."

"I understand," I said.

"She might be okay with meeting at the house, but she might feel more comfortable meeting on campus, or someplace in town," she said.

"Let me call you when I get into Santa Fe," I said, capitulating.

"That sounds good."

"Listen," I said, curious, "if you translate for Sinclair in her classes . . . isn't she holding a class now?"

"Right," Ligieia said. "But Bale teaches sign through their language department. Sinclair agreed to let one of the honor students translate for her today, as an assignment. So I got some time off to study."

"Are you studying sign language?"

"No, creative writing. I write poetry. But I had a deaf boyfriend all through high school, and that's how I learned to sign."

A group of noisy schoolchildren walked by the pay phones on their way into the library. I stuck a finger in my ear and turned away from them.

"Look, I hope I didn't make Sinclair sound standoffish earlier," Ligieia went on. "She's a really amazing person. I'm sure she'll be pleased to meet you."

I was going to have to make excellent time if I hoped to speak to Sinclair Goldman this same night, and I pushed my rental car up to seventy-five on the highway out of town. But nearly as quickly, I had to slam on the brakes at a traffic signal. The light was green, which was why I very nearly shot into the intersection and into a long black sedan. As I skidded to a halt partway into the crosswalk, I saw that the sedan was one of many like it, moving in a slow and sober chain. I looked to the left, the front of the procession. The very first car was a hearse, rolling through a wide stone gate behind which a narrow road wound through well-tended emerald lawns.

I hoped it was not a young person they were burying.

The mortuary where Kamareia's arrangements had been made clearly had overcompensated for the cold snap we'd been having; the interior nearly glowed with heat. Furthermore, my funeral dress—the one I bought and last wore when my father died—was wool, appropriate for wintertime. As Genevieve's family and friends trickled in and the room filled, I felt uncomfortably warm and wished I could slip away.

Shiloh was across the room in his dark going-to-court suit. I had taken a personal day to be with Genevieve and the family members who were staying in her house, to help her through the viewing, service, and burial. Shiloh had arranged a split shift so he could be here now, for the viewing.

That was a figure of speech in this case. The mortician could only do so much with a face battered like Kamareia's had been; the casket at the front of the room was expensive, gleaming, and closed. I stared at it a moment too long, then turned my gaze to the arriving mourners.

One of them arrested my attention immediately.

I'd heard Genevieve talk from time to time about her brief marriage. She was working-class white Catholic from the urban

North; he'd been born black in rural Georgia and was raised in the First African Baptist Church. When those differences doomed their marriage, he'd gone on to Harlem, then finally to Europe as a corporate lawyer, while she'd stayed to be a cop in the Cities that had been her family's home for several generations.

I'd never seen a picture of Vincent, but Genevieve described him to me once, early in our friendship. So when I saw him, there was really no reason for me to think, Who the hell is that? but I did, and then of course I realized.

It was my habit to categorize people I saw as the athletes they might have been in high school: linebacker, cross-country runner, swimmer, point guard. That wasn't possible with this man. Vincent Brown was six-foot-four and he had a powerful physical presence that was impossible to characterize. He was power all over, in a rich man's monochromatic suit, with something Aztec about his cheekbones and hawklike in his profile. His dark gaze reminded me not at all of Kamareia's light-hazel, wide-set eyes. It was difficult to imagine him as the father of that lighthearted, gentle girl, and equally difficult to envision him as Genevieve's husband, the two of them making a home together.

Vincent saw who he was looking for: Genevieve, among her family. He went to her side, and her brothers and sisters moved aside slightly at his approach. Genevieve raised her eyes to him, and Vincent kissed her. Not on the cheek or even the forehead, but on the top of her head, and he closed his eyes as he did it, a gesture of immeasurable tenderness.

Suddenly I saw what I hadn't been able to only seconds earlier: kinship. Belonging, despite everything that seems to argue against it.

Vincent spoke to Genevieve, and she to him. He turned and looked at me, and I realized I was being discussed. Caught staring, I glanced away, but already Vincent was moving toward me, so I turned back to acknowledge him.

"Sarah," he said.

"Vincent?" It was half a greeting, half a question. He didn't exactly shake my hand, but took it and held it a moment.

"You were with Kamareia, weren't you?" he asked. "On the way to the hospital?"

"Yes."

"Thank you," he said.

At the Salt Lake City airport I found a flight to Albuquerque that I could be a standby on. I laid down my credit card and bought a ticket.

If Shiloh's various statements—bank, phone, credit card— had shown no suspicious activity, I was leaving a paper trail that a child could follow: long-distance calls on my card, paperwork at a rental-car agency, plane tickets on the American Express.

But my name was not called, and I was left standing to watch the boarding agent close the door to the jetway. Behind the counter, the little red lights spelling out "Flt. 519— Albuquerque—3:25" went dead.

The 4:40 flight was more sparsely loaded. Our flight time was one hour, twenty minutes. At least, it should have been. As we neared the Albuquerque area, the pilot made an announcement.

"They're experiencing some delays in Albuquerque due to some heavy low cloud and rain there. We're not going to reroute; we expect to get you on the ground and on your way before too long, but we will be spending a little while in a holding pattern, waiting for clearance. Sorry for the inconvenience." The pilot's voice turned warm and avuncular. "Speaking of the weather, folks, you may want to factor in a little extra time for your ground travel this evening, due to the conditions. We like to see you stay safe so you'll be back to fly with us again."

I rested my head against the edge of the little porthole of the window, and listened to the impatient rhythm of my own heart.

The later I was, the more likely it was that Sinclair and Ligieia would put me off until tomorrow morning, probably for a meeting somewhere in town.

I didn't want to meet Sinclair in a café or diner. If I had to speak to Shiloh's closest sibling through a translator, at least I didn't want to do it in a busy public place that wasn't going to lend itself to a lengthy and comfortable conversation.

The surroundings in which Naomi Wilson and I had talked were ideal. In her own home, we'd had privacy and we'd had time to let the conversation go where it needed to. It probably wasn't going to be possible to re-create that with Sinclair, no matter what. But I wanted to go to her house, and it wasn't just so we'd have time and privacy to talk.

All of us have that one place we'd go if our lives fell apart. My conversation with his brother suggested that Shiloh's place might be wherever his sister Sinclair lived.

Shiloh's life had not been falling apart. Shiloh's life had been coming together. His career was taking off, his marriage was young and strong. And yet I had to satisfy myself that he hadn't, acting under stresses totally unknown to me, sought refuge in this remote corner of the country.

It would seem a strange coincidence, at least to me, if Santa Fe were indeed the place Shiloh had gone to ground. As far as I knew, he'd never been there, while one of my earliest memories was of Santa Fe.

I was perhaps four when Mother had taken me on a trip to the city, for some kind of shopping she couldn't do in the hinterlands. All I remember of it was that it seemed to be fall or winter. In my snapshot memories I see a cool rainy night and the warm inviting lights of the buildings; I remember eating a creamy soup made of pumpkin or squash in a restaurant and my child's satisfaction because it was only my mother and me at the table, and I had her all to myself....

The pilot's voice broke into my thoughts. We were cleared to make a final descent into the Albuquerque area. A stewardess moved smoothly up the aisle on the periphery of my vision, alert for tray tables still down or cell phones in use.

The plane sank down into a layer of cloud smooth as the surface of the ocean. At late twilight, the cloudbank was a very dark gray, night nearly fallen over the city. Droplets of water formed on my window and began to crawl sidewise across the pane. Wrapped in a charcoal mist, for a moment all of us on the plane were nowhere, between worlds.

It was ridiculous and I knew it, the prospect that I might surprise Shiloh at his sister's home in New Mexico. But I knew why I refused to reject it out of hand. In a weird and backwards way, it was attractive.

I'd once heard a widowed woman say that a month after her husband died in a car wreck, she began to console herself with a fantasy. The fantasy was that her husband wasn't dead, he'd just left her and was living in another part of the country. At the time, that hadn't sounded like a very comforting thing to think about late at night, but now I understood. That woman's love had been unconditional: she'd just wanted her husband to be alive and all right, with or without her.

Of the realistic choices I had to explain Shiloh's disappearance, this was the only remotely pleasant one.

White runway lights rose to meet the plane.

chapter **17**

I merged with a thin crowd of people on the concourse
leading to the main terminal. The things I had yet to do tonight
made me feel tired already. There was a bank of pay phones
right before me, but I already knew I wasn't going to call
Ligieia.

The kinds of city maps given out at car-rental counters
weren't going to be good enough for the directions I needed. It
was at a newsstand that I found what I needed, a map that included the whole state of New Mexico.

At the car-rental counter, I added to my paper trail, renting
a Honda. I unfolded the state map and pointed to the small
town where Bale College was. "How long should it take me to
get here?" I asked.

The clerk looked down to see where I was pointing. "An

hour," she said. "Maybe a little more, 'cause it's getting dark and you're new to the area."

"There's a full tank of gas in this car you're giving me?"

"Oh, yes, all our cars are filled up. You're responsible for returning them refilled or you'll pay a fueling fee—"

"What about a cupholder?" I asked.

"A what?"

"I'm gonna need coffee."

"I feel you," she said, a fellow caffeine addict.

But in the end I didn't want to take the time to stop, so I didn't walk back to the Starbucks in the main terminal, nor did I pull over anywhere. I just headed out of town.

A light mist fell steadily, and I turned the windshield wipers on to their intermittent setting. I hoped we weren't going to have a serious rain, because I was planning on letting my lead foot have its way. I was already going to be late enough to be rude; every minute counted.

I kept it at eighty-two as long as I was on the interstate. When the route to Bale College began to take me up into the hills, I eased off the accelerator, but not enough to be going at a legal speed. Then flashing lights turned the raindrops clinging to my rear window into the colors from a red-and-blue kaleidoscope.

I hit my turn signal immediately, telegraphing my intent to be cooperative, and eased onto the shoulder of the road.

The patrol officer who approached the side of my car looked about 20. He was Deputy Johnson by his name tag. "Do you know how fast you were going?" Johnson said.

"Well, I thought forty-five, but you're probably going to tell me it was more than that," I said, trying to sound good-natured.

"It was quite a bit more than that," he said, unsmiling. "I clocked you at fifty-seven."

"You got me, I guess. I'm in a strange car; sometimes they can fool you," I said.

"They can't fool you if you're watching the speedometer," he said didactically. "It's very important that people drive slow in a light rain like this. See, people think a light rain is better than a heavy rain, but there are oils in the asphalt that ..."

I'll pay the fine, I'll pay it twice, please just stop talking and write the ticket, I thought. But he was a kid; he took his job very seriously.

Deputy Johnson wrapped up his spiel about a minute later and took my ID off to run it through the computer. I began to leaf through my bag for my Hennepin County shield.

He returned and wrote up my ticket. I took it from him.

"Thank you for your courtesy," he said.

"Hold on a minute, will you? There's something I need to ask you." I held out my shield. "I'm with the Hennepin County Sheriff's Department. That's Minneapolis and the surrounding area."

His eyebrows went up, an expression both surprised and defensive.

"I'm not angling for professional courtesy with the ticket. I was speeding; I'll pay the fine," I assured him. "I'm here as part of an investigation. I was actually on my way to your department when you pulled me over. I have a phone number here without an address, and I was going to ask someone to get that for me tonight." I smiled at him to let him know he'd be doing me a favor. "If you could radio this in to your department in advance, maybe they could have it by the time I get there."

Deputy Johnson furrowed his brow. "You're from what jurisdiction again?"

"I'm a detective from Hennepin County. I can give you the

night number there for the investigation division, if anyone wants to check it out."

"This is part of an investigation?" he reiterated.

"A missing-persons investigation, yes."

It was beginning to dawn on Johnson that this was sort of an interesting break from manning the speed trap. "What's the phone number you're asking about?" he asked.

I gave him Ligieia's phone number and he went back to the radio.

"They're looking it up," he said when he returned, and gave me directions to the sheriff's substation. "Come back and talk to me if there's anything I can do to help you while you're in town, Detective Pribek," he said. It sounded as if his job wasn't keeping him too challenged.

It wasn't until I got to the substation that someone asked the obvious question, somewhat indirectly.

"Hennepin County must have a real budget surplus to be able to send its detectives around the country to look for missing persons," the deputy on duty said, lifting an ironic eyebrow.

"They don't," I said. "This is a rarity."

He gave me the address, written on a Post-it with the sticky part folded over onto itself.

"This is a special case?" he said.

"Kind of." I didn't feel like explaining. "Hey, is that coffee?"

Ten minutes later I pulled up in front of a low wood-shingled cottage, not far from where the map indicated Bale College was. At the end of the driveway was an outdoor light modeled to look like a Victorian gas lamp. Its hundred-watt bulb cast a bright light over the front yard. The garage was closed, and there was no nondescript clean vehicle parked outside that would have suggested a visitor's rental car to me.

I heard footsteps respond to my knock, but the door didn't open immediately. Instead, a curtain moved in a side window, reflecting a wise female caution. A moment later, the door swung open about a foot.

A young woman stood in the opening. She was about five-six, with two dark-brown braids stiff with repressed curls. A crop top over plaid pajama pants exposed her flat stomach, a shade or two lighter than cocoa powder. Her feet were bare.

"Can I help you?" she asked.

"We spoke on the phone today. I'm Sarah Pribek. I was going to call you"—I pushed ahead with my explanation before she could speak—"but my flight was delayed, and I was late getting in." That didn't mean anything, but in its way it sounded like an excuse. "And in a missing-persons investigation, time is really of the essence, so I came straight here."

Ligieia's deep-brown eyes studied me, and she wasn't saying no yet. I continued making my case. "I brought a legal pad along." I touched my shoulder bag, where the notepad rode. "You won't have to translate if it's not convenient for you."

She stepped back. "Come on in," she said, grudgingly. "I'll ask Sinclair if it's okay."

As she closed the door behind us, a little girl ran into the entryway. Her auburn hair was wet, and she was wrapped in a magenta bath towel held in place by her arms. She stopped alongside Ligieia and looked up at me, then she lifted her hands and began to gesture. The towel slipped to her feet.

"Hope!" Ligieia gasped, and knelt down to snatch up the towel and wrap the naked little girl again. Ligieia glanced up at me, and when she saw me starting to laugh, she began to laugh, too, rolling her eyes. It was the best icebreaker I could have asked for.

"Sinclair's daughter?" I asked.

"Yeah, this is Hope," Ligieia said. "The signing gives her away as Sinclair's kid, I guess."

I was looking down at Hope when I caught movement on the periphery of my vision. A tall woman stood behind Ligieia, her red hair loose. She trained a familiar assessing gaze on me from eyes that were just slightly Eurasian in their shape.

Sinclair. Ligieia hadn't noticed her presence yet. I straightened and nodded to her, and she returned my greeting in kind.

The exchange had a formal feeling for me, and not just because I couldn't speak directly to her. I had that feeling, like I'd found a missing person. Two days ago I hadn't really known she'd existed, at least not by name, and now she felt like someone I'd been trying to locate for a long time.

"Hold on to that towel, honey," Ligieia said to Hope, then she stood up and spoke to Sinclair, speaking and signing at once.

"This is Sarah Pribek." Spelling out my name slowed Ligieia down. "She says that time is very important in a missing-persons situation, so she came up early. She wants to talk to you tonight."

Hope watched the conversation silently. Sinclair lifted her hands and signed.

Ligieia looked at me. "Do you have a room in town?"

Damn, I thought, sensing a dismissal. "Not yet," I said.

Sinclair signed again.

"She says she's going to make up the spare room for you," Ligieia translated.

Sinclair scooped her daughter up into her arms and walked

back down the hall from which she'd come, while I stood taken aback by her unexpected display of hospitality. I was, after all, a total stranger.

Ligieia broke into my thoughts. "Why don't you come into the kitchen with me? I was going to make some tea."

"Look, I meant what I said about you not having to translate," I repeated, following her. "You look like you were on the way to bed."

"No," Ligieia said. "I'm just studying. I have to have Act III of *The Merchant of Venice* finished by tomorrow." She lifted a teakettle off the stove and shook it, checking the water level inside. "It seems kind of a waste of time. Hardly anyone performs *Merchant* anymore, and rightly so, because it's so horribly anti-Semitic. I don't think anyone even reads it anymore." She struck a match before touching it to the burner: it was a very old stove.

"Have you known Sinclair long?" I asked her.

"Three years," Ligieia said. "As long as she's been at Bale. I was assigned to be her translator right away, and started doing her readings shortly after that."

"Readings?"

"I perform her work at poetry readings and slams," Ligieia explained. "There's a lot of challenge in that, because I'm not just reciting her words. I'm translating the emotional content and trying to bring that across as well. I've had to really get to know Sinclair, to read her work like she would read it herself if she were a speaking person."

I turned at the sound of light footsteps behind me and saw Hope, her copper hair combed, wearing a white nightdress and looking up at me with a child's seriousness.

"Mommy says you're a speaking person," she announced,

but she signed it as well, just in case. Her voice was pitch-perfect, clearly understandable. Until that moment I had thought she was deaf.

"Your mother's right," I said.

"Is your name Sarah?" she asked.

Ligieia interrupted. "Hope, does your mother know you're in here?"

The girl looked at the floor. She didn't want to lie.

"You know what I think?" Ligieia went on, bending slightly to address Hope. "I think she already put you to bed and thought you were going to stay there." Ligieia straightened and pointed.

Hope ran from the kitchen, back down the hallway.

Ligieia shook her head, both indulgent and exasperated. "She's always got to be a part of everything," she said. Ligieia held a hand over the kettle's spout, feeling for steam. "The brainiest little kid I've ever seen. Sounds like a ten-year-old when she talks. Signs fluently. I'm sure when she's older she's going to do what I'm doing, reading her mother's poetry at performances. She's gonna be something."

"When did Sinclair divorce her father?"

Ligieia didn't respond. Her eyes went to a space behind me, and I turned and saw Sinclair.

Shiloh was like that. Walked like a damn cloud. Often I didn't hear him until he was right behind me.

"I was just about to pour," Ligieia said.

We settled in the living room, which was low-ceilinged and crowded with houseplants, marked by eclectic splashes of color. When I was seated in a rocking easy chair, I put my nose down into my tea, stalling. I'd gotten in here by saying that it was important that I speak to Sinclair tonight, and the truth was that I had no urgent questions for her. I'd come here to satisfy myself that Shiloh wasn't here, and it was plain to me that he wasn't.

It was Sinclair who broke the silence, not me.

"I'm glad you came," she said through Ligieia. *"I'm very curious about Michael. It's been years since I've seen him. I know you probably have questions for me first, though."*

I set my teacup down. "That was my first question: When was the last time you heard from him?"

Ligieia waited while Sinclair thought.

"About five, six years ago," she signed. *"I can't remember exactly. I was in the Cities to do a reading at the Loft and give a guest lecture at Augsburg College, then I was driving down to Northfield, to lecture at Carleton. I remember the Carleton visit well, because I got there several days after a terrible car wreck near the Cities killed three of their students. It was very sad. Things like that hit a small school hard."*

"Oh," I said. The anecdote struck a chord. "I remember that, too."

"Do you want me to check the exact date?"

"Not necessary," I said. "It was so long ago it's almost undoubtedly not part of whatever has happened now. I was more curious about how much you'd kept in contact with Shiloh. Did you actually see him in person when you were there?"

"Yes. We ran into each other on the street."

"You hadn't arranged to see him?"

"I didn't even know he lived there."

"Have you heard from him since: letters, e-mail?"

Sinclair shook her head.

"When you heard that he was missing, did any possibilities about what would have happened to him come to mind?"

Sinclair shook her head again. Her terse answers weren't meant to be unhelpful, I saw, but actually courteous: She was communicating directly with me.

"Why do you think he ran away, back when he was seventeen?" I asked her.

At this question she shifted her gaze from Ligieia's hands to my eyes, and ran her thumb across her fingertips quickly. I wondered if this hand motion was akin to a speaking person licking her upper lip during an interview, a temporizing gesture.

"I didn't hear about that until years later," Sinclair told me. *"But Mike didn't get along with our father any better than I did."*

"That's not what your brother and sister say."

There was a slightly longer pause this time, as Ligieia waited for Sinclair's hands to be still. Then Ligieia translated. *"They saw what they wanted to see. My family was accustomed to thinking of me as different, but they wanted Mike to be like them."*

"When you left home, where did you go?"

"Salt Lake City. I stayed with a group of friends who were . . . Jack Mormons?" There was a momentary hitch in the translation process as Ligieia stumbled on the phrase. *"Mormons who had fallen away from the LDS Church."*

It was a term that wouldn't have thrown me; I'd heard Shiloh use it before.

"When they went out of town for Christmas, I got lonely and went home. Michael slipped me into the house, through a window with a big tree outside it. It was the same way I used to sneak out."

She paused for Ligieia to catch up. *"We got caught, and my father was pretty angry. I was sorry that I got Mike in trouble. But he would have broken away from our family sooner or later."*

"Did Mike come to Salt Lake City and look you up after he left home?"

"No. As I said, I never knew about that until years later."

My questions, Sinclair's gaze, Ligieia's voice . . . I had a feeling like I was getting information through a system akin to an old rural party-line phone system. It felt slipshod.

"Why do you think he wouldn't have gone to you?" I said. There was something else I needed to ask, but it was best circled around to later.

Sinclair's gaze, so like Shiloh's, was very direct on me. She signed. *"Mike was always very independent,"* Ligieia translated. *"Can I ask you why you're asking about this? It was so long ago."*

I lifted the mug but didn't drink again. The strawberry tea had been a tantalizing clear pink color when Ligieia had poured, but when I'd tasted it in the kitchen, it had proved sour in a thin, watery way.

"History," I said. "I'm just looking for a pattern." I forced a little of the tea down. "But if you haven't seen him or heard from him in years, there's not a lot else I can ask you," I said.

In the moment that followed, it was neither Sinclair nor I who broke the silence. It was Ligieia.

"Does anyone but me want something stronger than this to drink?" Ligieia suggested. She glanced at Sinclair, who waffled a hand in the air with neither great enthusiasm nor disapproval. I was beginning to think that was the way Sinclair took everything, in stride, at peace.

Ligieia left the room. *Now we can really talk,* I thought, looking at Sinclair. But of course we couldn't. I would have liked to speak to Sinclair without the extraneous presence of Ligieia. The girl was nice enough, but she had never known Shiloh; she had no stake in the conversation.

"I couldn't sleep," said a pettish young voice at my side.

I turned to look where Sinclair was looking. Hope came into the room, wearing her nightdress, barefoot. Sinclair shook her head with maternal exasperation.

Ligieia returned with a bottle of Bombay gin in her hand and stopped short when she saw Hope. "What's this?" She looked to Sinclair. "Don't get up. I'll take her back to bed." She held out her hand to Hope.

But Sinclair shook her head and signed something. Ligieia laughed.

"Everyone hates to be left out of a party, she says," she explained to me. She looked at Hope again. "All right, baby, Mom says you get to stay awhile." She turned away and poured gin into Sinclair's glass, and then hers.

"Not for me," I said too late when she leaned over my mug. Ligieia was already pouring with a heavy hand.

"I'm sorry," she said. "I can get you more tea—"

"No," I said quickly. "No problem, I'm fine as is."

Ligieia put the bottle down and took her place on the sofa again.

"C'mere, Miss Hope, you want to sit between your mom and me?" Ligieia patted the space between herself and Sinclair.

But Hope climbed up onto the chair next to me, the chair dipping forward on its runners as she did so. There really wasn't much room, and Hope's weight settled against me, her head against my chest.

Ligieia's eyebrows shot up, and even Sinclair looked mildly surprised. She signed something.

"You make friends fast," Ligieia translated.

"Not usually this fast."

Hope looked up at me. "Is your name Sarah?" she asked again. She'd said she couldn't sleep, but I could see in her eyes and hear in her voice that sleep was hard on her heels. Mine, too, I realized.

"Yes," I told her.

Hope lifted a hand and began fingerspelling.

"She's spelling your name," Ligieia said. "She's showing off for you."

"Well, I'm very impressed, kiddo," I said to Hope. "We're gonna lean forward a little now," I warned. The chair tipped forward again as I reached for the cool tea and gin.

I swirled the liquid in the cup, a stalling gesture like bouncing a basketball at the free-throw line.

I had planned not to drink the gin; since I first realized Shiloh had disappeared, I'd been on guard against alcohol, even just one drink. One drink, I'd told myself, could lead to others; the warmth of liquor easing the fear in my chest and the tension in my shoulders, taking me away from reality, dulling my mind, slowing my search. All when my husband needed me to be clearheaded.

Then I drank anyway. I was so damn tired. The gin did improve the taste of the tea.

"It's your turn to ask the questions, I guess," I said.

Sinclair lifted her hands and signed. She got right to it.

"Is Mike in some kind of trouble?"

I shook my head emphatically. That was as close as I could come to being able to communicate in her language. "No," I reiterated. "Not that I know about. Something happened to him. I'm trying to find out what."

Sinclair gestured again. *"How did you meet?"*

"At work. We're both cops." As I said the evasive half-truthful words I felt a flicker of regret inside me. I almost wished I could tell the real story to Sinclair. Then the feeling passed. "It was a drug raid, actually," I said. Even if it had only been Sinclair and me in the room, the true story was too long and time-consuming to tell, and besides, it was a story I'd never told anyone before.

"What's Michael like now?"

I drank again, the action giving me time to theorize.

"Hard to summarize," I said. "Painfully honest."

There was a warm feeling spreading through the pit of my stomach. Back in the days when I really drank, it would have taken a lot more gin before I'd have felt its effects. I sipped from the mug again and began to push the floor lightly with my feet, rocking Hope and myself.

"How long have you been married?"

Ligieia, while translating, stood up to pour more gin into my cup. I let her.

"Only two months," I said. "Not long."

"Before that, how long did you know him?"

"About five years," I said. "We weren't together for all of it, though. We split up for a while."

Maybe the gin was doing it to me, but I'd lost the party-line feeling of being a degree removed from Sinclair. Particularly if I kept my eyes down on Hope, who'd fallen asleep, Ligieia's words seamlessly became Sinclair's voice.

"Why?"

"Shiloh and I had hit a wall." I spoke slowly, thinking. "It was professional, in a way. We weren't equals on the job, and that bothered me. When I was young I got angry easily. I was angry at him a lot of the time and I couldn't even explain why." *I'm drunk already, I should stop right here.* I didn't. "And besides that, he was so far away sometimes, and when I was young I grabbed at things I thought I needed, and I got scared when I felt there was a piece of him I was never going to have."

It was like I'd stepped barefoot on a shard of grief I hadn't seen before me. I put my face down in my hands as much as I could without waking Hope.

Sinclair came and stood before me and did something odd and lovely: she put her hand on my forehead like I might have a fever, then ran the same hand back over my hair.

"I miss him," I said quietly, and Sinclair nodded.

This time when she spoke to me, her lips moved as well as her hands, and I swear I understood even before Ligieia translated.

"Tell me something about Mike. Anything."

So I poured myself more gin and told her how Shiloh caught Annelise Eliot.

chapter **18**

Early in Shiloh's cold-case days, he'd gone on a fairly routine errand, out to Eden Prairie, a suburb of Minneapolis where several churches jointly ran a hospice. There a middle-aged man dying of AIDS needed to be reinterviewed, before his memories of an old crime winked out along with the sputtering candle of his existence. Shiloh sat by his bed, listened, took notes. And after the dying man slept, Rev. Aileen Lennox, who helped run the hospice, offered Shiloh what she self-deprecatingly called "the nickel tour."

He walked with the tall, plainly dressed woman and listened as she described with quiet pride the facility that had only been remodeled a year earlier as a way station for the dying. She pointed out the comforting, intimate touches; she spoke of the companies and individuals who'd donated time and money.

And as she did, Shiloh felt something akin to hair rising on the back of his neck.

She was, at that time, twelve years older than when she'd disappeared. Her high cheekbones had taken on softening flesh, there were crow's-feet around the glacial blue eyes, and her once-streaked blond hair was now dyed a lightless dun color. But Shiloh had seen it in her eyes, her bone structure, her carriage. Aileen Lennox was Annelise Eliot.

"I heard Montana in her voice," Shiloh told me that night, "but when I asked her about it, she said she'd never lived there."

"Bullshit," I told him. "You can't hear a Montana accent."

"Yes, I can," Shiloh had said.

Annelise Eliot had grown up there, a timber heiress, daughter of a land baron with logging operations and paper mills and extensive landholdings. Her name, with its European connotations, suggested an aristocrat, perhaps a touch neurasthenic, with a tracery of blue veins under paper-white narcissus skin. Little could be further from the truth. Anni, as she'd been known before notoriety fixed her in the public's mind as Annelise, had been tall, full-bodied, and strong. And if her fair hair was expensively streaked with paler blond salon highlights, well, her fingernails were also often a little dirty from caring for her horses herself.

From a young age, Anni had had fast Appaloosas that she barrel-raced in rodeos. After the age of 16, she'd owned a faster Mustang, and when her red 1966 coupe sped down the road, the radar guns of local deputies seemed stricken with an odd malfunction. Likewise, the stories about the Eliot summer place in Flathead Lake—excessive underage drinking, strip poker, and wild stunts—remained just that, stories about Anni and her friends told with almost wistful envy by adults grown too old and sensible for that sort of behavior. She was a tomboy with a charmed life.

Trouble finally came to Annelise when she was nineteen. She'd had a boyfriend, Owen Greene, for three years, and they were getting serious—the relationship had survived his decision to go to school in California. Greene was prelaw at UC San Diego, with a 3.9 average, well liked by professors and peers. Then Marnie Hahn, a pretty local girl in her senior year of high school, accused him of raping her after a party in the moneyed La Jolla area.

Hahn, an indifferent student and the employee of a pizza parlor near campus, had gone to the party of her own will. She had been underage and drinking. She was an unlikely girl to bring a rape case against a rich college boy; nevertheless, she stuck to her story.

Whatever Greene told Annelise over the long-distance wires shortly thereafter is unknown, but Annelise flew out to California in a public show of support. During her visit, Hahn turned up dead, bludgeoned with a heavy object never recovered or even quite identified.

Greene was firmly alibied. Annelise, on the other hand, was not. Evidence, circumstantial but inevitable as a snowdrift, began to amass. Witnesses had seen Annelise's rented car parked outside Marnie's house. A little of Marnie's blood, just a trace, was recovered from the driver's-side floor mat of that same car.

The police moved fast, but the Eliots moved faster. By the time there was enough evidence for an arrest, Annelise was gone.

The parents denied any knowledge of her disappearance. They lawyered up and made public appearances, calling on the police to investigate their daughter's disappearance as a kid-napping. However they were funneling money to Annelise—and the authorities all believed that they were—it wasn't traceable.

That was how the matter stood for years, despite the best efforts of the FBI and police in two states. Thousands of leads fizzled. Perhaps the most frustrating aspect of the case was that no set of fingerprints existed for Annelise. She'd never been ar-rested, and she was the kind of girl who always had a troupe of friends around her, using her things. There was no way any la-tent print lifted from any possession of hers could be proven to have been made by Annelise.

Her case had been news across the U.S., but it was particu-larly big in Montana, where an 18-year-old Shiloh followed it in the newspapers. He'd been employed by one of old man Eliot's logging crews—the magazine writers who'd done stories on the case had loved that particular detail.

But at first, when Shiloh believed he'd found Annelise Eliot in the Twin Cities, twelve years after her crime, his theory im-pressed no one. At first, it didn't even worry Annelise herself.

Like most investigators, he'd made narrowing circles around his target, pulling at the edges of her Aileen Lennox identity, discovering how thin and immaterial it was. As his courteous, relentless probing continued, her nerves began to fray. She tried a high-handed approach first, writing him a letter requesting him to cease his activities. Then she complained of harassment to Shiloh's superiors, as did some of her parishioners. And Shiloh's superiors had listened.

This is a law-abiding woman, they pointed out. More than law-abiding: a philanthropist, a clergywoman. This couldn't be

Annelise Eliot, they said. Everyone knew where Annelise was. She was living with other American expatriates in Switzerland. Or maybe in Cozumel, where her parents' U.S. dollars went a long way. She certainly wasn't in Minnesota, a cold midwestern state where she knew no one, a minister at a nondenominational New Age church, feeding the homeless and tending the dying.

And they pointed out that the Eliot case might be a cold case, but it wasn't a *Minnesota* cold case. Annelise had lived in Montana and killed in California. Back off, they said. Work your own caseload.

Shiloh had backed down, but only to retrench, looking into the life of Annelise, not Aileen. Shiloh talked to detectives in Montana. He'd begun talking to the FBI agent who'd headed up the Eliot investigation, who was polite but not very interested. And finally, he'd started talking to people who'd known Annelise. Not her close friends, but old acquaintances on the edges of her life.

It took a long time, an investigation crowded into the beginnings and ends of his workdays. But the day came when he had a long, friendly phone conversation with a high-school classmate of Annelise's. During the course of the woman's recollections, she suddenly remembered that during freshman-year biology, she and Annelise had been lab partners. They had typed each other's blood. And oh yeah, they'd fingerprinted each other. She'd never really thought about that before.

His voice calm, his heart slamming, Shiloh asked if she'd kept her old school stuff.

Maybe, she said. My parents are real pack rats.

That spring evening he came home from work a little late.

When I met him on the back step, he slid his hands up my rib cage and lifted me up off my feet as an exuberant young father might do with a small child.

Several days later, nearly a year after he'd met Aileen Lennox, Shiloh opened a Federal Express package containing patent fingerprints from Annelise Eliot. They drew a nineteen-point match with ones he'd had a fingerprint technician take months ago from the polite, annoyed letter Lennox had written to him.

Now Special Agent Jay Thompson of the FBI was interested. He flew to Minnesota. I'll never forget seeing him on our doorstep, a lean, leathery man in his late forties. He looked tired, sly, and happy, all things I'd never seen before on a federal agent's mien.

"Let's get her, Mike," he said.

It wasn't easy, even then. Thompson flew to Montana, where Annelise's mother, now a widow, still lived in a graceful old house on forty acres. Thompson and the detective who'd originally headed up the Montana investigation got a warrant to search the Eliot house; several officers went out to help them.

The widow Eliot was as tall as her daughter, and her blond hair was just beginning to be streaked with white. She'd had time to get used to follow-up visits from detectives, particularly the Montana man, Oldham. If she was alarmed that this time they had come with a search warrant—the first search in twelve years—it didn't show, Thompson later said. She offered the men homemade ginger cookies.

It was a good performance, but she must have known how futile it was. Although there was little in the house to betray her ongoing contact with her daughter—the paperwork on the phone bill, for example, showed no calls to Minnesota—there was a sealed and stamped letter with no return address on the old roll-top desk in the study. It was segregated from the other outgoing mail, as if Mrs. Eliot meant to drop it separately into a public mailbox in town. There was no receiver's name above the address, but it was going to Eden Prairie, Minnesota.

It was Thompson who'd found the letter, and he knew from that moment he had to move carefully. The letter hadn't been hidden; he doubted Mrs. Eliot would believe they hadn't seen it, even should he leave it behind unopened and in the same position on the desk. No matter what, the moment the police left her home, the widow Eliot was going to be on the phone to Minnesota.

No turning back. Thompson opened the letter. The salutation read, *Dear Anni.*

Thompson slipped the letter into his jacket, found Oldham, and told him to sit down with Annelise's mother for a reinterview. "Keep her occupied," he said.

While Oldham accepted ginger cookies and a cup of tea in a first-floor parlor, Thompson returned to the second-floor study and made two quick, quiet, and urgent calls to Minneapolis. The first was to a federal judge; the second was to Shiloh's cell phone.

"Today's the day," he said. "We're at the house. We got her, and the mother knows. I'm getting you a warrant. It'll be ready in twenty minutes." He looked out a wide window to where the Eliot land lay peaceful and white under March snow. "Go get her *now,* Mike."

Annelise had never truly believed Shiloh would catch her. When he came to her that afternoon, in her study at the church, she at first thought it was with more futile, probing questions. When Shiloh began to Mirandize her, she finally realized what was happening.

The look in her eyes, Shiloh said, must have been the same one that Marnie Hahn had seen just before she died, a rage born of frustrated, balked entitlement. Annelise Eliot had stared at him like that for a moment. Then she went for the letter opener. Shiloh had barely gotten a deflecting hand up in time.

"Did she really think she could get out of the situation by killing him?" Ligieia asked. Sinclair's hands hadn't moved. Ligieia had become interested in the story itself; she was asking out of her own curiosity.

"I'm not sure she was trying to kill him. It was just anger," I said. "She never really believed Shiloh was going to get any evidence he could use. And I think"—I paused, looking at Sinclair now—"that she really felt she'd paid her debt to society, through all the good she was doing in Minnesota. Maybe she even felt she'd repaid Marnie Hahn's memory."

Sinclair was signing. *"And when Mike wouldn't let it go at that,"* Ligieia translated, *"when she knew he was really going to make her pay, she got angry again. Just like she got angry at Hahn, years ago, the girl who was ruining her life."*

"Yes," I said, nodding. Sinclair had Shiloh's broad, contextual intuition. And in addition, I thought, she understood her brother as well. She saw that he'd been angered as a teenager by Marnie Hahn's cold-blooded murder and had stoked and fed that long-banked anger during a long, seemingly fruitless investigation that had finally caught fire.

And then I told Sinclair and Ligieia the rest, the part that I thought of as the coda to the story.

Marnie Hahn, Shiloh had told me late the night of the arrest, was a poor man's lamb.

"Mmm, that's a biblical thing, right?" I asked. The reference itself wasn't familiar to me, but Shiloh's way of making allusions was.

"In the Old Testament," Shiloh said, "King David desires a married woman, Bathsheba, and sleeps with her. And Bathsheba becomes pregnant, and when David realizes there is no covering up for his sin, he sends the husband to the front in the war. He sends the man to certain death. And it works, the man dies.

"To make him understand that his actions were wrong, the prophet Nathan tells David a story about a rich man who has a whole flock of sheep—that's King David, metaphorically— who kills the only lamb his impoverished neighbor owns rather than give up one from his own flock."

"Was Marnie the Hahns' only child?" I asked him.

"Yes," Shiloh said. "But that's not really the point. Annelise is an only child, too." He fell silent for a moment, then explained. "Annelise and Owen had just about everything. Marnie had almost nothing. And what little she had, they took."

That night, I'd heard in his voice the unflinching right-and-wrong creed of his youth, and I wondered if such a great ideological expanse had, after all, separated Reverend Shiloh and his son.

When I finished the story, Sinclair signed *Thank you*. For the story, I supposed. I wanted to thank her for letting me tell it. It had restored my lost equilibrium.

She rose and crossed to me again, looking down at her

daughter's flushed, sleeping face. She bent to take Hope into her arms. Standing, she nodded toward the hall in invitation. It was time to sleep. Ligieia had gone ahead of us into the hallway.

Before Sinclair looked away, I spoke without preamble, facing her directly so she could read my lips. "Did you ever know Mike to use drugs?" It was the question I hadn't asked earlier.

Sinclair furrowed her brow in what seemed to be genuine bafflement, and she shook her head, *No*.

Just before I slept, I thought I heard the old-fashioned clatter of a typewriter, but I couldn't quite bring myself to get up and find out, and then the sound was fading to nothing, like the sound of a passing train receding into the distance.

chapter 19

"Run it by me again?" I said to Sorenson, the watch commander at the Third Precinct in Minneapolis. My bare feet were cold on the kitchen linoleum at home. Minnesota seemed to have plunged ahead into near-winter cold while I had been in the warmth of the West.

"A vice guy brought a hooker in on a soliciting bust. She wants to trade some information, but she says she won't talk to anyone but Detective Pribek."

"Information on what?"

"Major felony is all she'll say." Sorenson coughed. "I know you're supposed to be taking some personal time, because of the situation with your husband, but she's asking for you."

"It's all right," I said. "I'll come down."

I'd expected a skinny drug user scarcely out of her teens,

hardly attractive, ready to drop the dime on her pimp for something he'd done. Someone far different waited for me in the interrogation room. Her age was hard to judge. She had the perfect skin and lustrous hair of youth, but her gaze and especially her poise reminded me of an older woman.

She'd shed a fur-lined coat to reveal a white leather dress that bared her arms. The heat in the Third Precinct building was generous, although my feet were still cold.

"I hear you've got something to tell me," I said.

"Got a cigarette?" she said.

I was inclined to say no, to exert some control over this meeting. But looking at her, I got the feeling that she wasn't nervous at all. She might very well refuse to proceed until she got her cigarette.

In the hall I flagged down the third-watch detective, a born-again Christian I had a casual acquaintance with. "I need a smoke," I said, and he nodded. "Matches, too."

The hooker said nothing when I returned with her cigarette. She took the cigarette and matches and lit up, making a prodigious cloud of smoke. Then she took one drag, exhaled, and stubbed out the cigarette.

"Thanks," she said throatily.

A power trip. *Fuck her information.* "It's been real," I said. "Enjoy your ninety days."

When I was at the door she said, "Don't you want to hear about your husband?"

I stopped and turned.

Her hard eyes traveled me like mine did her, from my wool hat and gray T-shirt down to my salt-stained winter boots. I hadn't bothered changing into my on-the-job clothes, since it was the middle of the night, and if she'd asked for me specifically, she obviously knew who I was.

"I killed him," she said, and crossed legs encased in hip-high boots.

I took a seat across the table from her. Standing was a position of greater authority, but I wanted to get my hands out of her line of sight in case they started shaking.

"I doubt it," I said mildly. "Can you prove it?"

"I have ads in the weekly papers. He called me," she said. "Looking for sex. When I got here tonight, I recognized him from the picture hanging up on the bulletin board."

"I said proof, not circumstantial details." *Why are my feet still so goddamn cold?*

"I can tell you where he's buried."

"Bullshit. If you got away with murder you wouldn't be here confessing."

"Great in bed, wasn't he?"

"Knock it off. You read about Shiloh in the *Star Tribune* and decided to have some fun jerking the cops around with a fake confession."

"No, I wanted to get a look at you. He told me that you once picked up a rattlesnake and killed it by breaking its neck. Is that true?" she asked.

"Yes." Now my hands really were shaking. She shouldn't have known that.

"I asked him why he was out looking for strange pussy with a woman like that at home," she said. She leaned forward to speak confidentially. "Your husband told me you could never really let go in bed because of what your brother did to you when you were young."

The slamming of my heart woke me. It took a moment for me to remember where I was. A poster advertising the Ashland Shakespeare Festival brought it back: I was in New Mexico, Saturday morning, in Shiloh's sister's home.

I'd slept on the couch in Sinclair's study, with motley blankets wrapped around me. My feet, bare and escaping the covers, were cold.

Stiff as an old dog that had slept on a hard floor, I threw the blankets back and rose. Limberness returned slowly as I folded the blankets and stacked them as neatly as possible on the couch, placing the pillow on top. Then I bent to gather up my things. As I did, I rooted through my duffel bag to find Shiloh's Kalispell Search and Rescue T-shirt, suddenly feeling a desire to wear it today.

When I came out into the kitchen wet-haired from the shower, Ligieia was at the table, reading *The Merchant of Venice*. She looked up at my approach.

"Is Sinclair still here?" I asked Ligieia. Already I sensed that she wasn't.

"No," Ligieia confirmed. "She had some errands."

Reaching into my shoulder bag, I took a piece of paper from the legal pad I'd brought and tore it in half. On the top half I wrote my home phone and work voice-mail numbers and my work e-mail address. "In case she thinks of anything else, you can call me, or she can send me a message," I explained.

Then I hefted my duffel bag onto my other shoulder. "Thanks for everything. Tell Sinclair I'm sorry I didn't get to say goodbye."

Ligieia followed me to the front door. "If you don't mind my asking, what are you going to do now? About your husband?"

"I'm going back to Minneapolis," I said. "I've got some more leads I can follow up there."

"Well," she said. "Good luck."

On the drive back down to Albuquerque, I kept my speed down under the posted limit.

And really, there was no reason to hurry. I would catch the first available flight back to the Cities, but I had little idea what I should do when I got there.

I'd been a cop so long that it was second nature for me to lie when a civilian like Ligieia asked how an investigation was going. No matter how badly an investigation is going, cops simply don't say they're at a dead end. They say, *Leads are coming in every day, and I can't comment any further than that.*

That was nearly always true, for what it was worth. Missing-persons cases, homicide cases, bank robberies—every serious crime generated leads from the public. A vast percentage of them were worthless, though: visions from psychics, lies from anonymous pranksters, honest citizens who'd seen something that turned out to be nothing.

Vang, though, had promised to follow up on any leads and leave me a message if anything looked promising. So far I'd heard nothing from him.

At a bank of pay phones in the Denver airport, I did the first of my twice-daily message checks. Today, the recorded voice told me I had one message. To my surprise, it was Genevieve. The message was unrevealing.

"It's me," her voice said simply. "I guess I'll call you later."

I played it again. There was a muted anger in her tone. I

couldn't imagine what she wanted from me. Well, I'd call when I got back to the Cities, I thought. If she had urgent news, surely she would have left details in her message.

On the plane east, I scribbled copious notes—if not particularly articulate ones—in my legal pad. I was trying to identify what came next.

Reinterview all the neighborhood witnesses? Were this some sort of exercise in my police training, that's the answer I would probably have written down, fairly confidently. Shiloh's trail seemed to be freshest in our own neighborhood, where he'd bought food at the Conoco the day he disappeared, where Mrs. Muzio had seen him walking and looking "angry" on a day that had most likely been Saturday, the day of his disappearance.

But already I had a hopeless feeling about it. If the most useful information I had was that Shiloh was walking somewhere and looking purposeful on Saturday, then really I had nothing. I understood nothing about how or why Shiloh had disappeared.

Genevieve's ideas had been the simplest and the most likely. Somehow he'd walked to his death somewhere in the neighborhood. Suicide on a bridge. Murder at the hands of some prostitute or her pimp.

Fucking Genevieve. She'd all but planted in my head the dream I'd had last night. Shiloh and I had always been nothing if not physically compatible; I'd never had any worries on that account. But "strange pussy" had been Genevieve's phrase, and the prostitute in my dream had quoted her.

Genevieve's theories of adultery or suicide didn't square with what I knew of Shiloh. It was disrespectful to his—to *him*, damn it, not to *his memory*—to entertain them.

I closed the notepad and slid it back into my shoulder bag.

As I did so, I felt my hand brush a rectangle of paper smoother and stiffer than the random papers I'd shoved into my bag for the trip west.

It was a letter-size envelope, and clearly it contained more than one sheet of paper inside; it was nearly pillowy. On the address side, in an unfamiliar hand, was one word: *Sarah.*

Sinclair, I thought, and opened it to find a small sheaf of pages inside. As I unfolded them, a yet smaller envelope, three-quarters the size of the one I'd just opened, fell out. It was cream-colored, sealed, unmarked.

I set the little envelope on the unoccupied seat next to mine and directed my attention to the typewritten letter before me.

Sarah,

I have a feeling I'm going to be up and out of the house before you get up today. I wish we'd had more time to talk. Thinking about what we talked about, I realize that none of it seemed to be germane to your search for Mike. But I gather from what you said that you feel a need to understand where Mike came from, and maybe I can help with that. I've only known you a very short while, but Hope likes you, and I've found my daughter to be an excellent judge of character.

I'm not sure I can tell you all that much about life at home while Mike was growing up. I spent a lot of my childhood away at school. Mike and I didn't get to know each other well until we were both older, when I came home to live. Those days stand out in my memory because they were difficult ones.

When my parents sent me away to school, they did it with misgivings, first because ours was a close-knit family, and also because they worried about me being in a secular environment. To compensate, they sent me away with a Children's Bible, and when I was older they mailed me books of devotions and daily prayers. When I went home on term breaks, I always went to church with them and prayed with them around the dinner table. But in the end, their fears were well founded.

I had a lot of freedom at school. There was no mandatory church or chapel attendance. I could read whatever I wanted to in the school library. And the other girls came from many different cultures, and we often discussed our religious backgrounds and beliefs. I never questioned the schism between my two worlds. Home was one kind of place, and school was another.

I loved my family, of course, and I was happy to come home full-time when my parents arranged it. But actually being there was a shock. Church services on Sunday morning, youth group on Sunday evening, Bible study on Wednesday night. No television, no secular movies. The most difficult thing, though, was that no one at home could use sign language as well as people at school did. Both my older brothers were rusty, and Naomi and Bethany were too young to be fluent. My parents encouraged me to speak aloud, but I wouldn't. Some of the girls at school described how other kids made fun of the way deaf people spoke, comparing it to the bleating of sheep or the sounds made by dolphins. So pride made me insist on signing.

A great deal of what I did back then was either rooted in pride or a grab for freedom. Suddenly I was out of my cloistered private school and into the wider world, yet I

*felt, if anything, more boxed in. By my parents' rules and
my family's lifestyle. By the averted gazes of hearing kids
who were afraid to make eye contact with me for fear that
I'd try to communicate with them and they wouldn't
understand. By the unwanted touches and hugs from
people in the congregation who thought that being disabled
made me "special" and childlike and morally pure. I
started to feel panicky, like there wasn't enough oxygen in
the air.*

*During this time, there was only one person who made
me feel like the person I'd been at school. That was
Michael.*

*By September, I'd been home all summer, but I hadn't
seen him. In fact, I hadn't seen him in over a year. I'd
spent the last term break at the school, and then by the time
I got home in June, he was already away on a summer
service project to do with the church, building homes on
an Indian reservation. We'd just kept missing each other.
And he was late coming home in September, too, because
he'd broken his arm falling off a roof he was working on.
They let him stay where he was and miss the first week of
school so he could get the cast taken off instead of traveling
with it.*

*Then one night in the first week of school, I was
working on a book report and I got that somebody's-
behind-me feeling—you become fairly good at that when
you're deaf—and I turned around and it was Mike.*

*For a minute I thought it was one of Adam's or Bill's
friends. Mike had grown three inches since I'd seen him
last; he was taller than me all of a sudden. And when he*

asked me if what I was reading was any good, I realized he could really, honest-to-God sign, and I was terribly relieved.

After that we spent a great deal of time together. We'd been apart so long, and changed so much in the interim, it was like getting to know a stranger. We used to have these long conversations. Mike knew the Bible incredibly well; he could debate like a seminarian, but when I told him all the things I didn't understand or couldn't believe about God and the Bible, he never judged me. I realized that he was losing his faith, too. I never meant to push him in that direction, but I just couldn't lie about how I felt. I had to have one person with whom I could completely be myself, and that was him. Apostasy was hard for Mike; it's harder to lose your faith, like him, than to realize you never really had it, like me.

Things with my parents just got worse and worse. I wanted freedom, and I took it in the places young people usually do—in drinking and sex. I'm not entirely proud of how I behaved back then, but I was young. My parents resorted to tighter restrictions, earlier curfews. I started sneaking out of the house, but after I got caught a couple of times, I stopped trying. I knew I just had to wait until I was 18 and could leave, and until then, Mike made living at home bearable. He was the oxygen in the air when I couldn't breathe.

I know none of this will help you find him. I just wanted you to know it. Mike has his own life now, and I have mine, but he'll always be special to me. When you talked about him last night, I could see what he means to

you, and without even talking to him, I know how much
you must mean to him, because Mike is a fiercely loyal
person. He's very lucky to have you. I know you're going to
find him, and when you do, I want you to give him the
message I've enclosed.

Sinclair

After I read the letter, I felt strangely light, the way I did
when I'd received an unexpected kindness. I picked up the little
envelope from the seat next to me.

Open it. That was my first instinct; this was an investigation and every piece of information counted.

Don't be ridiculous. I realized the next moment that the
idea of Sinclair sealing up important information in an envelope like some kind of test was obviously ludicrous. She wasn't
going to play games with her brother's well-being at stake.

The sealed note was a gesture of faith, twofold: it said she
trusted that I would find her brother, and that she knew I wasn't
going to open and read a personal message to him without his
permission. It was a kind, subtle, clever gesture. I slipped it into
the pocket of my leather jacket.

Genevieve, Shiloh, now Sinclair . . . if there was a God, it occurred to me to wonder why He chose to surround me with people so much more intelligent than I was, and then to make so
much of what was happening to us depend on me.

chapter 20

Perhaps because of the dream I'd had that morning, the first place I went back in Minneapolis was to headquarters. I wanted to walk its corridors in the sane and normal light of day and reclaim them as my territory. And to check in with Vang in person, see if he'd heard anything he might not have thought important enough to call me about.

But when I got downtown, Vang was out. I checked my voice mail at my desk. There were no messages. But I hadn't yet returned Genevieve's call.

"What's going on?" I asked when she picked up. "You called me earlier today."

"It's him," Genevieve said without preamble. "That bastard Shorty. He's got the luck of Satan himself, the goddamned prick."

This was amazing language, coming from Genevieve. "What happened?" I asked.

"He stole that old man's truck, but he's not going to get busted," Genevieve said.

"Wait," I said. "Back up, okay? What old man's truck?"

"Everyone thought there was an old guy missing," Genevieve said. "They found his pickup smashed up by the side of the county road outside Blue Earth, and they thought he must have walked away from the accident disoriented."

"Yeah, I remember that from the news," I said.

"The old guy turned up two days ago. He was in Louisiana visiting a friend, and his truck was stolen from the Amtrak parking lot while he was gone. So they dusted it for prints, and guess whose name came up?"

"Royce Stewart."

"Damn straight," Genevieve said. "They got partials off the door. But he fed them this bullshit story. He said that he just stumbled across the wrecked truck on the way home from town. He'd been drinking in town, of course. As always."

"Mmm," I said.

"He said he checked the truck out up close, to make sure no one was hurt inside it. When no one was there, he said he figured everything was cool and went on home. A real saint, is our Shorty."

"Does he have an alibi for when the pickup was stolen?"

"They don't know exactly when the truck was taken," Genevieve said. "Because the old man who owned it left it parked in the Amtrak lot. So that muddies things for the cops. But it's just the sort of thing he'd do. He didn't have a ride, he saw one he liked, he stole it. And he's going to get away with it."

"Is that the only reason you called me?"

"Isn't it enough?" she demanded. "Why can't anybody but me see what this guy is?"

"I know what he is, too, Gen," I said. "But there's nothing we can do. His time will come."

There was silence on the line, and I knew my answer didn't satisfy her.

Then she said, "Should I ask how the search for Shiloh is going?"

"No," I said.

I sat at my desk for a moment after we'd hung up. I thought of people I'd met, relatives of the permanently missing. They checked in with Genevieve or me at increasingly infrequent intervals. They tried to interest reporters in "anniversary" stories. Waited for someone out there to drop the dime on a cellmate or an ex-boyfriend. Holding out hope for little more than that someday there would be a proper funeral, a gravestone to visit.

How soon would those days come for me?

I had learned nothing, virtually nothing, in five days of investigating Shiloh's disappearance. I couldn't think of a single case I'd made less progress on.

On the ground-floor hallway, a sign shaped like an arrow caught my eye. BLOOD DRIVE TODAY, it read.

Shiloh was O negative. He always gave religiously.

Ryan Crane, a records clerk I knew, rounded the corner and approached. He had a bright pink stretch bandage on the crook of his elbow; he'd donated.

"Going to let 'em stick a needle in you, Detective Pribek?" he asked cheerfully.

"I hadn't thought about it," I said, caught flat-footed. "I just came down to—"

"Oh, hell, I forgot," Crane said. "Have you heard anything about your husband?"

"No," I said. "Nothing. I'm still working on it."

He nodded and looked sympathetic. He was 22 at the most—I'd never asked—but I knew he was married with two kids.

Crane moved on, but I didn't continue on my way to the parking ramp.

I had A positive blood, which was common, but not as useful as Shiloh's. But Shiloh wasn't here to give any blood at all, and that fact was nagging at me, like it fell to me now to act for him.

Besides, the Northeast reinterviews were going to be a tired round on a cold trail. They weren't urgent.

The blood-bank people had set up in the largest of the conference rooms available. There were four reclining chairs, with rolling stands next to them from which hung plastic bags, some filling with blood, others empty.

All the chairs were occupied. That didn't surprise me. I'd heard the lectures before, when I was in uniform. Despite the fact that most cops got through their careers without serious injury, sergeants and captains liked to lecture uniforms about how the blood they donated could easily save the life of a fellow officer injured in the line of duty.

While I waited for a chair to open up, a white-coated phlebotomist read me a list of improbable conditions that would disqualify me: Did I or anyone in my family have Creutzfeldt-Jakob disease? Had I ever paid for sex with drugs or accepted drugs for sex? Had I had sex with anyone who'd lived in Africa since 1977?

She rewarded all my "no" answers by stabbing me in the finger with a tiny lancet.

"Go ahead and take that chair," she said. "I'll get back to you when your hematocrit is done."

I lay back next to a grizzled parole officer with whom I had a slight acquaintance.

"How are you?" he asked.

"Full of blood," I said lightly. For all that I hate doctors' offices and exam rooms, needles have never bothered me, particularly in blood drives at work, a place where I feel most at ease.

"Take this," the young white-coated woman said, returning to my side.

She gave me a white rubber ball. "We'll get you started. Make a fist and squeeze."

I did, raising a vein. She painted the inside of my elbow with antiseptic, put a strap on my upper arm, and then I felt the bite of the needle. She taped it down. A clamp on the line kept the tube clear.

"Keep squeezing the ball," she advised. "Not too hard, not too soft. This should take about ten minutes."

She took the clamp away and the clear tube turned red, blood racing away from my body as though it were eager to escape.

The parole officer was absorbed in a copy of the *FBI Law Enforcement Bulletin*. I'd brought nothing to read. I closed my eyes and thought back to my conversation with Genevieve and what she'd said about Shorty. When I thought about it, his alibi sort of made sense.

When someone stole a car, the most likely place to look for a good, usable fingerprint was the rearview mirror. Everyone has to adjust it getting into an unfamiliar car. Even thieves. But Gen had said the police in Blue Earth had only found partials on the door.

I imagined Genevieve saying, *So?* She'd been my longtime partner in this kind of deduction, and it was natural for me to imagine discussing it with her.

So, I thought, partials on the door are consistent with him checking out a wrecked vehicle, not stealing one. He touched the door going in. He didn't touch the mirror because he wasn't going to drive anywhere.

He wore gloves, Gen said succinctly. In my mind I heard the annoyance she would bite back that I was taking Shorty's part.

Why would he touch the door bare-handed and then carefully put on gloves to adjust the mirror? I thought.

Because he acts on impulse. He doesn't plan ahead.

Then why would he put on the gloves at all? And if he acts on impulse, why would he go out of his way, to a train station, to steal a truck?

He stole the truck from the Amtrak station because he knew it wouldn't be missed right away, with the owner out of town.

But that suggests planning ahead, which you said isn't like him. Plus, what's he going to do, drive it around for a few days in the same area where it was stolen, where everybody can see him behind the wheel? That doesn't make any sense. That kind of theft would only make sense if someone were going to use it for a few hours and abandon it.

I opened my eyes, seized by an impossibility.

"No way," I whispered, sitting up abruptly.

A car is a weapon, Shiloh had said.

The world swam gray before my eyes. When I heard a cry

of alarm near me, I thought the same revelation had struck all of us at once. The chair began to tip beneath me.

"Put your feet up." It wasn't Genevieve's voice in my mind anymore; it was a real voice somewhere beyond the fog I was in. "Can you hear me? Move your feet, roll them in circles. Big circles."

I opened my eyes, or maybe they were already open. Either way, the grayness was abating and I could see my feet. I responded to the command, wriggling them.

"Okay, that's good. Keep them moving." The phlebotomist who'd set me up was standing by my side. Another was approaching with a brown paper bag. She opened it with a crisp snap of her arm.

"Here, breathe into this," the second woman said.

"I'm all right," I said, trying to sit up again. As soon as I did, I got dizzy.

"Lie back. We'll tell you when it's okay to get up. Breathe into this."

I took the bag from her and did as she said. I needed a moment to think, anyway.

There was nobody I could call yet. There wasn't anything I could prove. I'd have to do the legwork myself.

Maybe twenty minutes passed before I was allowed to leave. First they let me sit up on the side of the reclining chair, and after a few minutes of that, I was allowed to go to the recovery area, a folding table and chairs with orange juice and Fig Newtons set out. They felt my face and watched me walk, before I was finally released to go down to the parking ramp and my car, a bright green gauze wrap around my arm. I'd given about half the usual allotment of blood.

I felt mostly recovered, just a little tired, when I kicked open the stubborn kitchen door at home, my duffel bag slung over the shoulder of my unpierced arm. I dropped the bag unceremoniously on the kitchen floor. There wasn't time for unpacking.

At the phone I dialed one of two numbers I'd come to know by heart: the one from the back of Shiloh's plane ticket. I dialed it with the 507 area code. That number had reached the bar, and at the time I'd figured it didn't mean anything.

But there had been way too much southern Minnesota karma in my life of late, and none of it had been good.

"Sportsman." It was my friend Bruce again. Crowd noise in the background.

"This may seem like a stupid question," I said, trying to sound light and at ease, "but where exactly are you guys?"

"Right on the west edge of town," Bruce said.

"West edge of what town?" I asked.

"Oh, you really don't know where we are," he said, sounding surprised but still jocular. "Blue Earth."

Blue Earth.

"I need directions, then," I said.

"Where are you coming from?" he asked.

"Uh, Mankato," I said, stumbling on the lie.

But Bruce didn't notice the hesitation in my voice. He quickly rattled off the directions for me in a practiced way, then he asked, "Are you coming all the way from Mankato for a drink? Boy, we're all fun guys to drink with here, but I didn't know our reputation had got around that far."

"Is Shorty there?"

A beat passed before he answered me, and his voice was more puzzled now than flirtatious. "No. Who is this?"

I hung up, thinking, *I knew it.*

Blue Earth would be a long drive, about three hours, but time was on my side. The problem was that Bruce of the Sportsman sounded pretty tight with the "fun guys" at the bar, and he was liable to tell Shorty that a strange woman had called asking about him, and had hung up rather than give her name. He might even remember the call from Sarah Pribek, who'd left her name and number days earlier. Shorty might have a rare wised-up moment and leave.

The Lowes' number was the second one I'd carved into my memory, and I didn't have to look it up this time. Deborah answered.

"Hi, Deb, it's me." By now she surely recognized my voice. "Can I talk to Genevieve?"

Genevieve came on the line. "What's going on?" she asked, but her voice was incurious.

"I need something from you." I didn't answer her question. "You know Shorty's address, right?"

"What?" More alert now.

"You've been keeping track of this guy for a while. You must have his address. I need it."

"What's going on?" she asked again.

"I just need the address."

"I have to go look for it." She set the phone down.

The subject of Shorty was the only thing that I'd ever seen rouse Genevieve from her depression, and now, true to form, she was showing signs of interest. When she gave me the address, she'd probably realize I was going down there. She might want to meet up with me, come along.

In a way, I would have liked to have her with me, but it was a bad idea. Maybe I'd need to reason with Shorty, make nice with him. I didn't think I could do that with a maternal avenging angel riding shotgun.

Genevieve came back on the line and gave me the address. It came as no surprise that he lived on Route 165.

"What's going on?" Genevieve asked again.

"Maybe nothing," I said. "I'll call you tomorrow."

"Are you going down there? What did he do now?"

"I'll call you," I repeated.

"Sarah—"

I hung up on her. I didn't have time for my twinge of guilt, instead collecting the things I needed: my keys, jacket, my service weapon. I was itching to be on the road. Just like Shiloh had been.

chapter **21**

Every time I drove 169 south, and this was my third time
in a week, I did it faster than before. It was a testament to the
unhappy acceleration of my life in the past seven days. When I
reached the Mankato city limits, I saw I'd shaved nearly thirty
minutes off my last time. Amazingly, there wasn't a single speed
trap along the way. It wasn't much longer before I was cruising
through the quiet streets of Blue Earth.

Would Shorty be at home, or at the bar? People liked to say
that barflies were in their favorite watering holes "every night,"
but that was usually an exaggeration. For all I knew, Shorty
could have stayed at home tonight.

I wouldn't have long to wait to find out. Already I could see
ahead a bright neon duck, flying away from a low building with
tinted windows. I didn't have to cruise past to know I'd found
the Sportsman.

If I were smart, if I were careful, I would wait for tomorrow. I would approach Shorty at his job, in the sober light of day, under the full color of my authority. But I'd never been smart, and what I'd painfully learned about being careful was drowned out under the relentless drumbeat of my need to know.

The place wasn't busy for a Saturday night. The Timberwolves were on the TV, and the jukebox was so low you could actually hear the play-by-play. Shorty was at the bar with two friends. Well, barroom friends at least. They might not even like him in daylight.

I walked directly to him, and virtually everyone in the bar watched me do it.

Shorty had seen me on the stand at his pretrial hearing, where I'd been established as Kamareia's friend and as the main prosecution witness against him. And of course, Shorty had known I was a cop. Now, when he saw me coming his way, his eyes widened. He looked so alarmed for a moment I thought he might just bolt for the back door.

Then he got control again, remembering that the case against him was dead. His face hardened from alarm into contempt and he didn't take his eyes off me.

I stopped a foot from his bar stool and said, "I need to talk to you. Outside."

That was my first mistake, specifying "outside." He only had to refuse and I would lose face. He looked at his friends and started to smirk. "Uh-uh," he said.

I looked at his friends, making them for more-or-less law-abiding types. I took my badge out and laid it on the bar, not opening the holder until it was down on the bar. I didn't want everyone to see me flash it around. But Shorty's pals saw it and looked back up at me.

"Leave," I said succinctly.

They got up, carrying their steins, and went to a booth. The show of authority took the edge off Shorty's good mood; his expression was moving toward being a scowl. I slid onto a stool one of his drinking buddies had vacated.

"So what do you want?" he said.

"Tell me about Mike Shiloh."

Unease wiped the last of the smirk away. "I don't know who that is," he lied. Then he took a sip of his beer, the mug a symbolic foxhole for him to dive into.

"Yeah you do. You can tell me about it now, or I can get a warrant for your arrest." It was my turn to lie. I didn't have anything near probable cause.

"You're harassing me," Shorty said. "Everyone will know it's because of that stuff in the Cities. They won't listen to you."

That rape and murder, you mean, is that what you mean by "stuff"? No, don't antagonize him or you'll never get what you need. Easy.

"Tell me what happened now, before this gets any deeper," I persisted. "It'll be easier that way."

"Easier than what? I beat you last time. It couldn't get any easier than that."

Then Shorty realized that what he had said was dangerously close to an admission. The case against him was dismissed for insufficient evidence, but double jeopardy didn't apply because he hadn't actually been found not guilty in a trial. Shorty didn't know, in light of that, what was safe to say and what wasn't.

"Do you really want me on your case, Shorty?" I demanded. "If you do, keep on like you're doing. Keep your mouth shut and don't tell me what you know."

"I already told you what I know," he said sullenly. "Jack shit."

I got off my bar stool and walked to the door, not looking back to see if he was watching me or not.

Outside the bar I made an illegal U-turn and headed out of town. It wasn't long before I pulled over on the side of the road. I was there so long, trying to think, that I finally switched off the Nova's idling engine.

Shorty would not tell me what I wanted to know. There was no reason for it. Neither would he let me look inside his home, which was what I wanted to do next.

While I thought, I was trying to chew on the nail of my middle finger; biting my nails was a bad habit I fell back on at difficult times. I also realized that I couldn't really get any purchase under the edge of the nail, because they'd still been too recently clipped. Not by me, but by Shiloh, who'd sat on the edge of our bed and held my hands in his and pared my nails for me.

Prewitt had cautioned me that he expected me, in the course of my investigation of Shiloh's disappearance, to consider myself a representative of the Hennepin County Sheriff's Department. By that he certainly did not mean breaking and entering.

All my thinking on the roadside wasn't really thinking. I was justifying a decision I'd already made.

The darkened road that the Nova ate up so greedily was the same highway that Shorty walked to get home from the bar. It wasn't terribly far from town to his house, but it wasn't what most people meant by "walking distance." Surely it wasn't just the alcohol that led Shorty to walk it late at night, even in wintertime and early spring. He could have drunk more cheaply and conveniently at home. But it wouldn't have been the same. Shorty would probably have gone without groceries before giving up the cost of tap-drawn Budweiser with his buddies.

Shorty's "house" was nothing more than a garden shed behind a two-story farmhouse. I cut off my headlights, gliding past with only parking lights on. The lights in the front house were off, the windows dark as sightless eyes. Even so, I rolled gently into the yard as though my Nova could tiptoe if I were light enough on the gas.

Following the rutted dirt, I drove all the way around the back of the shed, where my car wouldn't be visible from the road. I killed the lights, then the ignition. When I got out, I left the door cracked so it would make no sound in closing, switching off the dome light first so it wouldn't drain the battery.

I held the flashlight under my armpit while I laid out the tools I'd need for the lock. The door actually looked flimsy enough that it would have come down under a couple of kicks, if I had the luxury of being so obvious.

As soon as I touched the knob, I knew I wasn't going to have to pick the lock. The door was already unlocked.

Something about that struck me as wrong. But I told myself, *Come on, relax. What does a guy like Shorty have that's worth stealing anyway? Everything's fine. What are you waiting for?*

Then I stepped inside and switched on the flashlight.

A figure rose up in the beam, close and fast. I went for my .40.

"Sarah, wait, it's me!" The shadow before me was already dropping to the ground.

"Gen?" I pointed the flashlight down. She squinted up against its glare, one hand coming up against the flashlight's beam. "What are you doing here?"

"Waiting for you," she said. "I had a head start. Don't shine that thing in my eyes."

Later I would realize how changed she was at that moment, how revived in comparison to the zombie of weeks past.

My heart started slamming belatedly. "Are you crazy? I almost shot you!"

"Could you get the light off me?" she said again. "There's something you should see."

As she got to her feet, my light played over her hand. She was holding something.

"What is that in your hand?" I asked.

Wordlessly she held it into the light and tilted it. Something flashed: the holographic seal of the State of Minnesota. It was a driver's license. Michael David Shiloh's driver's license.

I'd been sure, but I hadn't been ready to face it, not really. I don't know how long I would have stared at his license if she hadn't spoken again.

"What the hell is going on?" she demanded.

"Where'd you find this?"

Genevieve pointed. I followed her hand with the flashlight's beam.

There was a backpack on the floor. Also Shiloh's. He'd used it sometimes when he'd had to go to the library for research and bring home a lot of books. He'd taken it out infrequently enough that I hadn't even missed it in my search of the closet.

I walked over to it and knelt. Inside was a railroad atlas and a bruised, cidery apple. And the billfold, empty of money.

"Shorty," I whispered. "That son of a bitch."

"Yeah," Genevieve agreed. "But what happened? How'd you know to look here?"

I pointed the flashlight up at the white ceiling, so we'd both have ambient light to see each other in.

"You were wrong," I said quietly, and my voice was steady enough. "Shorty didn't steal that truck. Shiloh did."

"Shiloh?" She was incredulous.

"He came down last week, while I was visiting you. As soon as I was out of town, he jumped a freight."

"A train?"

"He and his brothers used to ride freights over short distances, for kicks. He knew how. And that's why he didn't leave a trail: Greyhound, Amtrak, nothing. Nobody saw him, nobody picked him up hitchhiking. The train took him right to the Amtrak station, where he could steal a vehicle that no one would miss for a while. Afterward he could ditch it and get a freight back home."

"But why?"

"Kamareia," I said, and was about to go on when noises from outside distracted me, the creak and slam of a gate very like the one between this property and the road. Genevieve heard it, too, and went to the dirty, unshuttered window, pressing her face close to the glass to see what could be made out in the dim night.

"Looks like Shorty's done drinking for the night," she said rather mildly.

I got to my feet. "We can't be here," I said. "Legally."

"I'm not going to run from that murdering prick. Are you?" she challenged me.

"No," I said. "Hold the flashlight. Point it down low."

Genevieve did, sitting on her heels to get it close to the ground. I moved to the door. Gravel crunched underneath footsteps, and we both watched as the doorknob turned counterclockwise.

As soon as Shorty was through the door, I sent my fist as

hard as I could into his solar plexus. As he doubled over, I grabbed his hair and pulled his face down into my rising knee. He hit the floor with a hiss of painful breath.

"How they hanging, Shorty?" I said. "I felt a little unsatisfied with where we left things at the bar."

Genevieve was still holding the flashlight down. "Why don't you turn on the overhead light?" I suggested.

She pulled the string and we had light.

It was a shitty little place. A bare bulb overhead, a narrow cot. A card table, a folding chair, a cheap dresser. A bathroom through the doorway; I caught a glimpse of an old freestanding tub, an ancient sink on one porcelain leg. The kitchen was a sink and a hot plate.

But Shorty had his skills. He was obviously converting the place into a residence. I saw plumber's tools on the bathroom floor, a wrench and some pipes. In the main room were things he most likely used in his day job: housepainter's things, coveralls, a wallpaper shaver with a foot-long handle and a sharp, asymmetrical blade.

Shorty rolled onto his side to look at Genevieve. When he saw her, he looked like a man getting a visit from the harpies.

"Tell me about Mike Shiloh," I said, as if we'd never left the bar.

"Fuck you," he muttered. He'd been afraid to say that to a cop earlier, but clearly he saw that things had changed.

"You've got his backpack, his very empty billfold, and his driver's license. That looks bad," I said.

Shorty sat up. "I found them. In a ditch."

"A ditch where?"

"On the county road."

"Pretty near where you put your fingerprints all over that pickup?"

"This is illegal," he said. "You broke into my place. What do you think a judge is gonna do with anything you find here? This is a fucking illegal search."

Shorty knew a little about the system, like a guy with his rap sheet should have. And in his face I saw cunning that can, for a while, substitute for true brains.

I pulled out my gun again and pointed it at him. "Nobody in this room is thinking about the courts," I told him. "Except you."

Shorty stood up and faced me. He looked pretty tough for a guy with blood all over the lower half of his face. He said nothing. Somehow he'd seen the truth in my face: that even after everything he'd done, I wouldn't pull the trigger. Just a little bit of the bar smirk came up to his lips.

Then he turned to Genevieve and said, "Your daughter *loved* fucking me."

His eyes went back to me, to see how I was taking his little joke. That was his mistake. He was mostly paying attention to me. He hadn't searched Genevieve's face to see what could be read there.

"Gen, don't!" I yelled, but I was too late. Her arm was a blur as she embedded Shorty's own wallpaper shaver deep into the arteries of his neck.

Shorty made a sound like a cough, and I couldn't jump back in time to keep his blood from splashing me. He stumbled backward, eyes rolling toward Genevieve. She lunged again, digging the blade yet deeper into his neck.

"Gen!" I caught her arm. Shorty fell away from both of us,

his hands on his throat. They were already red, arterial blood coursing from underneath them.

"Call 911," I said.

Genevieve looked at me and I knew what she was thinking. If Shorty died and we covered our tracks, we were all right. If not, both our careers were over. Our freedom as well. All for a rapist and murderer. I didn't expect her to do it.

She said, "There doesn't seem to be a phone in here."

Shorty, on the floor, made a gurgle that didn't seem promising.

"The front house, then. Wake them up," I said.

Genevieve looked at Shorty, looked at me, and then she turned and went out the door.

The blood on the floor of Shorty's sad home was truly amazing. There was a lake of it. From the floor, Shorty's eyes met mine.

"Keep pressure on your neck," I said.

"There's nobody home," he said, his voice raspy.

"In the front house?" I asked.

He couldn't nod, afraid of opening the wound in his throat any more than he already had. But assent was in his eyes.

I knelt, despite the blood that soaked my legs from knees to feet.

"Then this is probably the ball game for you," I said. "You know that, right?"

"Yeah," he said.

"I just want to know how it happened," I said. The blood was soaking through to the skin of my legs, unpleasantly warm. "If I can, I want to bring him home and bury him. But even if I can't, I need to know what really happened."

A bubble of blood appeared at the corner of Royce Stewart's mouth. He coughed.

"Please," I said.

He was silent so long I thought his heart was hardened against me. Then he spoke.

"I was walking home, it was late," he said with effort. "This truck drove by me. A big Ford. A lot of the guys I work with drive trucks just like it."

I nodded. A big pickup, with a strong engine, a solid body, and a high grille. The kind of vehicle in which you could—if you were angry enough, and fearless enough—run down another human being and not be seriously injured yourself.

Royce took a shuddery breath. "Maybe five minutes later I heard the engine again, getting louder, like the truck's coming back. But I couldn't see it anywhere. Then the lights came on, out of nowhere. He'd been driving with the lights off and he was goin' real fuckin' fast on the wrong side of the road. My side.

"I di'n know who it was but I knew he was coming for me. I started to run and fell. It'd been raining and then froze over. There was ice on the road. I sat there looking up at the headlights coming. I thought I was dead." His hands tightened on his throat.

I remembered seeing the black truck on the news. Undamaged, on the road, headlights like cold white fire...it would have looked to Shorty like Death had come.

"Then the guy pulled out," Shorty went on, "back to the center of the road. He went by, and then that truck hit some black ice and skidded out. I don' think he even got a chance to hit the brakes before he was off the road and into that tree.

"For a couple minutes I waited for someone to get out, or

another car to come along. But nothing was happening, so I went to see what was up." He drew in an unsteady breath. "There was only one guy in the pickup. His eyes were kinda open, but he wasn't seeing me. He was messed up. So I took his shit and left."

"When you left, he was still in the car."

"Yeah. He was bleedin' pretty bad, but he was breathing and all. But I wasn't going to call anyone to help him." Shorty's eyes searched my face. He was watching to see how I'd react to this part of his story. "He'd been laying for me. It was his fault he was that messed up."

"When you say he pulled away and went past you, are you sure that wasn't when he lost control of the truck?" I needed to be sure. I held Shorty's eyes, the better to watch for truth. But I believed what Kilander had explained: the dying were past needing to lie.

"It was on purpose," Royce said. His voice was getting fainter, thinner. "He lost control because he pulled out at the last minute. It was two different things."

I had nothing to add; Genevieve failed to reappear. Shorty coughed again. "I wanted," he whispered, "I wanted to..."

He never did finish that thought. He started it five or six times, then his eyes glazed over, and I got up and went outside and lost track of time.

When Genevieve returned, I was sitting under the willow tree, looking up at a waning moon that had appeared over the trees. I was finally distracted from the night sky by Genevieve waving her hand in front of my eyes. She was saying something, but I couldn't make it out. Then her hand was a black blur on the periphery of my vision and she slapped me.

"What?" I said, and rubbed the stinging spot on my cheek.

"That's better," Genevieve said. "Shorty's place has got to burn," she explained. "You were smart enough to wear gloves, but I wasn't." Moonlight glinted off the metal can in her hand. "You can stay there if you want, for now. Do you want any of Shiloh's things?"

"His things?" I echoed.

"The stuff we found in there. Try and stay with me, Sarah. I can do most of this myself, but I can't drive your car and mine both when we leave."

"Your car? Where—?"

"My car's right there." She pointed. "You didn't see it when you first got here, and neither did Shorty, because I parked around the side of the main house. I didn't know why exactly you were coming to Shorty's place, but it didn't seem smart to advertise that we were here."

She walked to the shack and went inside. Her step was light and energetic. A moment later she came out again. "I'm going to light it up in a minute. We should get out of here pretty quick after that, okay?"

"Okay," I said dully.

"You'll follow me back to my sister's place, all right?" she prompted.

"Yeah." I couldn't bear to ask her if she'd made any attempt to find a phone and call 911 before committing to her plan. I was already sure I knew the answer.

We stayed to make sure Shorty's place was truly going to go up in flames. Maybe we stayed a little longer than we needed to, watching the spectacle of it. We were drawn to destruction, just like it seemed it was drawn to us.

Genevieve was in the lead as we drove back toward Blue

Earth, but she stopped when she saw my car pull off the road at the tree that loomed in the dark.

In the headlights of my car, I looked down into the wet and matted grass until I saw what I was looking for: a small piece of broken glass.

Sitting on my heels, I picked it out of the dirt.

Genevieve came to stand behind me.

"You were right all along, Genevieve," I said. "He's in the river. He probably made it as far as the Blue Earth River; if not, they would've found the body already when they were looking for the old guy who owned the truck."

"It's best if someone doesn't drive by and see the two of us here. Or our cars," she said gently. "We don't need to be placed in Blue Earth late at night."

"His body is probably in the Minnesota River by now. Nobody will ever find it."

"Sarah, come on. I'm not kidding," she said. But my feet seemed to be frozen.

Genevieve took me by the hand and led me back to the Nova.

She pulled back onto the highway first, and I followed her red taillights on the road back to Mankato.

Could I know for certain that Shiloh was dead? Not yet, maybe never, if his body had been borne away in the river as I'd suggested to Genevieve. He'd walked away from the wreck; what Shorty had said made that clear. But Shiloh had been missing now for seven days, and now that I understood what had happened to him, I knew that seven days were about six days too long. The area around Blue Earth was rural, but it was no vast wilderness for a person to lose himself in, even someone with a head injury. If he hadn't found his way to help, or at least been seen by the people searching for the presumed-missing Thomas Hall, he was dead.

From counseling the families of the missing, I knew that it took a long, complex legal process before the system would accept a missing person as a dead one. A more important turning point, totally unwitnessed by the world, was the silent, awful recognition of the missing person's husband or wife, lover, parent, or child; that moment when the still, small voice said, *He's dead.*

Genevieve killed her headlights as she pulled into the yard of the Lowes' farmhouse, and I did the same, creeping to a stop nearby.

As I put my keys into the pocket of my black leather jacket, I felt the stiffness of paper and drew out the three-quarter-size envelope that Sinclair had given me. It had ridden in my jacket since early this morning, when I'd opened Sinclair's letter on the plane.

Instead of getting out of the car, I looked out at Genevieve, now on the steps of her sister's home. I was expecting her to be impatient again, to hurry me along as she had by the tree at the side of the highway. But now that we were safely away from Blue Earth, on private property and unseen, she seemed re-laxed. In the dark she was only a silhouette, but I could see ease in the way she lounged against the porch railing, studying the night sky.

I opened the car door a fraction so that the dome light illu-minated the front seat, slipped a fingernail under the flap of the cream-colored envelope, and slit it open.

Sinclair had sealed this envelope believing Shiloh would open it. It was her gesture of faith. And I'd left it sealed, not yet ready to hear the still, small voice inside myself.

Sinclair's message was brief enough to make the small slip of paper she'd written on look expansive by comparison.

Michael,

I'm so glad for you and Sarah.

Please be happy.

S.

Genevieve and I stayed awake for more than an hour after we'd crept into the house like thieves. Deb and her husband, quite fortunately, had not awakened.

While the washing machine in the basement removed the stain of Royce Stewart's death from our clothes, if not our hands, Gen and I got our story straight. I had called Genevieve from the Cities, asking if I could come down. Phone records would bear that out, if it came to the point that anyone checked. I'd gone to Blue Earth first, to talk with Shorty, who refused to talk about the car theft and wreck Gen and I both still found suspicious. When he wouldn't talk to me, I drove back up to Mankato. Genevieve had stayed up to meet me and let me in, which explained why I hadn't rung the doorbell and woken anyone else in the house.

Later, we talked in low voices, like college roommates, in the twin beds of the Lowes' guest room. There I recounted for Genevieve the story that Royce Stewart had told me, how Shiloh had turned away from his murderous course at the last minute.

"Does it comfort you at all?" Genevieve asked.

"Does what comfort me?"

"Knowing that Shiloh couldn't go through with running Shorty down," she said.

"Yeah," I said. "It does. But it's weird, too. Everything I used to know, or thought I knew, was wrong."

I paused, thinking that it was going to be hard to explain what I'd just said, and that Gen was going to want an explanation for a cryptic statement like that.

But Genevieve's eyes were closed, her breathing slow and steady. She was asleep.

Everything I knew was wrong.

Around the department I'd had a reputation as impulsive, a *wide-open girl*, as Kilander had put it. It was me who'd jumped into the Mississippi after a kid. Genevieve had a reputation for patience, for getting even hardened perps to unburden themselves to her in interrogation rooms.

Of the three of us, Genevieve and Shiloh and me, it was me who I would have voted the most likely to give in to the dictates of a murderous shadow self. After that I would have said Shiloh, and gentle Genevieve last.

But it was Genevieve who had put a wallpaper blade into the throat of an unarmed man, and later all but whistled as she torched the crime scene. It had been Shiloh who had laid plans for murder, acting on an anger I'd never seen building inside him. And yet, at the final moment, he hadn't been able to carry out his plans. It had been me who'd sat with a dying man, an inveterate hater of both women and cops, and coaxed him to tell me what I needed to know. It was me who'd prayed in Salt Lake City with Shiloh's sister.

I looked over at Genevieve. She was a murderer now, but she slept in a peace that passed all understanding.

Sleep did not come so easily to me. I was still awake when

the first rays of sunlight stole under the sheer white curtains of the Lowes' guest room, and the rooster in their henhouse crowed.

Genevieve stirred and opened her eyes. When she saw me, she said "Sarah?" as if she'd forgotten the events of last night altogether.

Then she reached across to my bed. I gave her my hand and she squeezed it.

We got up when we heard Deborah and Doug moving around outside our door. There were mild exclamations of surprise at my presence.

"Sarah had some business down this way," Gen said. "She called kind of late. You probably didn't hear the phone. I got it on the first ring."

"Oh," Doug said, rubbing his jaw, and if he or Deborah had questions about the vague and brief explanation, they didn't voice them.

"Are you two hungry? There's coffee on, too," Deb said.

"I could use some coffee," I said, and I realized that I could probably eat a little bit, too.

About fifteen minutes later, the four of us were sitting around the Lowes' kitchen table, having linguica and eggs and coffee. As near as I can reconstruct, that's where I was when Shiloh walked into the police station in Mason City, Iowa, and turned himself in for the murder of Royce Stewart.

chapter 22

Memory plays tricks, the police psychologist who inter-
viewed Shiloh said. Shiloh's belief that he'd killed Royce Stewart
was a product of retrograde amnesia. Like many crash victims,
he couldn't remember the moments surrounding the wreck.
But in his case, his mind had supplied the details, details that
turned out not to be true. Shiloh had unintentionally seen to
that.

In preparation for Stewart's murder, Shiloh had gone over
and over the scenario, rehearsing it mentally, steeling himself to
go through with it. In the violence of the accident, somehow,
imagination became memory.

"I saw it in my mind," Shiloh told me. "When I thought
about it, I could see him go down. I felt the impact when the
truck hit him. It was so real."

Shiloh couldn't clearly remember all the time between the

wreck and his visit to the police station. He knew he had a head injury and a fever, but did not seek medical help. He was paranoid, convinced the police were looking for him, a misconception supported by the fact that a helicopter was crisscrossing the skies, looking for the presumed-missing Thomas Hall.

He went deeper into the countryside, irrationally moving south, not back up toward the Cities where he had people who might have sheltered him.

One morning, after a particularly long sleep, he woke up feeling more clearheaded and knew he had to give himself up.

It took a while, though, before all the parties involved sorted out the details.

At 7:20 A.M., the desk sergeant in Mason City was enjoying a Sunday-morning cup of coffee and the last forty minutes of his watch when Shiloh walked in and made his confession.

What Shiloh actually said was that he was the guy who'd run over Royce Stewart in Blue Earth, Minnesota. The last part of his statement was "Don't handcuff me. I'm not going to resist and my arm's probably broken."

The desk sergeant treated him with the caution due a man who'd identified himself as a murderer. He put Shiloh in a holding cell while he conferred with his supervisor. It was clear to both of them that Shiloh was probably sick as well as injured, and they assigned an officer to take Shiloh to the hospital, where his broken arm was set and he was treated for a head injury and a fever of 103.

Beyond that, the Mason City cops turned the situation over to the Faribault County Sheriff's Department.

Shiloh's identity was fairly easily confirmed. He'd had no ID with him when he turned himself in, but just from his name, Faribault County found out that not only did he have no priors and no warrants, but he was a missing person who also happened to be a cop.

The phone rang at Minneapolis police headquarters at 9:45 A.M. About twenty minutes later my voice mailbox taped a message from the daywatch commander on duty at the MPD.

If it hadn't been the weekend, and the agencies involved had their regular clerical staff, Royce Stewart's whereabouts might not have baffled everyone so much. Genevieve's courthouse friend, after all, had known his current address. But when no records showed that Royce Stewart was a murder victim, or even dead, it was a slow process for the local deputies to find out whether he was among the living.

Qwest had no listing for a Royce Stewart.

The Department of Motor Vehicles had an address from the last time he'd had a driver's license. It turned out to be his mother's home, outside of Imogene. Contacted by a detective, Mrs. Stewart explained her son's living arrangements. Royce, always good with tools, had struck a bargain with a couple he knew. He would live, rent-free, in a small outbuilding behind their farmhouse, in exchange for fixing the place up into a livable in-law unit. It was an informal agreement with no paperwork involved.

The outbuilding, in the early stages of renovation, had no phone line. Mrs. Stewart explained that she called her son at the phone in the main house. She only knew the first names of the husband and wife who lived there: John and Ellen. She didn't have their address.

It took a bit of time on the phone with weekend staff at Qwest before the Faribault deputies could match an address to the phone number Mrs. Stewart had for her son. Then Deputy

Jim Brooke drove out to the home of John and Ellen Brewer. Brooke didn't even get as far as the front door before noticing something was obviously wrong.

He had been told that Royce Stewart lived in an out-building, but there wasn't one as far as he could see. He stood in the Brewers' driveway and looked, dumbfounded, at a large patch of blackened wreckage, still smoldering.

Sometime around the time Deputy Brooke was making his discovery, I was standing around in the Lowes' guest room, watching Genevieve pack. She'd decided to come back to the Cities with me. Although we had separate cars, I waited to drive with her.

Packing up took her a long time. She'd been downstate for about a month, and her possessions had begun to drift to different places in her sister's home.

In the hallway outside the guest room, I was pacing a little, but I wasn't restless. Now that Shiloh was dead—and that was truly what I had come to believe—I wasn't in any hurry anymore. My state of mind was calm, on the edge of numb.

Even so, I decided to check my messages up in the Cities. It had become a habit. My voice mailbox held one message, from Beth Burke, the daywatch commander in Minneapolis. Before, I would have been curious about what Lieutenant Burke wanted. It was only a sense of duty that made me call down the hall to Genevieve.

"I'm gonna make a toll call up to the Cities. I'll leave a couple bucks to cover it." I didn't expect Gen to respond, and if she did, I didn't hear it. I was already dialing.

The next few moments probably rank as the most tongue-tied of my life. At first, I thought Lieutenant Burke was telling me that

Shiloh had turned up in Iowa and confessed to last night's murder and arson. I didn't even understand what was going on well enough to know what lies to tell. I said "What?" a lot and finally resorted to "I don't care what he's done or hasn't done, just tell me where he is."

When I hung up the phone I yelled for Genevieve.

Around midmorning, fire investigators removed a body from the ash, timber, and water that had once been Shorty's home. In light of Shiloh's confession, that was considered suspicious. Two detectives from Faribault County went south to Mason City to talk to Shiloh, beating Genevieve and me there by about thirty minutes.

"Have a seat," the desk nurse at the hospital said. "The police gave orders when they went in that no other visitors could be admitted until they're through talking to him."

"What room is he in?" I asked. "So I'll know, later."

"Room 306," she said.

"Thanks," I said, and instead of returning to the lounge, walked past her desk and into the hall.

"Hey!" Her protest followed me. I held up my shield for the uniform outside the door of 306 and he didn't try to stop me.

Both detectives looked up as I entered. Only Shiloh looked unsurprised to see me.

"You need a lawyer," I told him, ignoring his interrogators. My voice sounded hard.

"You can't be in here," one of the detectives said sharply. The pair of them resembled each other, both in middle age and white, each a little heavyset. One wore a full mustache, the other was clean-shaven.

"He was in a car wreck," I said. "He had a concussion. Anything you get today could be inadmissible because of that."

The other detective stood up to put me outside. "You've got to go, babe," he said.

"I'm his wife."

"I don't care."

"And a cop."

"I don't care," the detective repeated, taking me by the arm.

"No." Shiloh spoke for the first time, sharply enough that both men looked at him, the one next to me stopping with his hand still under my elbow. "We're done here."

"We have more questions—"

"We're done here," Shiloh repeated.

They glanced at each other. "You're getting a lawyer?" the first one asked.

It wasn't what Shiloh had meant, but it put things in terms they could understand. "Yes. I'm getting a lawyer."

The seated detective glanced at his partner, and then they packed up their notepads and left. The door swept shut, leaving silence in its wake and Shiloh and me inventorying each other from six feet apart. He was gaunt and unshaven, closely resembling the undercover narcotics officer I'd met in an airport bar years ago. For a long moment, I could think of nothing to say. He broke the silence first.

"I'm sorry," Shiloh said.

That was when it hit me: this was Shiloh, he really wasn't dead, I was looking at Shiloh again. I went to the bed, buried myself against his neck and shoulder, and wept.

Shiloh held me so hard it would have hurt me under normal circumstances. I felt the weight he'd lost in the prominent bones, hard against my flesh.

"I'm sorry, baby, I'm so sorry," he said again and again. He stroked my hair, whispering small endearments and reassurances, holding me as though he were the strong one and I was weak.

Shiloh stayed in the hospital for two days while doctors discerned the extent of his head injury and decided he didn't need to be under a physician's care. Then he was taken back to Minnesota and booked into the Faribault County Jail.

While no one could corroborate his location the night of Shorty's death, Shiloh's story and the physical evidence that accompanied it—his injuries—were compelling enough to rule out the possibility that he'd gone back to Blue Earth to kill Shorty. Auto theft, on the other hand, was a charge that was going to stick.

At the arraignment, his lawyer made a case for bail, saying that Shiloh was a first offender, and employed in law enforcement with an excellent professional reputation. The judge pointed out that Shiloh was not currently employed in law enforcement, was highly unlikely ever to be working in law enforcement again, and had already proven himself able to evade justice even under difficult circumstances. Bail was denied.

There was nothing I could do in Faribault County. I drove back up to the Cities to keep from going crazy, then found that a change of location was no antidote for the nervy restlessness that refused to be exhausted by exercise or distracted by television. My first day back I called Utah and left Naomi a message explaining that Shiloh had turned up alive and in reasonably good health. Then I wrote a short note to Sinclair and dropped it into the mail.

Naomi called the next afternoon, wanting details, and I did the best I could to explain my husband and his actions. The conversation wasn't a short one, and outside, the sky lost its light and deepened in color. After we hung up, I sat on the couch and thought unproductively about the future, and as I couldn't bring myself to turn on a lamp, twilight fell in our living room as it did outside.

Ten minutes later I was on the 94. I wanted to see how Genevieve was settling in, back in St. Paul. More important, I wanted to know when she'd be ready to go back to work. Myself, I was rather desperate to get to the distractions of the job.

But when I got to Genevieve's house, it wasn't she who answered the front door.

"Vincent," I said.

"Sarah," Genevieve's ex-husband said. His heavy-lidded gaze had weight: I felt it deep in my spine.

Genevieve appeared in the light spilling from behind him. I noticed anew how much her once-short hair had grown: It was chin-length now, long enough to swing a little when she moved and shine when it caught the light, and she'd tucked it behind her ear on the right side, revealing the subtle silver flash of a small earring.

"Come on in, Sarah," she said. "I'll make some coffee."

"That'd be good." It was a cold evening, but still it hadn't snowed. Gusts of sharp wind chased the few remaining fallen leaves around the sidewalks and streets.

"Take a break, sit with us awhile, Vincent," Genevieve suggested.

"No, I'm fine. I'm going to keep working." He moved to the stairs as I followed them in.

In the kitchen, I asked Genevieve, "What's he doing here?"

"He's cleaning out Kamareia's room," she said.

That answer didn't clear things up, but I sensed that it was a preface and waited for the rest to come out.

Genevieve took a package of ground coffee from the door of her freezer and spooned it into a paper filter. "We're working on clearing out the whole house, actually. I made my resignation final at work."

"You did?" My voice was higher than usual.

"When Vincent goes back to Paris, I'm going with him." She lifted a diffident shoulder, poured water into the coffeemaker.

"You're kidding."

"No." She turned to face me.

"Why?"

Genevieve shook her head. "I can't live here anymore," she said. "Not in this house, not even in St. Paul. I can learn to live without Kamareia, but not here."

My only partner as a detective. My partner of two years and friend for much longer than that. All those cold mornings we'd fantasized about running away to some faraway paradise, like San Francisco or New Orleans. Now Genevieve was really doing it. She was going farther than even we'd imagined. Permanently. Without me.

You can't go, I thought, like a child.

"You want a splash in that? Vince brought these from the flight." She held up a single-ounce bottle of Bailey's; another one sat on the counter nearby, next to an equally small bottle of gin.

The first time I'd ever been to Genevieve's home was after work on a midwinter night, and she'd done almost exactly the same thing; she'd made us coffee. Then she'd said, "You're off duty, you want me to make that special for you?" and had poured some expensive white-chocolate liqueur into both mine and hers. I remembered how pleased her generosity had made me, how disarming it had been to be in the home of someone who had a big kitchen and a liquor cabinet instead of a studio apartment and Budweiser in the refrigerator.

I doubted she knew how much she'd meant to me even back then.

"This thing with Vincent," I said, "isn't it kind of sudden?"

"Sudden and long overdue. There was a reason why I never remarried or even dated." Her voice was happy, a joyful knell for our partnership. She took two heavy glass mugs down from the cupboard and poured out the coffee. She laced one of them with the first bottle of liqueur and pushed it in my direction. "He had business in Chicago and came up here afterward, and we both sort of realized . . . you know."

I was glad for her newfound happiness, but her behavior was a little too upbeat. Maybe she was laying Kamareia's memory to rest at last, but Royce Stewart's death was something else again. That memory was still raw and bloody, and Genevieve was trying to bury it in a hasty, unmarked grave she would never visit in her mind. She was simply turning her back on her actions, and maybe that was the best way to deal with it. Maybe she'd been right the first time. Maybe closure was overrated.

"Oh, God, I'm sorry." Genevieve looked closely at me, then came to my side. "I didn't even ask about Shiloh. How is he?"

She'd misread my unvoiced thoughts. I took a sip of the coffee. "It's hard to say," I explained. "He wants to plead guilty and do his time; his lawyer's trying to talk him out of it. She thinks that, procedurally, she can poke holes in the way his confession was obtained, make something of the head injury and how it might have affected him. Get enough to throw the case out."

"Do you think Shiloh will go along with that?"

I turned to give her what was probably a dry, deadened look. "No," I said. "He won't. He wants to..." I had to search for the right word. "...atone for what he did." It was such a gentle word, *atone*. To put it more honestly, Shiloh wanted to punish himself: for giving in to murderous impulses, yet failing to avenge Kamareia; for ruining his career and putting me through a week of anguish and uncertainty.

"Maybe the judge will be lenient," Genevieve suggested. In her own happiness, she sought to hold out hope to me.

"No," I said again. "He'll do time." I couldn't afford to kid myself.

"What about the two of you?" Genevieve asked. "Have you talked about the future?"

I shook my head. "You've never had a real jailhouse conversation, have you?" I asked her. "In the room where wives and girlfriends and relatives have to do it? It doesn't lend itself much to serious discussions about the future."

"So what's going to happen?" Genevieve said, pressing me.

"What's going to happen? Shiloh's going to do time," I told her, again.

"For auto theft," Genevieve said. "That's a pretty light sentence. When he gets out, what's going to happen between the two of you?"

I didn't have an easy answer for her. Stalling, I looked out the window, at the frozen silver of early-evening moonlight between the branches of neighborhood trees.

As the judge had pointed out at the arraignment, Shiloh would never work in law enforcement again. For all his adult life, he had done virtually nothing else, from the days when he'd searched for lost kids in the rugged Montana terrain until he'd arrested a nationally known fugitive. When, at some point in the future, Shiloh walked out of a prison gate, everything he'd worked for would be gone. I'd still be a cop, and he'd be an ex-convict. Inequities like that had the potential to poison relationships. Slowly. Painfully.

Whenever Shiloh and I spoke, these things hung between us, impossible to forget, but too heavy to be acknowledged.

"We'll cross that bridge when we come to it," I said.

My right hand was resting on the countertop, and Genevieve now laid her own hand over it, gently.

"What about you?" she asked me. "Are you okay?"

"I'm not sure I know," I said honestly.

I stopped in at work to tell Vang I'd be back on the job tomorrow, and that Genevieve wouldn't ever be again.

"I heard," he said. "News travels fast around here. Which reminds me," he said, his tone brightening, "they busted the guy who was making those calls to the wives and girlfriends. Remember?"

"Yeah," I said. "The killed-in-the-line-of-duty calls?"

"Right. Sergeant Rowe told his wife about it. She had a phone jack that lets her tape calls, and she set it up just in case." He shrugged. "It sounds paranoid, but it paid off. The guy called her and said Rowe had been killed in a shootout. She pretended to freak out, and he stayed on the line for a while, giving her these fake details. Then Rowe brought the tape in and passed it around for people to listen to."

"And it was someone in the department?"

"No, the medical examiner's office, actually. None of us even knew this guy, either, his name is—"

"Frank Rossella," I finished for him.

Vang looked at me, surprised. "How'd you know?"

epilogue

Shiloh was sentenced to twenty-two months in prison. It was a stiff sentence for a first offense, by Minnesota's standards. The judge had departed upward, he said, in light of the public trust that Shiloh had borne and failed. The truth, I believed, was that the conspiracy-to-murder charge that Shiloh had escaped, the intent with which Shiloh had stolen the car, was in the back of his mind.

It was clear the court didn't view Shiloh as a sympathetic figure. However, Shiloh had made cases against a number of serious and violent felons; those men were serving time in all of Minnesota's prisons. Shiloh's safety was a concern the judge couldn't overlook. He referred the matter to the Bureau of Prisons, which arranged to have Shiloh serve his time across the state line, in Wisconsin.

He was transferred immediately after the sentencing; I

went to see him about a week later, in early December. The first snow had fallen the night before. The fields and barns of Wisconsin were ridiculously lovely in the fresh whiteness.

I don't know if it was professional courtesy, but they let me talk to Shiloh in a small, private interview room. He was clean-shaven again, but he'd never regained the weight he'd lost in the countryside. His work shirt hung loose on him.

"How are you?" he asked immediately.

"I'm fine," I said.

"Are they treating you okay at work?"

In truth, I missed Genevieve terribly already, partly because she alone would have treated me normally. Everyone in the department had been shocked to learn what Shiloh had done; they didn't know what to say when they saw me. Almost to a person, my fellow officers dealt with it by never bringing it up.

"Sure," I said.

Shiloh heard the lie. "Really," he said, "how are things?"

"Everyone's treating me okay," I insisted. "I came to talk to you about something else."

I looked around. As private as the room seemed, I doubted there wasn't some kind of electronic surveillance in play, and therefore I had to choose my words carefully.

I waited so long that Shiloh spoke again. "Look, Sarah," he said. "I understand that what I did in Blue Earth might have changed the way you feel about me—"

"No, no," I said. "It's not that."

"Go on," he prompted me, gently.

"I met her," I said. "I know why you left home. I know what you were doing on Christmas Eve."

I'd said the last thing in the world that still had the power to alarm him. In Shiloh's lynx eyes, in the sharp way they focused in on me, I saw all the confirmation I needed. I hadn't really been sure, not until that minute.

"She *told* you?" Shiloh said.

I shook my head.

Sinclair hadn't told me the truth about her troubled relationship with her brother, not with words, anyway. She'd done so with her silences, relating her life story with the most important aspect in the unfilled blanks.

She and Shiloh had been extremely close, yet after leaving his family he hadn't sought her out in Salt Lake City. He'd fled the other way, north to Montana.

They'd run into each other when she came to Minnesota, and Sinclair had made no mention of a fight or disagreement, yet said they'd never gotten in touch again after she left.

Mike without a last name in the bar at MSP, five years ago, just out of a *very brief, very wrong* affair.

The connection had simply come to me, unwilled, on the flight home. Sinclair had referred to last seeing her brother in Minnesota in winter, just around the time a wreck had taken the lives of the three Carleton students. I wouldn't have been able to place it, except that I had been one of the patrol officers on the scene, an icy secondary highway outside Minneapolis in frozen late January. That had been only days before I'd learned of my father's death. Days before my quick trip west, at the end of which I had met Shiloh, drinking and trying to forget a sexual entanglement about which he had shared no details. I had been willing not to ask. In the months and years that followed, I never had.

Small wonder he'd been able to keep his intent to go to Blue

Earth a secret from me. Shiloh had learned long ago how to hide his heart. I'd never even known that he knew sign language.

He and Sinclair had both tried very hard to forget; that much was clear. They'd spent their adult lives avoiding each other, an estrangement that had grown to encompass their entire family. Shiloh had brushed aside even Naomi's innocent, questing attention, when she'd crossed a cardinal, unseen line in suggesting he come home.

Shiloh couldn't go home, for the same reason he'd been unable to go to his father's funeral: He couldn't bear the prospect of looking in his older brothers' eyes and wondering what they knew, never knowing if they had been told nothing or were feigning ignorance because the truth was too terrible to acknowledge.

He needn't have worried. Shiloh's brothers and sisters lived in a fog of self-deception. Naomi never wondered what the Christmas Eve disaster was all about. Bill had possessed all the pieces of the mystery but never quite put them together. *Mike was there and suddenly he wasn't there,* Bill had said. *My father said God could forgive anything, but not until He is asked.* Bill had never considered the prospect that Mike and Sara were guilty of more than everyday human sins. He never let himself wonder how a single instance of teenage drug experimentation could have permanently ruined his brother Mike's relationship with the entire family.

I wondered how much it had hurt Shiloh's father, by all accounts a truly godly man, to lie to his children about what Sara and Mike had really been doing that long-ago Christmas Eve.

Perhaps I would have missed all the signs as well—I had

even more reason than they did for self-deception—but for Sinclair's message. *I am so glad for you and Sarah. Please be happy.* Short as a haiku, both a greeting and a farewell, every word weighted with a lover's bittersweet kindness and gentle regret, nothing like what a sister should have written.

I'd brought the note with me and handed it silently over to him.

Shiloh studied it longer than the simple text seemed to merit. When he finally spoke, his voice was so low it was barely audible.

"God knows I've tried to make sense of it. I never have. Sometimes things just go wrong in your head."

But he tapped two fingers not against his temple, indicating the mind, but against his chest, indicating the heart.

"I was fifteen when she came home. She was like a stranger to me. But we understood each other. I could talk to her. Not just because I knew sign language. I could *talk* to her." He was looking down at the floor, not at me. "We got really close, too fast. One night we were on the roof, during the Leonid meteor shower. I asked her if I could hold her hand and she let me. We didn't realize we were opening a door that we were never going to be able to close."

He fell silent. It wasn't the end of the story, but it was all of it, essentially.

In my mind's eye I saw her again, Shiloh's sister, perhaps the most beautiful woman I'd ever seen. I couldn't bring myself to hate her. She'd had that same inner light that had drawn me to Shiloh from the first moment I'd seen him. He was right. They were the same kind of people.

What was it I had said to Sinclair? *I was scared there was a part of him I was never going to have.* I'd been talking about the early days of our relationship, but it had never stopped being true. And I'd been right to be scared.

"All this time, I never realized," I said softly. "I could never have measured up."

"That's not true," Shiloh said vehemently.

Suddenly the room seemed too small. "I'm sorry," I said. "I shouldn't have come." I jumped to my feet.

But Shiloh had always been as quick as I was and he was up, too, holding me hard by the upper arms, near the shoulders. "No, Sarah, wait," he said.

"Hey, hey, that's enough! Take your hands off her!" Two uniformed guards were pulling him off me.

"Are you okay, ma'am?" one of them asked. I realized that Shiloh's chair was tipped over on the floor, so fast had he gotten up. It must have made an alarming picture.

"I'm all right," I told them.

"Time to go, buddy," the other one said, guiding Shiloh to the door of the interview room. In the doorway he turned to look at me again, and then he was gone.

I'd just crossed over the Minnesota state line again when my cell phone shrilled. Keeping my eyes on the road, I picked it up with my free hand, not thinking about the times I'd lectured drivers about pulling over to answer the phone.

"Pribek?" It was a smooth, familiar voice. "This is Chris Kilander. I've been meaning to talk to you," he went on. "Where are you?"

"I'm, uh, a little ways out of town. Like twenty-five

minutes. I wasn't planning on coming in today," I said. It was late afternoon; the sun had already set.

"That's fine," he said. "Actually, I could meet you outside. At the fountain. Say, in thirty minutes?" He meant on the plaza outside the Government Center. "This won't take long."

I parked at a metered spot near City Hall and walked mostly against the crowd, up toward the courthouse. Across the street, at the plaza's edge, people waited for the city buses, wrapped in their gloves and scarves. At the end of the day, the bus-stop lines grew surprisingly long, like a crowd of people waiting for concert tickets.

Up by the fountain, Kilander stood, not pacing. He wore a long dark coat, looking every inch the lawyer. I loped across the street in a break in traffic and went to his side.

"How are you, Sarah?" he asked.

"I'm all right."

"Glad to hear it," he said. "Where were you coming back from?"

"Wisconsin."

"The prison?"

I nodded.

Kilander did not ask after Shiloh. Instead he sat on the fountain's edge and gestured to the space next to him. The dark, speckled surface was not only devoid of snow, it appeared dry. I accepted his invitation to sit, waited for him to speak.

Kilander's eyes went to the crowd of office workers at the bus stop, then he looked back at me. "No one in the department has suggested to you that you shouldn't be back on the job, have they?"

"No," I said.

Kilander nodded thoughtfully, one of his courtroom temporizing gestures. "Shiloh's confession of attempted murder raised a lot of interest in how Royce Stewart actually did die."

"Really? How did he die?" I said, trying for his brand of archness.

"They're still figuring that out," Kilander said. "Arson investigators sifted through that jumped-up kennel he lived in. They're saying now the fire doesn't look like natural origins."

"Yeah?"

"And there were apparently a lot of tire tracks around that place, the main house and the outbuilding, considering that the homeowners were away and Shorty had one car that didn't run. They're looking closely at those tire prints."

My tracks. And Genevieve's. Genevieve was leaving in two days for Paris. She was wasting no time in pulling up her roots here, and now I was happy about that.

"And Stewart's friends say that the night he died, a woman cop came to the bar in Blue Earth to talk to him. A very tall woman cop in a Kalispell Search and Rescue T-shirt. She doesn't fit the description of anyone in that jurisdiction."

I had not done a good job of covering my tracks, and neither had Genevieve. We would have been more careful, had we known we were going to kill Royce Stewart. But we hadn't gone to Blue Earth with the intent to kill. Royce Stewart's death was unplanned, very nearly an accident. I had to think of it that way; I couldn't stand to think of my partner as a murderer.

And that wasn't the way the world would likely view her, either, I realized. The evidence did not point to Genevieve as Shorty's killer. Nobody had seen Genevieve in Blue Earth. They had seen me.

And further, Genevieve was a very well-liked veteran who'd left the job and gone somewhere that would require extradition, which in turn called for paperwork, negotiation, international cooperation.

Of course, these things shouldn't matter, but I knew the reality. They would matter. I, meanwhile, wasn't as well-known as Genevieve. While I had no enemies that I knew of in the department, mostly I counted as friends patrol officers and working detectives. To those in higher places, the administrative jurymen, I was just a name, a young detective tainted by my marriage to a man who'd proven himself a rogue cop.

And I wouldn't be in Paris. I would be in Minneapolis, not within arm's reach of the system but in its very heart, working right under the watchful and suspicious eyes of my superiors as the investigation went forward.

"I see," I said quietly.

He laid a gentle hand on my arm. I did not object. In the past I'd seen Kilander as a pleasant lothario, to be enjoyed at arm's length but not trusted. It surprised me now to realize that I thought of him as a friend.

"Have you ever heard the saying 'The mills of the gods grind exceedingly slow, but they grind exceedingly fine'?" Kilander asked.

"Yeah," I said. I hadn't, but I knew what he meant.

He stood, and I followed his example. As close as we were standing, I keenly felt every one of the six inches he had on me. He laid one hand on my shoulder, and with his other hand, Kilander tipped my face up toward his and gently kissed me on the mouth. A chain of streetlights flickered on, like lightning in the periphery of my vision.

Kilander released me and stepped back. "The mills of the

gods are grinding, Sarah," he said. There was no irony in the words, just like there had been no sex in the kiss.

Two buses had come along and vacuumed up the waiting people at the curb, so the crowd was gone. There were a few people still on the plaza, coming and going, ghosts and abstractions in the gathering dark. I stood and watched Kilander as he walked back to the Government Center, the hem of his long coat swirling slightly in a gust of wind that made the jets of the fountain flinch. He did not look back, and I watched until he disappeared into the lighted atrium of the Hennepin County Government Center, the tower of light and order where he worked.